SISTERS OF THE SOUTHERN CROSS

JEAN GRAINGER

To D-daw and Barb, what an adventure we had.

PROLOGUE

 *ctober 1, 1933*

BISHOP'S PALACE
   Brisbane
   Queensland, Australia

SISTER CLAIRE,

   *I hope this letter finds you well, my dear niece, and that you are contin-
uing to enjoy your work at St Catherine's. I am hearing wonderful things
about you and your fellow sisters and the progress you are making in the
school there. I'm sure the children of Cork City are blossoming under your
tender care.*

   *I am very much looking forward to my visit home. I can hardly believe it
has been five years since I was last there for your final vows. A wonderful
day for the whole family. Such a pity your granny didn't get to see it. She
would have been bursting with pride to see her little granddaughter joining
the Ursuline community.*

1

Your father and I have a lot to catch up on since neither of us are great men for writing letters, even if it is to one's only brother. Your mother writes every month. If not for her, I'd have no idea what was happening back in Macroom at all.

Life here in Queensland is busy and hot as always, so I dream of the lovely Irish breeze, especially as the summer is coming here. I'm arriving into Cobh – how strange to no longer call it Queenstown – on the fifteenth of December, God willing, and I was hoping to call on you at the convent if it would be convenient? I have a proposal that may interest you.

Of all of my nieces, you are by far the most audacious, and I have a role here that might whet your appetite for adventure, as well as be a unique opportunity to do God's work.

You probably know that Queensland is an enormous state, and while I am based in Brisbane in southern Queensland, I am 1,500 miles away from the Cape York Peninsula in the tropical north of the country. The area I mention, Cape York, is badly in need of a Catholic school. The town I have in mind is called Jumaaroo, and it is a thriving town as a result of gold mining, which was then followed by logging, sugar cane production and food growing.

There are many Catholic families based there now, Irish primarily but Italian and Polish as well, and there is no school to accommodate them. The parents face the upset of sending their offspring hours away to be educated, and even then, the school is a Protestant one. So you can see, Claire, there is a need.

I propose that you lead a group of sisters to set up a Catholic school in this town. I know you are young and have never taken on such an onerous task before, but I have faith in your abilities.

This is a young country. It is a place where the societal constraints of age, experience, class and family do not hold such sway as they would at home, and you will be accepted and welcomed with open arms.

There is a local man – well, he's originally one of our own as they say – a Corkonian called Joseph J McGrath, who has very generously offered to build a convent and a school, entirely at his own expense. The gesture is a very welcome one. He is himself a devout Catholic and is anxious that the many people in his employ have access to a quality Catholic education for their children. Thank God for such men.

He is also the mayor of the town, and so you would have his full support. He is married to the daughter of a prominent Catholic family – also of Irish extraction, settlers though, not convicts – here in Brisbane, so the family's credentials could not be higher. And so it would be with complete confidence in your safety and happiness that I would place you in the care of Mr and Mrs McGrath.

Claire, on a personal note, I genuinely think you would love it here. This is an incredible place, with animals and birds and all manner of divine creation that you would never otherwise see. While I know you had a desire to go on the African missions and do God's work there, and in this role it will be white Catholics who will receive the benefit of your skills and grace, I promise you this position would fulfil you in a way dealing with natives – regardless of where in the world you would be sent – could never do.

There are natives here too of course. The Aboriginals, as they are called, are managed by other denominations largely, though of course there are Catholic missions as well. But you need not concern yourself with them.

There is a mission, I believe, quite near the town, run by the Seventh-day Adventist Church. They have said terrible things about our faith and are essentially a cult of some description, and so are best avoided. I do not know what they do there, nor do I want to. Our sole concern is for the Catholic families that are at this point without the necessary spiritual guidance that I hope you and the sisters that would accompany you out here can bring.

I know it is a daunting prospect, but I hope I have appealed to your sense of adventure and your deep commitment and vocation to spread the word of our Lord throughout the world.

Fond regards and God bless you,
Rev Bill
The Most Reverend William McAuliffe
Archbishop of Brisbane

CHAPTER 1

 eptember, 1934

SISTER CLAIRE MCAULIFFE watched as the brass band sweated through 'Faith of Our Fathers' in the blistering Queensland heat. She felt sorry for the poor musicians in their elaborate royal-blue and gold woollen costumes, colourful and regal but entirely impractical. They'd been bussed in from Cooktown for the occasion, God love them.

That said, the long black nuns' habits she and her sisters wore weren't much better. Their heads covered in tight veils, she and her four fellow sisters sweltered. The people of Jumaaroo had gathered for the spectacle – the arrival of the nuns off the Cooktown bus this morning – and so to wish the ceremony could be over quickly and they could all move to the shade and get something cold to drink seemed churlish. It felt like they'd left Cork years ago. The journey had been demanding, and she longed for a meal, bath and bed. Mrs McGrath, the mayor's wife, had invited the nuns for afternoon tea once the speeches were over, and Claire couldn't wait. She was so hungry. But people seemed to have gone to such trouble, so she would force a smile on her face and endure the ceremony.

She sat demurely on the podium erected for them, feeling rather like a specimen in a museum placed there for gawping purposes. To her right up the hill was the brand new school, and according to Mayor McGrath, who'd walked up from the bus stop with them, it was built with every convenience in mind. It was going to be a wonderful place to work. She couldn't wait to see it for herself. There were apparently five large classrooms and four smaller ones. She was to have an office on the second floor overlooking the school playground on one side and facing down the hill to the town on the other. And there was a hall with a stage, a large playground and, beyond it, even a playing field.

Rev Bill, as she'd always called her uncle, now Bishop of Brisbane, had warned her that Jumaaroo was nothing like Cork, and he wasn't wrong. It was vast, hot and dusty, and so far she'd seen so many things she'd never before encountered. She couldn't wait to write home and tell them all about it. She could just imagine her father's sardonic smile at her descriptions of her new world.

The town consisted of one street, about a quarter of a mile long. The shops and businesses traded under a canopy that stretched out over a raised wooden boardwalk footpath, which shielded shoppers from the relentless tropical sun and kept their feet dry from the flooding rain during the wet season. There was a hotel and a grocer's, a shoemaker and a draper's, and a large hardware shop that had everything from a needle to an anchor, as the proprietor had informed them when Mr McGrath took them on a tour of the town before the ceremony began.

Beside her, Sister Mary seemed enraptured with the band. Anything musical delighted her, and Claire knew she couldn't wait to get her instruments unpacked and her music classes set up. Claire didn't get to choose the sisters who accompanied her on this mission, but if she'd had a choice, she would have chosen Mary. Mary was a sweet girl from Skibbereen in West Cork who missed her mother desperately when she first came to the Ursuline convent in Cork City, but she'd soon settled and realised her vocation was real. Claire and Mary had taught together at St Catherine's. Mary was slight and short, with the sweetest smile and a tinkling laugh. A natural musician, she loved children and music in equal measure, and the grating noise of early days in violin lessons, or the endless *plonk, plonk, plonk* of a piano, didn't seem to bother her in the slightest, though Claire admitted she herself often had to suppress a wince.

Claire wished she could say the same of Sister Gerard, who bristled at the end of the row. The fact that she was so overweight didn't help her in coping with the heat. She was as sour as Mary was sweet. The Reverend Mother had confided to Claire that the order had proposed the taciturn nun for the move to Australia because she'd slapped the wrong child with the leather rather too severely, drawing the little girl's blood, and the parents were threatening all sorts. Claire had never met her before that day on the quayside, but throughout the journey she'd been most disagreeable.

Gerard, now in her fifties, was too old for the missions, but the child she attacked had powerful parents and so she had to be removed. She'd complained ceaselessly since the day they left Cobh: It was too hot, she was seasick, the food was horrible, nothing was right. Claire knew she would be the most difficult to manage. Already she was refusing to accept that Claire was the school principal, as appointed by her uncle, the archbishop, and was making executive decisions without consulting anyone.

Sister Helen, who sat beside Gerard, was a mystery. She had come from a convent in East Cork and seemed serene, but she said very little and watched everything. She had pale skin and thoughtful hazel eyes, and there was a serenity to her, a kind of stillness that should be restful but wasn't for some reason. She was devout, as they all were, and she prayed constantly the entire journey.

Sister Teresita was full of fun. She was from near Claire's home of Macroom, but about seven miles outside the town, and her accent was so thick it was hard to imagine how the Australian children would have the faintest idea what she was saying. Claire could understand her – she used to hear her father talking to people with that accent at the fair in Macroom every month – but even to the townspeople they were hard to understand. So far, Teresita's hilarity had been met with blank stares. Claire felt so sorry for her. She was so kindhearted, but it was going to be a struggle.

One of many.

Mr McGrath stood to the side of the stage, awaiting his introduction by a member of the town council. He was tall and handsome, and Claire noted with amusement his charismatic influence on her fellow sisters. Mary blushed when he spoke to her, and even Gerard lost her dour expression and smiled at him. He was very good-looking, she supposed; she was not a great judge of these things, but his dark wavy hair creamed back from his high forehead and twinkling blue eyes were pleasant. She'd been surprised at his accent. She'd assumed he was of Irish extraction by his name, but he wasn't the son or grandson of immigrants or even convicts – he had been born and raised in Cork. His accent was odd, not city or county but cultured. His perfect blonde Australian wife, Assumpta, was dressed impeccably, with a powdered face and pink lipstick. She was pretty but seemed cold somehow. She looked as if something unpleasant was directly below her nose at all times. They had three children, a toddler and twin babies.

'Ladies and gentlemen, Reverend Father, Sisters, boys and girls.' The short bald councillor addressed the gathered crowd. 'It is my great pleasure to introduce to you all a man who needs no introduction in Jumaaroo. As we all know, our town, this school and indeed everything that makes Jumaaroo the envy of the state is down to this man. So without further ado, I invite Mayor Joseph McGrath to the stage to officially welcome our community of Irish nuns.'

This was greeted by enthusiastic applause.

Joseph McGrath took the stage, and the spectators instantly hushed.

'Ladies and gentlemen, Reverend Father.' He nodded and smiled at Father Bruno, the priest from Strathland, the nearest town over forty miles away. 'And of course, the Ursuline Sisters, for whom this special occasion is a warm welcome to our town.' He smiled at them. 'As you all know, it has long been an ambition of mine to build a school for the children of Jumaaroo. For too long, we have had to send our little ones to board at the wonderful – but very far away – Saint Xavier's, and broken several mamas' hearts here in Jumaaroo.'

This last comment produced indulgent smiles and a ripple of laughter from the crowd.

'Well, that is no more, as Sister Claire, along with Sister Mary, Sister Gerard, Sister Helen and Sister Teresita, will provide quality Catholic education, not just for the townspeople of Jumaaroo but for the many families in the hinterland. Archbishop McAuliffe has taken a personal interest in our little town, and we are so grateful to him for that. Between us, we have made this school a reality. St Finbarr is the patron saint of Cork, the home not just of Sister Claire and her sister nuns but also of my own family, so it is a source of tremendous pride to me personally that Finbarr, himself a scholar, should have his name remembered here, as far from his home as it is possible to be.

'And so all that remains is for me to welcome the sisters, to thank them for making the arduous journey and to pledge our support and dedication to their mission.'

The band struck up again as Joseph McGrath cut the ribbon in front of the brand new school building, and the crowd cheered even louder.

They walked in procession to the McGraths' house, Claire almost fainting from hunger and heat. Everyone wanted to say hello, to welcome them. It was lovely, but Claire longed to get inside and drink something cold.

Her sister Eileen had suggested that she would lose weight in Australia, something that had eluded her thus far, and something she cared not a jot about. Her sisters were forever trying to be thinner, but she loved her food and had enjoyed years of her mother's cooking followed by many more at the hands of wonderful sisters whose life's purpose was feeding the nuns in the convent.

Eventually they reached the large house at the opposite end of the town to the school. It sat on a hill and seemed to watch over Jumaaroo. The McGrath house was so luxurious, and the nuns were lavish in their praise as they were led into the drawing room. Assumpta had a nurse and a governess to help with the children, as well as a cook, two maids, a housekeeper and a selection of groundkeepers and gardeners. The kitchen and laundry were in a separate building, for fear of fire, she explained, since everything was made of wood. The house was like nothing they'd seen in Ireland. It had a green copper roof and was built on stilts, which allowed air to flow around it and keep it cool. Inside, there were paintings and fine carpets and all manner of ornaments and antiques. There was a pianoforte, a full baby grand, which Claire could see Mary was itching to get her fingers on, and the walls were adorned with photographs of several generations of McGraths, she assumed, all glowering aggressively from their frames. Though none of them seemed to bear a resemblance to the mayor in any way.

The mayor had been charming and funny on the walk over, but once they arrived at the house, he took his leave – allowing the ladies time to chat, he explained – and withdrew to his study.

Claire's heart sank when she saw the meagre spread laid out on a beautifully ornate marble table. There were tiny fancies, beautifully iced and presented, but she knew that they would be like a daisy in a bull's mouth to her. And there was one plate of delicate cucumber sandwiches with the crusts cut off. To add to her disappointment, they were serving hot tea in tiny china cups; she so longed for a long drink of something cold.

Several other ladies had arrived as well and were all sitting expectantly but respectfully silent as Assumpta explained to the new arrivals various aspects of the town, from the weather to dealing with the creepy-crawlies. At the mention of funnel-web, redback and huntsman spiders, the gathered ladies dutifully shuddered. Every time Assumpta stopped speaking, the air in the room seemed charged with the musty anticipation of her next pronouncement.

In one of those pauses that seemed interminable, Claire couldn't help herself. She gushed about how fabulous the scenery was, how they'd seen kangaroos and a huge snake on the way up from Cooktown. She could tell that the audience were humouring her.

It was one of her many failings, the inability to endure social awkwardness. Her Reverend Mother had pointed out that her need to fill silence with chatter when she was nervous was a most un-nun-like trait. Sisters were supposed to be serene and contemplative, but Claire was impulsive and chatty and often ended up saying too much and cringing afterwards.

'We even saw an Aboriginal man throwing a boomerang! He was too far away to see his face, but it was so fascinating to watch. It really is a remarkable place – I'm so excited to explore it. Do you know any Aboriginal people, Mrs McGrath? I'd love to meet one.'

Before Assumpta could answer, Gerard interjected. 'I don't think any of these ladies would mix with the natives, Sister Claire.' She turned to the others and gave a saccharin smile. 'Forgive my sister. She's never been abroad before and doesn't know the correct way of dealing with, well...those people.'

'Quite, Sister Gerard, but I'm sure you'll be a help,' Assumpta agreed. 'To answer your question, Sister Claire, I don't. My husband employs some of them, caretakers and odd-job men, that sort of thing, but to be entirely honest with you, they are generally unreliable and often untrustworthy. He has employed one to care for the grounds at the convent and the school, and he would have handpicked him. They are not like us – they can't settle to anything, they wander off mid-task, and following even the simplest instructions is entirely beyond them.'

During another awkward silence, Teresita shot Claire a glance of friendly solidarity. 'So there are enough Catholic families in the area to fill a school, are there?' she asked, changing the subject.

Claire exhaled slowly.

'Oh, yes, indeed. At one stage, when Joseph first came up with the idea, he thought there might not be, that we would have to admit the Italians.' This elicited a slight eye-roll and a titter from the ladies. 'But thankfully, it won't come to that.'

Claire sipped her tea and bit her tongue. Rev Bill might think Mrs McGrath was a pillar of the community from a well-got family, but Claire was finding her hard to warm to.

CHAPTER 2

*C*laire dragged herself out of bed, exhausted after another night of interrupted sleep. The stifling heat, biting insects and very different food were playing havoc with her body. The other nuns were suffering too, and all anyone seemed to say was that they would get used to it. She tried to put on a brave face for the others, and their days were filled with preparations for opening the school, but it was exhausting.

Three days ago, she and her sisters had moved in and were shown around by Mr McGrath, who was charming as always and smelled like expensive leather and wood.

'So I hope you'll be comfortable here, and if you need anything else, please just call.'

As they'd rounded the corner into the garden, they had almost collided with an Aboriginal man. Gerard had screamed, but Mr McGrath was quick to reassure her. 'Please, don't be alarmed, Sisters. This is Daku. He's part Aboriginal, and he works here. He won't hurt you, and he'll stay outside.'

Claire was mortified. He was speaking about this man as if he weren't there. No introductions were made. She tried not to look alarmed.

The powerfully built man just stood before them and remained still. His thick dark hair, with what looked like copper-coloured ends, was swept back from a high brow and fell in unruly curls to his shoulders. His deep-set, almost-black eyes were wide apart, intelligent and intuitive beneath straight black brows. His skin was the colour of chocolate, and he was clean-shaven. He wore ragged trousers held up by a length of rope, but his chest was bare. He had markings on his upper body and arms that looked like they were drawn with white chalk or something. It was hard to determine his age.

'Let's get on, shall we?' Mr McGrath said, ushering the nuns past Daku.

'It's nice to meet you, Daku,' Claire said, feeling foolish. She didn't even know if he spoke English.

Did he give a ghost of a smile? It was hard to tell. As she passed him, he slightly inclined his head.

'So that was a native, or an Aborigine,' Mr McGrath explained as they gathered in the kitchen after the tour, where Mary made him a cup of tea. 'Best to avoid them generally if I were you. They can be a bit… Well, let's just say they take a bit of management. The old one who runs them here, well, he's a bit daft to be honest. They are big into spirits and spooks and goodness knows what. But if he comes round, just let me know and I'll have it dealt with. They don't have any skills, and they have no concept of industry or development. I mean, they've been here for thousands of years and they've done nothing, achievements are literally zero, so educating them is a priority for the government.'

He took the tea and smiled, making Mary blush again.

'So will they be coming to this school?' Claire asked innocently, already knowing the answer.

'Good Lord, no.' McGrath chuckled. 'You're joking. Do you want my poor wife to have a heart attack?' He sipped his tea. 'No, there's a place out at the coast, a few miles out of town, that looks after them. You needn't worry.'

They chatted about this and that for a few more moments until he announced, 'Well, I'm sure you ladies would like me to take myself out of your way so you can set about putting this place together as you'd like it, so I'll be off.'

Claire saw him out, and as she went to close the door, she noticed a very old Aboriginal man, with long grey hair and a very long grey beard, approach the mayor.

'McGrath,' he called, his voice husky.

Mr McGrath sighed and turned towards him. 'Yes? Can I help?'

The man stood four-square before Joseph McGrath. Though the Irishman was taller, there was an agility and strength to the older man. His sinewy arms were bare and his feet shoeless, but the speed of his movement and the way he squared up to McGrath belied his years.

'You know what you can do.' He spoke quickly, almost staccato, and with a heavy accent. 'You can stop driving my people off our land, you can stop blocking the dam. I know what you are doing, McGrath, and I'm warning you, you need to stop or there will be consequences.'

'I don't know what you're talking about.' McGrath spoke slowly and loudly as if the man were either deranged or hard of hearing or both. 'But if you want to make an appointment, then of course you can come and talk to me.' He turned on his heel and walked back to his car, raising his eyebrows at Claire and giving her a conspiratorial smile.

This must be the man he mentioned, she thought.

He drove away, and when she'd turned back, the elderly man was gone.

* * *

WITH A SIGH, Claire threw back the covers. She had been woken – like she had been every morning – by the incessant arguing of some birds outside the window. She thought she'd seen birds at home, but nothing prepared her for those in Australia: the cockatoos that swooped so close to her head; the kookaburras, so cheeky with their laughing call and the way they flew down and plucked the food from your plate; the enormous jabirus that looked like they were too big to fly and yet they could; the tiny Jesus Christ birds that could walk on water. And she would take to her grave Mary's blood-curdling scream when, as she was setting up some music stands, a huge prehistoric-looking creature – a gigantic bird over six feet tall with sleek black feathers, a colourful head and huge fat feet – stalked by. Claire had come running at the sound of the other nun's distress, but one of the children who had gathered to watch the schoolhouse being prepared explained that it was a cassowary. They found the nun's alarm amusing.

Claire normally loved nature, but the birds outside drove her daft with their loud calls that started at daybreak or before. Mynah birds, galahs, lorikeets and curlews – there were so many varieties, and they were all so loud. She tried to marvel at God's creations, but it had been weeks since she'd slept the night through and she was exhausted. The voyage had been long, and she'd felt ill for a lot of it, and now that they were here, it was hot, itchy and noisy. At least in bed she wore the linen nightdress of the order. It was white and cool, and despite the oppressive heat even at night, she felt like she could breathe. During the day, the black habit was a trial; they longed for a breeze, even a tiny puff of wind, as respite from the relentless heat.

She sat on the side of her bed as the dawn streaked the morning sky and decided she may as well get up. There was no priest in the village – the nearest one was forty miles away so he only came for special occasions – but she and her sisters rose and prayed together before the day's toil began. Then they would breakfast together, simple bread and tea and sometimes a boiled egg if one of the townspeople's chooks, as they called hens, was feeling particularly bounteous. Morning prayers would be at seven and the big old alarm clock told her it was five thirty, but there would be no more sleep for her.

Dressing in her heavy black habit, she noticed she had become thinner. Even as a child, her grandmother used to say she was like a ball of butter, but now that she was here, for the first time in her life, she was shrinking. *Though by anyone's standards* – she smiled ruefully as she dressed – *I am still a short, fat nun.*

She checked herself in the mirror and felt no satisfaction at what she saw there. She was no beauty, that was for sure, and she knew her father

15

and mother were proud but also a little relieved when she said she had a vocation. Finding a husband was much easier for her pretty sisters. Her mousey hair was cut short under her veil, and her brother used to tease her that she had a face like a currant bun. Luckily such things mattered not at all to her; she had no vanity in that regard. Her body was a functioning thing, she could walk and even run if necessary, and she could teach. She was sure that her vocation was real. God had called her, and she felt immense gratitude to him for his divine intervention in her life.

She crept downstairs and saw that Mary had soaked the sheets and towels overnight, so she could hang them out on the makeshift clothes line recently erected by Daku. She carried the heavy enamel basin out to the line and realised she had no clothes pegs. She sighed. She could drape the larger things, but the little ones would surely blow away in the breeze that had thankfully arrived.

She stood, wondering what she should do, when she saw him, standing in the back yard of the convent, gazing intently at her. Feeling self-conscious but unsure of what to do, she carried on with her task. She hung up the sheets and towels but left the smaller things in the basin. Immediately, a gust caused the tea cloths to fly from the line onto the dusty ground. She sighed and retrieved them – they would need to be washed again now.

He was still there, just staring at her, a rake in his hand. She smiled at him and gave a little wave. She gathered the laundry that had fallen in the dust, acutely aware of his presence.

'Good morning,' she called, but he remained where he was, totally still.

Quaking inside, she approached him, crossing the garden as the sun was rising. 'I am Sister Claire,' she said slowly. He was only feet from her but still gave no reaction. He wasn't nervous or aggressive; he was still, watchful.

She pointed at her chest and said again, 'Sister Claire.'

Daku leaned the rake on a hedge and walked past her. Without saying a word, he bent down under a tree in the yard and picked up several round nuts about the size of a plum from the ground. Claire watched him and was fascinated by the agileness of his movements. Like the older man, he was supple and strong. The nuts had all naturally split on one side, and he carried them to the clothesline and wedged several over the clothes as very effective clothes pegs. Claire had never seen anything like them used before, and she was fascinated. The clothes were now secure and blew merrily in the early morning breeze.

Daku's feet were bare and dusty, and that slight smile she recognised from the first day played around his lips. It felt like he was laughing at her. She couldn't blame him. She must look ridiculous to him in her totally impractical habit.

Long seconds passed. Just as she was about to try again to thank him, he spoke, his voice gentle and clear. 'Hello. I know who you are. Joseph McGrath told me your name.'

His English was accented in the way of all Australians, but she was astounded to hear him speak English fluently.

'I'm sorry, I thought you...' Claire was flustered now and embarrassed.

'Reckoned I couldn't speak English?' he asked. No hint of sarcasm accompanied the words.

'Well, I didn't know,' she said truthfully.

'I can. I was taught in a mission, a Catholic one like yours, but I left, came home. They called me a whitefella's name, but when I came back to country' – he glanced around – 'I was Daku again.'

She longed to ask him so many questions, but something about him told her he wouldn't appreciate it. 'Thank you so much for your work, making the place look so nice for us. Is there anything you need?' she asked, steering the conversation away from his origins and her assumptions about him.

'No. I don't need anything from you.' Again, it was a simple statement, and there was no belligerence in his tone.

'Oh, right. Well, thank you very much. And if there is...or you need a drink or some food or anything...' She was babbling again, she knew it, and she felt her face flush. 'Well, just come up to the convent. You

17

are welcome there. And thank you for the clothes peg solution – I would never have thought of using those.' She smiled.

'You're the stranger here, not me. My people have lived here since the Dreamtime. All you whitefellas' – he waved his hand down the hill towards the town of Jumaaroo – 'it's not your country.'

Claire didn't know what to say. The land for the school and adjoining convent had been donated by Mr McGrath, but she imagined he was referring to the general colony rather than that specific piece of land. 'Well, Mr McGrath donated this land to the Church. I think a school is badly needed for everyone around here, so I hope we can do some good.'

His dark eyes held hers. Clearly, he had no sense of the awkwardness of such an intense stare. 'Not for us. The mission out at Trouble Bay is good enough for us. *Mr* McGrath sees to that.'

Claire knew she wasn't imagining the sneer in his voice as he said the mayor's name. It was all very confusing. Hadn't Mr McGrath given Daku a job? Singled him out as a trustworthy person? And yet she could swear Daku's tone suggested he didn't like him.

Claire remembered the old Aboriginal man and the things he'd said to Mr McGrath as he was leaving. Surely it was a misunderstanding, or perhaps they didn't fully understand what his plan was. She hoped so.

Rev Bill had mentioned the Seventh-day Adventist mission twelve miles away out at the coast. Apparently it was run by a teacher and his wife, and by all accounts, he was a force to be reckoned with.

'Do you live at that mission?' she asked.

He laughed, a loud guttural sound from deep in his chest. 'No. I live here, in my country. When I was a kid – I told you already – whitefellas took me away, far south. But I got back. I wouldn't stay there.'

She nodded, unsure if her question had offended him. His words were blunt with none of the deference she was used to; in fact, he could be interpreted as borderline rude, but he delivered his comments with no malice. She'd never met anyone like him.

'And do you think it's a good thing? The mission school?' She knew from her uncle and snippets she'd heard about the mysterious Seventh-day Adventists their take on Catholicism, and the terrible names they called the Holy Father. Truth be told, they kind of frightened her.

Daku shrugged. 'The best thing would have been for whitefellas to never have come here, to leave us alone. But now that you're here, well, at least it's somewhere for us to go, for the kids to learn – and he's OK, Russell Gardiner, who runs it. He's kind and he's making space for more and more every day as they are driven off the land. McGrath is the biggest problem, not Russell.'

Just as Claire was about to ask him exactly what he meant, Daku picked up his rake and strolled away. The bush, which seemed a blanket term for all of the wild tangle of trees and hard spiky bushes that covered every bit of land not wrestled from it by human hands, bordered the property, and he just walked off into it, seemingly oblivious to the dire warnings they had been given about snakes and all manner of things that could kill you that lived in the undergrowth.

It was the oddest exchange. He just spoke as he found. In lots of ways, his manner reminded her of people at home in Macroom. They didn't soft-soap anyone; they said what they had to say bluntly, and tough luck if you were offended.

Later, at breakfast, she described her encounter to her sisters. Mary and Teresita were fascinated, but as she spoke, Helen interjected. 'Daku is Black Cockatoo – that's what the ocean-going Aboriginals call themselves.' Noticing the look of surprise on their faces, she smiled. 'I was speaking to him yesterday about the fruit trees. He was telling me when the different trees would give fruit. He is so knowledgeable about nature and how things work here.'

Gerard sniffed, her disapproval seeping from every pore.

'What is the matter, Sister Gerard?' Claire asked gently.

'Nothing. Why should anything be the matter?' the older nun snapped.

'You just seem annoyed, that's all.'

Claire knew that Mary, Helen and Teresita were watching and observing. Since they'd left Cork, there had not been one pleasant exchange between Gerard and the others. Claire had tried her best to be friendly and gentle, but it fell on deaf ears. More than once, Gerard had snapped at poor Mary about the space her instruments took up, and she'd told Teresita her voice was giving her a headache.

'I'm not one bit annoyed. I just don't think it's befitting a nun to be conversing alone with...well, with someone like that.'

'Someone like what?' Claire asked, her voice light. While she was anxious not to antagonise the other nun, she also knew she would have to stand her ground.

'You know perfectly well what. Don't make me spell it out.' Gerard's eyes glittered with disdain.

'I don't, otherwise I wouldn't have asked you to explain.' Claire smiled.

'Fine. A native, a savage. Look, we are here to teach the children of the Catholic families who have settled in this dreadful place. I think we should stick to the job at hand and not involve ourselves with anything else. The likes of him are catered to in some other place, and they are presumably doing whatever is needed to tame them or whatever. I think we should stay out of it and stay away from them.'

Gerard's tone suggested she was issuing a decree from on high that she expected everyone else to follow without question. Claire knew that if she didn't establish herself as the person in charge now, not only would Gerard get worse, but the other three nuns in her care would be confused as to who to follow.

'I disagree. We are, as we know, all God's children regardless of where we come from or what colour our skin is. Jesus did not discriminate against anyone, and we are trying to follow in his footsteps, so I think opening our hearts to all people is how he would want us to behave.' Claire tried to stay conversational but firm.

Gerard coloured, a wash of dark crimson creeping up from her neck. Mother Patrick back at the old convent had warned Claire that Gerard was not a person to be trifled with nor underestimated, so her reputation preceded her. Claire didn't know if Gerard understood that she was aware of her history of violence towards the children in her care. It was apparently not a one-off incident either. 'Spare the rod and spoil the child' was the motto of many Reverend Mothers, so Gerard's behaviour must have been very far beyond the pale to have warranted, in effect, exile.

It had appalled her as a novice to see her fellow nuns beating children. She was sure that she could never do such a thing, and once she was qualified, she didn't. She was determined that it would not happen here. She knew there was a culture of physical punishment in schools, but in her heart of hearts, she knew it wasn't necessary. Little children wanted to please their elders, and as her mother used to say, 'You get a lot further with wine than with vinegar.' Praise and encouragement were the methods she used to teach, and they had served her well up to now. She hoped to instil that way of teaching in all the staff, even the bad-tempered Gerard.

'Well, *Sister* Claire' – Gerard's emphasis suggested Claire was not a Reverend Mother and therefore in no position of power – 'you can do what you wish, but I will not be engaging in any such interactions with anyone but the decent God-fearing people of this town.' She eyeballed Teresita, Mary and Helen. 'And I would suggest you three do the same. The McGraths, who have done so much to make us welcome, would not like it, and I'm sure the bishop would be horrified to think we were fraternising unnecessarily with people who have nothing to do with the job we came here to do.' She pushed her chair back and stood, indicating the conversation was over.

Claire wasn't going to let her win. 'Bishop McAuliffe' – she used her uncle's formal title – 'mentioned the Bundagulgi people to me on several occasions, and he feels strongly that they should be protected and cared for.' Claire knew she was stretching the truth a bit, but she needed to win this. 'And as for the McGraths, while we are very grateful to them, we must now paddle our own canoe, as it were. Daku seems like a very nice person, and I've told him he is very welcome here.'

'Yerra, 'tis true for you, Sister Claire. Sure aren't they grand people the same as ourselves?' Teresita had decided which horse she was backing. Claire gave up a silent prayer of thanks.

'I've never met a dark-skinned person before, but one of our missionary sisters wrote home often explaining about their customs and how they were so gentle and kind,' Mary chimed in.

'Those are Africans.' Gerard corrected her as if speaking to a particularly slow five-year-old. 'An entirely different continent.'

Mary blushed to be spoken to like that and mumbled, 'I did know that, I just meant...'

Helen placed her hand on the younger nun's arm and glared at Gerard. 'I'm sure the message of the Lord is as welcome here as it is in Africa. I served plenty of years in India and in Ghana too, so I know you're right. Those people were the grandest you'd ever meet. They had almost nothing, but they'd share what they had. And I'll tell you something for nothing – they never moaned or groaned the way we do, only got on with it. I've great time for them, so I do.'

Three on her side. Claire hated that it had come to a power struggle like this, but that's what it was.

CHAPTER 3

Claire pored over the school roll book, arranging the children into different classes. School would begin in four days' time, and all of the sisters were busy preparing their classrooms. Sister Mary would teach the younger classes; she was sweet and gentle and the little ones would love her. She would also teach music to everyone. Sister Helen would teach the middle group, those aged eight to eleven, and Sister Gerard would have the eleven- to thirteen-year-olds. Sister Teresita would have the high school–age children, those thirteen and up. Many children, Claire was told, would finish school around age fourteen and go to work for Mr McGrath, seemingly the area's sole employer. She had not given herself a class yet – she would oversee the operation and decide where she was most needed once they were up and running for a while.

Since the discussion about Daku, things with Gerard were even more frosty to say the least of it, but Teresita more than made up for it. She was waging a one-woman war on the rainbow lorikeets, beautifully colourful and cheeky birds that insisted on having loud screeching matches outside her window before dawn even broke. The nun's cells were individual, and each had a small bed, window, locker and wardrobe, but Teresita could be heard through the thin partition walls admonishing the birds that were utterly oblivious to her displeasure. It made Claire smile to hear her. So far Teresita had trapped several gruesome-looking spiders and removed with a stick a treacherous snake from outside the front door, and Claire was glad the older nun seemed fearless in the face of creatures that made her shudder.

'Sure, wasn't I brought up on a farm?' Teresita explained, though she pronounced it 'far-um'. 'I was forever catching rats and mice, so a few auld spiders and oversized worms aren't going to put the kibosh on me!'

She'd chuckled when Claire called her to remove a huge hairy spider out of the sink. Claire's family were farmers too, but her father didn't really expect the girls to do awful things like catch rats.

There was nothing Teresita couldn't do. She was, as Claire's father would have said, 'as handy as a small pot'. Daku was around often and was really obliging, and they could have asked him, but Teresita said not to bother him. She fixed anything broken and devised ingenious devices to make their lives easier. Like the other day, when they discovered that there were parts of the music stands missing – a packing case hadn't arrived – and Mary was distraught, Teresita came to her rescue, fashioning metal pins out of some wire she found, and now all the stands were fully assembled.

When Claire visited Gerard's classroom, Gerard refused offers of posters and pictures for the walls, and so her room looked drab and forbidding. There was only a blackboard onto which she had written the rules of the classroom; presumably the children would have to transcribe these into their exercise books. Apart from that, she had a particularly terrifying representation of the Shroud of Turin on the wall, a sepia and brown image of the face of Jesus as he carried the cross, a crown of thorns on his bleeding head. Though Claire felt such pity and pain at the idea of Jesus being treated like that, she wasn't convinced it was the most conducive-to-learning image that could have been chosen. But she let it go. With Gerard she would have to choose her battles wisely. Inexplicably, the only colour on the walls was a map of Ireland. Surely Gerard wasn't planning on teaching Irish geography to the children of Jumaaroo?

It wasn't until Claire noticed a leather strap with ominous bulging at the end – suggesting it had been reinforced with small metal balls to inflict maximum pain – hanging on a hook beside the blackboard that she felt compelled to say something. Dreading another altercation, she tried to inject authority into her voice. 'I don't anticipate a need for that, Sister Gerard,' she said, glancing at the strap.

'Don't you?' Gerard replied, busily stacking chalk and other school supplies in a cupboard, her offhand tone indicating exactly what she thought of Claire's opinions.

'No, I don't, and I'd rather you put it away actually.' Claire was quaking inside but determined not to back down.

Gerard stood and fixed her with an insolent glare. 'Would you rather that?' she asked, each word dripping sarcasm.

'Yes, I would. And as the principal of this school, I'm asking you to remove it. I do not want the children in our care to be physically reprimanded at all, and I certainly won't allow that leather strap to be used.'

Claire held Gerard's gaze. Gerard reminded her of one or two of the nuns that had taught her, women who seemed to enjoy inflicting pain on children. Most of her teachers had been kind, and while slapping was very much part of the school day, it was not usually hard and generally just with a ruler or a bare hand that didn't really hurt.

'I will use whatever disciplinary means I deem necessary in my own classroom,' the other nun said belligerently.

'Sister Gerard, are you questioning my authority? Because if you are, let me remind you, I have been appointed by the –'

'The Bishop of Brisbane, your uncle. Yes, we all know.' Gerard's tone was dismissive.

'On whose authority I run this school.' Claire ignored the implication that it was nepotism and not merit that had got her the position. 'So I'll ask you again, are you questioning my authority?'

Gerard smiled, the first Claire had seen in days, although it was more of a smirk than a smile. 'Oh, I wouldn't dare, *Sister* Claire. As you wish.' Gerard swept past her, her dark habit swishing on the polished timber floor. She removed the strap and placed it in a trunk behind her desk. It wasn't gone, and Claire was in no way confident she wouldn't use it, but for now it was at least out of sight.

'Thank you,' Claire said. 'It's important that the children learn in an environment where they're not afraid. Jean-Baptiste de La Salle, the patron saint of teachers, wrote that you cannot teach through fear, you can only teach through love. His writings are worth reflecting on, Sister, if you get time.' Before Gerard could retort and have the last word, Claire left the classroom.

Across the hall, Helen's room was as different from Gerard's as it was possible to be. She had covered the walls with paintings of her favourite book covers and brought an entire trunk of books with her, which she used to create a wonderful library in her classroom. Nuns took a vow of poverty; each of them was allowed only one trunk and a shipped tea chest, but Helen had far more than that. Several chests of books were waiting for her when they arrived, sent on from Ireland. She had all the classics, and even some modern children's books as well. Her classroom was arranged in a most interesting way. She had placed all of the desks in a circle around the room, rather than in rows facing forward. When Claire had popped her head round the door and registered her surprise at the layout, the other nun merely nodded and said she preferred it that way, that she liked to sit in the middle of the room, the class gathered around her.

'My goodness, but you've a lot of books. The children will be delighted to see so many stories to enjoy, I'm sure.'

'I hope so,' Helen replied, returning to her alphabetising. Her voice was quiet and gentle, and Claire wondered how on earth she would manage a class full of exuberant boys and girls who would much rather be outside playing or raiding the peach tree that grew in the schoolyard than sitting reading Charles Dickens.

'Well, the best of luck. You have the eight- to eleven-year-olds, and seeing some of them around the village in the past week or so, well, it looks like you might have your work cut out for you.'

'Active minds and active hands have no time for misbehaving,' Helen said with a gentle smile.

'These paintings are beautiful. Where did you get them?' Claire pointed to the walls where the covers of *Just William*, one of the books in the Doctor Dolittle series and *The Children of Odin* had been reproduced on canvas.

'I did them,' Helen replied quietly.

'Really? They are remarkably good. God bless your talent.'

'I love to paint. Always have, even since I was a child. I'm hoping I can take the children outside and do some life painting. Daku mentioned the Dreamtime art of his people, using the colours of nature to represent the time before memory. It sounds fascinating.'

'It really does. I'm sure the children would love that.' Claire looked around the still chaotic classroom, with books and art supplies, rolls of paper and pencils piled everywhere.

'How did you manage to get so many boxes out here? We only brought one box each?' Claire knew she was being nosy, but she was intrigued.

'My brother sent the books from our library at home, and some friends donated the art things.'

That was as much of an explanation as she was willing to give, it would seem, so Claire bade her good day and went on.

Teresita's room was the least organised. Bright sunshine flooded the space in a lovely warm, buttery light, and the desks and chairs were arranged all higgledy-piggledy. Pencils, T-squares and pots of glue were everywhere, and in the midst of it all, the nun was busy sawing some wood.

'Ah, Claire, 'tis yourself. Ideal. Hold that for me, will you?' She handed Claire a level and a hammer.

Claire suppressed a smile as Teresita pulled a pencil from her veil at the temple and marked the piece of timber she was cutting.

'What's that?' Claire asked, pointing at the project.

'More bookshelves. Sister Helen has so many books, and they are still in trunks because she has nowhere to put them, so I said I'd put a few bookcases together for her.'

The idea that Teresita's time might be better employed putting some kind of manners on her own classroom seemed lost on her, so Claire tactfully withdrew, leaving her to it.

Since everyone seemed busy with their own tasks, she decided to take a walk around the town. She took the opportunity whenever she could since arriving, and she was gradually getting a feel for Jumaaroo and its people in their day-to-day lives rather than as they were on the welcome day, all in their best clothes and on best behaviour.

She left the convent grounds and walked down the hill. As she made her way down towards the town's only street, she observed the bushland that pressed insistently at the edges of the settlement. It was all so very different to Ireland, which was lush and cool and green. This place with its red earth, strange tropical plants and colourful birds was as alien to her as the moon, but it had a beauty all its own and she was committed to making it work. There was a rawness to this place – the night sky lit up with stars in a way she'd never seen before, and the wildlife was incredible – but the heat was so hard to cope with. Everything was humid and dusty and so very hot.

As she mentally ticked off jobs in her head ahead of the opening day, something caught her gaze. Right before her was a kangaroo, the first she'd seen close up, and in the creature's pouch a curious little joey poked out, its ears twitching. The mother stood and stared, unafraid of a human so close by. Claire marvelled at the beauty of the creature. Of course she'd seen pictures in books, but they hadn't prepared her for how lovely kangaroos were – a gentle, pretty face, soulful eyes and such graceful movement. The creature's hindquarters were powerful, but when she loped off, it was slowly, seemingly taking her weight on her tail. Claire just stood and observed her, this majestic creature, so gently taking care of her baby. She felt a lump in her throat. Was this really happening? Here she was, a girl from Macroom, County Cork, in this wild, most strange place, as far from home as it was possible to go.

She walked on, and soon there were houses on either side of the street. She passed a garden with a beautiful tree, and the masses of delicate flowers blooming on it filled the air with fragrance. Inside the fence, a woman was on her hands and knees weeding.

'Good morning,' Claire said, and the woman looked up from the seedlings she was transplanting.

'Good morning.' The woman's English was accented. She looked friendly. She had dark hair and olive skin, and Claire judged her to be in her early thirties.

'That tree's fragrance is just glorious.' Claire pointed at the tree with its delicate flowers curling prettily outwards. 'What is it called, do you know?'

'Frangipani,' the woman answered.

'It's beautiful. So many new plants and flowers and animals here, it's like a different world.'

The woman stood and placed her hands on her lower back, stretching after being stooped over for so long. 'It is a different world, Sister, in more ways than you can guess.' She grimaced as she stretched. 'I was going to have a cold drink. Would you like one?'

'I would love it,' Claire said immediately.

The woman opened the garden gate and led her to the veranda on the other side of the wooden house. Though more modest than the McGraths', this house too was up on stilts.

'My name is Cassia. I am from Greece.' She held out her hand and Claire shook it warmly.

'My goodness, I've never met anyone from Greece before. I'm Sister Claire and I'm from Ireland.'

'I know.' Cassia smiled gently. 'I was at the parade to welcome you.'

'Ah, right.' Claire felt a little embarrassed that so much fuss had been made. 'Mr McGrath was very welcoming – everyone is.'

'It will take some time to adjust, but I'm glad you are happy so far.' She went inside the house, then emerged a minute later with a jug and two glasses.

Claire accepted a glass of lemonade, which looked wonderfully tart and cold. 'Mmm.' She sipped the drink gratefully, the cold lemon refreshing her. 'This is delicious.'

Cassia nodded. 'My mother made it for us when we were children

– we had a huge lemon tree in our garden – and now I make it for my boys.'

'So have you lived here long?' Claire asked.

'Yes. I married Stavros when I was eighteen and came here. He came back to Greece for a wife.' She winked and chuckled. 'He was born here, but his family and mine have known each other forever.'

'And how long did it take you to adjust?' Claire asked ruefully, aware of her red, sweating face.

'Oh, I don't mind heat. Greece too is hot. But here, ai, it is so sticky. Many years and some days still, and when I was pregnant with my boys, oh, it was so…urgh!' She flapped her hands and made a dramatic face to match her gesture. Claire liked her instantly.

'And how old are your boys now?'

'Darius is ten and Max is eight.'

'And where do they go to school?' Claire saw the shadow of loneliness cross Cassia's face.

'They have to board at Koraki Creek. It's a six-hour journey each way, so they stay there, but I miss them so much and they are so unhappy there. My husband wants to take Darius out next year, take him to work, but I want him to have a proper education and I don't want him to leave Max alone.'

'But surely the new school will solve that problem? Then the obvious thing is for both boys to attend our new school, and they can come home each evening.'

'I know, it would be.' She sighed. 'But the McGraths won't allow it.' Cassia seemed sure.

'But why ever not?' Claire asked. 'And why is it up to them?'

Cassia gave her a look that she couldn't decipher. 'None of the families that are Russians, Greeks, anything else are welcome. We're Greek Orthodox. They thought they might allow the Italians since they are Catholics, but it seems not. Assumpta has spoken and word has got around – nobody but Irish Catholics need apply.'

Claire stood up and placed her glass on the table. 'Well, that's just ridiculous. I was under the impression that the reason it was a school for Catholics was because the town was made up of Catholics, but if there are other Christian religions here as you say, and there is no school for miles, then we must open our doors to everyone. We are all Christians, so I'm sure it won't be a problem. Cassia, please do not worry. It's just a misunderstanding. I will sort this out.'

Cassia shook her head. 'I don't think you can. I have asked already.'

'Cassia, I'm happy to welcome all children –'

'With respect, Sister, you may be, but the McGraths decide. They have made it very clear, before you even got here, that it was for Catholics only, and only Irish too in reality.'

'But that's nonsense,' Claire said. 'I am the principal of the school, so I will decide who can attend, and I say any Christian children in the region are welcome. The Protestant school accommodated Catholic children until such time as a Catholic school was available, so we'll extend the same hand of friendship now. I'll contact the bishop imme-diately, but I'm quite sure he'll support me. He wouldn't like to hear of unnecessary hardship when we could alleviate it, I'm sure of it. It would be different if we were in a large urban situation where there were several options, but that isn't the case here.'

Cassia shrugged. 'I'd love it if you were right, of course I would, we all would, but...'

Claire drained her glass. 'I'm going to sort this out, Cassia, don't worry. Thank you for the delicious lemonade. Perhaps someday you can show me how to make it? I think we have a lemon tree on the convent grounds.'

'I'd be happy to.' Cassia grinned and took the glass.

CHAPTER 4

*A*ssumpta McGrath fumed. She'd sent Lockie, the useless imbecile Joseph had employed to do odd jobs, up to the school to see if what people were saying was true, and it seemed – incredibly – that it was. That small dumpy nun had set up a table and chair on the path outside the school with a sign saying, 'St Finbarr's School, Jumaaroo. Open enrolment today. All Christians welcome.'

Lockie had come back with news that all sorts were lining up to enrol. Greeks – that annoying Cassia especially – those Italians with all of their loud and wild children. Even the Russians from out beyond the creek had come in, putting their offspring's names down for the school. It was an outrage. What did that nun think she was doing?

Assumpta had made it very clear who would be attending the school. Joseph didn't care as such, but when the time came, he wouldn't want his children educated alongside all sorts, for goodness' sake. She knew that fat little bee, Sister Claire, was trouble when she met her; there was just something about her. She was barely five feet tall and just as wide, with a round face. She looked like a sweet little innocent nun, but Assumpta didn't trust her. The way she kept going on about the Aboriginals at the tea party was frankly embarrassing.

She'd tried to get her off the unsavoury topic, but she was relentless. And now this.

The only reason they even had a school was because of all Joseph had done to get it built. And the nuns showed up here with their stupid accents, surely put on for effect, and decided they could change everything? Not a shred of gratitude or understanding of how things were? Well, she wouldn't stand for it and that was that.

She bided her time all day, inwardly seething as the lines at the school grew longer as word got round. Joseph had to be approached with caution.

He came home after six, and Alice made him a drink. He'd changed into his relaxing clothes and was reading the paper on the veranda awaiting dinner. Assumpta made sure Alice had made his favourite, shepherd's pie. Kitty, the nanny, was bathing Julia and the babies, so for once the house was an oasis of calm. Now was the best time.

He didn't even look up when she joined him on the veranda. Even now, he took her breath away. He was easily the best-looking man in Jumaaroo, as well as the wealthiest and the most powerful. She loved how the women admired him and the men respected him. She might hate Jumaaroo, but Joseph McGrath was a prize worth winning. She bent down and kissed his cheek. He smelled of his woody cologne.

'Hello, dear, how was your day?' she asked.

'Fine,' he replied, never taking his eyes off the newspaper. He barely acknowledged her existence. Assumpta hid her hurt well; she was used to it by now. She longed for the amorous young man of their courtship, but Joseph was different now. It broke her heart to know that she had all the trappings of wealth and privilege but her husband behaved as if she was invisible. He didn't find her interesting, or charming, and no matter what lengths she went to with her looks, he never noticed.

He did take his conjugal rights twice a week, but even then, there was no intimacy. Joseph wanted something, he took it, and that was all there was to it. He was charming and funny to all he met out on the street, and he was universally adored, but he seemed to have none of that *bon vivant* left for his family when he got home. He often ate in his study, and though he patted the children on the head if he passed them, she knew that they didn't interest him either.

She feared he had other women. If he was discreet, then she would have to endure it, but she saw how he looked at that Greek woman, Cassia Galatas. She was so obvious. Her dresses were far too revealing and figure-hugging, and she was so rounded you could say she was overweight, but Assumpta could see the lust in men's eyes when they watched her at her stall on market day, selling the fruit she grew in her garden. Not that she did anything about it; she seemed devoted to that Stavros, who was a total dullard as far as Assumpta was concerned.

She'd written to her mother for advice in the early days, complaining about how backwards Jumaaroo was, telling her that Joseph seemed to have gone off her, but she got short shrift. Her mother adored Joseph even more than anyone else did, and flirted embarrassingly with him whenever they met. She of course had just told Assumpta to buck up – her answer for everything.

'Could I have a word about something, dear?' She tried to keep her tone light.

'Hmm?' he replied, still focused on an article in the paper. She read over his shoulder – it was something about Australia preparing for war. Seemed like nonsense. There wasn't going to be another war; it just made men feel important to speculate. Her brother Pius was in the army and was forever droning on about it. It was all anyone talked about these days. She found it so boring. As if anyone would be mad enough to invade Queensland. The spiders, snakes, sharks and jellyfish would drive them out long before an army could.

'It's about the school,' she said.

'What about it?' he asked, but she knew she only had a fraction of his attention. She thought quickly.

His profile was chiselled, and his dark wavy hair oiled back from his high forehead. His skin took the sun well, not like most Irishmen, and he stayed fit and lean. He took care of himself and enjoyed the admiring glances he got from both sexes, so she would appeal to his vanity.

'Well, you know how you built it for our community? I mean, without you, everyone would still be sending their children to board at Koraki Creek, and I know the mothers are so grateful to you for making a way for them to keep their little ones at home.'

He didn't respond, just began writing in the notebook he kept permanently in his pocket, transcribing something out of the newspaper.

'But there is a problem,' she continued, praying she'd timed it correctly.

He put the newspaper down and turned to her. 'What kind of problem?' he asked, the weariness in his tone suggesting she was boring him.

Assumpta swallowed. The next part of the conversation was crucial. 'Well, the nun, Sister Claire, is enrolling all of the children in the area. Greeks, Italians' – she played her trump card – 'even the Russians.'

'But she can't. It's a Catholic school,' he said smoothly.

Assumpta inwardly sighed with relief. He was on her side. 'Exactly. And that nun is deliberately going against your wishes for St Finbarr's by allowing all sorts in. I thought you'd want to know.'

He picked up the newspaper again. 'I'll have a word.'

She knew from his tone that the audience was over, but she had achieved her objective. 'Do you want to dine out here, or at the table with us?' she asked, trying to sound placatory. 'Alice has made shepherd's pie and Julia wants to show you –'

'In my study,' he replied, returning once again to the newspaper.

AFTER DINNER, Joseph sat back and poured himself the last glass of Midleton Very Rare, emptying the bottle. The whiskey distilled in County Cork was the finest in the world. He swirled the amber liquid round and round in the Waterford cut-glass tumbler, enjoying how the sunlight caught the glass, illuminating the whiskey inside, making it almost luminescent.

He only drank Irish whiskey – it was his only nod to patriotism – but this bottle was kept for very special occasions. He'd had a glass when Assumpta told him she was pregnant, not because he was thrilled to be a father or had more than a passing interest in her, but to celebrate his way in. The Prendergast family were well-got. The father, James, was a banker, and they had a nice house in Brisbane. He smiled at the memory of himself, suitably shamefaced, confessing his crime to Assumpta's father, throwing himself on the man's mercy, apologising and looking mortified and begging for the darling girl's hand in marriage.

The two men had sat opposite each other, this very desk he now had in his own office between them, as James Prendergast accepted his sincere apologies and proposal of marriage to his only daughter. The deal was sweetened with an envelope of cash. He'd heard of Prendergast's gambling debts before he set about seducing his daughter.

After that, it was easy. He'd married into one of Brisbane's leading families, Catholic too. It was just a matter of cleverly and unobtrusively climbing the ladder; the first rung was all he'd needed. And all it had cost him was the thousand dollars he'd taken from the pockets of a lucky punter at the races, some stupid young pup with more money than sense. He'd fought back, but not hard enough. Too much champagne in the winner's enclosure probably, and anyway, few men were a match for Joseph – he'd had enough experience over the years to dispatch any opponent. Thankfully, these days those skills were never called upon. Joseph had left the man bleeding in an alleyway.

Old James Prendergast used that thousand dollars to pay his debts...only to accrue more, of course. It was helpful that his father-in-law was so weak. Addicts were an easy mark.

Now he was free of his debts to the Prendergasts, James was dead, and Assumpta served him well enough as a wife. She did the necessary. And actually, on the subject of the school, she was right for once. If that nun needed to be reined in, he'd enjoy doing it.

* * *

JOSEPH MCGRATH KNOCKED on the convent door the following Sunday morning. He liked to call to his adversaries at odd times when he had a power struggle to win; it put them on the back foot. He'd had doubts about this little nun from the beginning – she seemed too young – but the bishop had insisted. She was his niece or something, so Joseph could understand that. It was how the world worked; you looked after your own. But he would need to nip this nun in the bud before she started getting too many notions of herself.

He heard footsteps, and then the door opened to reveal another nun, the little mousy one. He'd forgotten her name.

'Ah, good morning, Sister. I wonder if I might have a word with Sister Claire?' He crossed the threshold, stood in the hallway and removed his hat, hanging it on the hook of the antique hallstand. The builders he'd employed had done a nice job on the convent. It was bright and allowed for lots of air to flow through, and the nuns had decorated it with statues and holy pictures. It smelled of beeswax, and there was a hushed, reverential atmosphere, just as he remembered about the institutions from his own childhood.

'I'll go and find her, Mr McGrath,' the nun said, and he was gratified to hear the note of deference in her voice. She knew her place.

'Thank you, Sister, I'd appreciate it.' He smiled warmly and she returned it, blushing. His charm even worked on nuns.

He mused as he waited, examining the holy pictures on the walls – how did nuns manage to make their places smell the same even thousands of miles apart? It was weird. All convents, monasteries, churches, they all smelled the same no matter where in the world you were.

Uninvited, he opened the door of the first room on the right, a reception room where there were some armchairs, a sideboard and an oval mahogany table. He went in and strolled around. He was examining the small library of books when he heard Sister Claire enter. Deliberately, he finished reading the blurb on the back of a book, only returning it to the shelf when he was finished. Then he turned the full beam of his attention on her.

'Ah, Sister Claire, I trust you are all settling in well?' He wanted her to be under no illusions as to whom was hosting who here. She might have notions of upperosity, but he'd soon put an end to that.

'Yes, thank you, Mr McGrath, very well indeed. The convent is most comfortable, and the school is taking shape nicely. How can I help you this morning?'

'Oh, I hope it's I who can help you, Sister.' He chuckled. 'Might we have a cup of tea?' He thought he caught a slight hesitation. Was she ready for him? Did she know what was coming? She was hard to read.

'I'm afraid breakfast is long over and we all have much to do before school opens tomorrow, so if you don't mind, we might just get on. I hope you understand?'

Joseph never allowed the smile to slip. 'Of course. No problem.'

She waited expectantly for him to speak.

This wasn't how he wanted it to go. 'There seems to be a bit of a mix-up, so I wanted to come and clear it all up in person.'

Her face was inscrutable, and still she said nothing.

She was infuriating all right. A quizzical smile, nothing you could find fault with. She might be a small chubby nun, but if her current demeanour was anything to go by, she was shaping up to be a bit of a challenge. No matter. He'd soon have her eating out of his hand, one way or another.

'Regarding enrolment. This is a Catholic school, as you know, and is under the auspices of the diocese, so it is only right and proper that the enrolment would reflect that. I'm sure you understand.'

She paused, and then spoke, her tone unequivocal and with no trace of the deference he was used to. 'What I understand, Mr McGrath, is that this school is badly needed. There are so many families that have no option but to send their children away to boarding school. But now that we have this magnificent building here, then I don't see why we cannot offer a quality Christian education to all who need it and spare families the heartbreak of being separated unnecessarily.'

He was going to have to play this differently. She wasn't going to be charmed or intimidated, so he would have to pull rank. 'Yes, of course, that is why it was built. For Catholic families. Look, Sister

Claire, you are new here, and you are a long way from County Cork now, so please let yourself be guided by me in this matter. This place is wild frontier land. It works because we have found a way to live side by side. All the people of this earth have come here to make their fortune, and it is successful only because everyone knows their place. Upsetting that delicate balance can only lead to strife – believe me, I know.'

Nothing in the nun's demeanour changed; she was still pleasant and businesslike. 'And people's places are set in stone, are they? Is the role of the Church not to nurture those in it and to offer an alternative to others? Their inclusion in this school may result in many of them converting to Catholicism, and would that not be a blessing? And even if they don't, they are all Christians, followers of Jesus Christ, so surely that unites rather than divides us?' She asked gently, 'Are we not all created equal in the likeness and image of God?'

'Next thing you'll be telling me you want to let the Chinese in.' He laughed.

'If they are Christian, I don't see why not?'

That's when he heard it, the slightly unsure note. She was on shaky ground there and she knew it.

'Have you ever even seen a Chinaman, Sister? If you had, you wouldn't be so sure of that, unless God's suddenly got slitty eyes.' He chuckled at his own joke, but she remained impassive.

She spoke quietly but firmly. 'All men, women and children are beautiful in the eyes of the Lord, Mr McGrath, and I will be offering places at St Finbarr's to all who want them. Travelling so far and children being away from their parents when it is unnecessary is a hardship we can alleviate, and as a man who is serving the people so diligently, I'm sure that is something you would endorse. Now, if that's everything, I must get on.'

Joseph did not like this woman, and he was not going to be undermined by her. He felt his fury rise. He'd had nothing but adversaries all of his life, and he was damned if he was going to be beaten by a tiny round nun.

'Look,' he said, straight-talking now, no more charm. 'This school is not to be opened to anyone but Catholics. Irish families are to be given preference, and only when and if there is space – and I have calculated the numbers, so I do not anticipate there being any space – could another Catholic family be enrolled. As for the rest of them, they'll have to make their own arrangements. Am I making myself clear?'

Sister Claire's brow furrowed. Something was confusing her it would seem.

'But, Mr McGrath, this school is in my control, not yours. You donated this very generous gift to the Church, and now the Church runs it.' Her tone suggested she was explaining something perfectly obvious to someone who wasn't really capable of comprehending it. 'And I answer to the Bishop of Brisbane, who has expressly stated in a telegram to me that he is more than happy to accommodate all children who wish to attend. Yes, we are a Catholic school, and our teaching will reflect that absolutely, but did Jesus not say, "Suffer the little children, to come unto me, for theirs is the kingdom of heaven"? Bishop McAuliffe feels as I do that exposure to the Catholic faith can only be a good thing, and perhaps the inclusion of other Christian children may result in conversions. But even if it doesn't, I do not think, Mr McGrath, that our Lord meant only specific children from a specific place when he said that. So I'm afraid I cannot comply with your request. Now as I said, I must get on, lots to do. And I'm sure you wish to get back to your family.' She waddled past him out into the hall and opened the front door.

He should have been furious, but instead he found himself amused. So rarely these days did anyone dare defy him. It was kind of refreshing. He'd break her, for sure, but it wasn't going to be as easy as he'd first thought. And if she had the bishop backing her, he'd have to tread carefully. He'd met William McAuliffe several times and realised he was a man not to be trifled with. Not only was he powerful in his own right, but he was on very friendly terms with Cardinal Mannix of Melbourne. Joseph chose his enemies carefully when he could, and taking on senior Church figures was not a smart move, so he knew he would have to be careful. She might be the bishop's dumpy niece, but there was more than one way to skin a cat and he had not achieved all he had by being impetuous, so he would make a tactical withdrawal for now.

'Indeed I do, Sister, indeed I do.' He put his hat back on. 'Good day to you.' He gave her a smile and a nod and walked out the door.

CHAPTER 5

The early weeks at St Finbarr's flew by, and the children were settling in nicely. Sister Mary ensured there was an almost constant cacophony of music, though Claire had to admit that sometimes it sounded much less than melodic. The children seemed very happy to be playing all of the instruments she'd shipped out or that had been donated by the grateful families whose children were now happily attending St Finbarr's, so there was almost a complete orchestra now assembled in the school hall.

Sister Helen's classroom door was always closed, and Claire didn't want her to think she didn't trust her, so she was letting her get on with things. She observed the children as they came and went to her lessons, and they seemed very happy.

This morning, however, she faced two difficult tasks. Several parents had approached her, and there were two major issues, neither of which she had any idea of how to solve.

The first was Sister Teresita. The children loved her, but they had absolutely no idea what she was saying most of the time. The mothers who approached her were very quick to explain that they liked the nun very much, as did their children, but when they were doing their homework, they didn't understand it because they couldn't make out the nun's thick accent.

Claire stood at the window, looking out at the playing field, and thought about how best to bring it up without hurting Teresita's feelings.

Teresita was in her fifties and had spoken like that all of her life. She made sense in mid-Cork, just about, but out here she might as well be from Japan. The mothers and their children weren't exaggerating; she'd seen it with her own eyes as Teresita explained how to play hurling. The nun was a huge fan of the game, her brothers all being county players of the national Irish sport, and so she'd actually made the hurling sticks she needed to have two teams and was delighting the boys and girls with her instruction, even if they were mostly mystified.

'Aren't you supposed to use ash for hurleys?' Mary had asked Teresita one evening over dinner.

'Yerra, you are, but sure 'twill have to be somethin' else because there's no ash out here that I can see. Daku gave me this other stuff. I don't know what it is, but sure 'tis better than nothin'. 'Tisn't as springy as our ash, but 'twill do right enough. 'Tis trying to find bits long enough is what has me rightly vexed. They need to be three feet long at least, and 'tisn't easy to find. Daku is on the lookout for another kind of tree, I forget what he called it now, some Aboriginal name, so we might have a cut off that if he can find it.'

'Daku showed me how to make paint from nuts. It makes the most beautiful ochre colour,' Helen interjected. When all eyes turned to her, surprised at her interjection, she blushed, saying, 'He knows everything about the bush.'

Mary had taken on the role of cook, and they were delighted. She had a really light hand, and her cakes and breads were delicious. 'He's marvellous. He gave me some vegetables yesterday. I'd never seen them before, but I'm going to cook them tonight.'

Meals and prayer were the only times they got together as the school day was so busy, so Claire wanted those occasions to feel as relaxed as possible.

She gazed down at the playing field from her office. After her showdown with McGrath, she had no option but to admit anyone who came claiming to be Christian. She had no idea whether the Chinese children were or not – she'd heard a rumour they were Buddhists or something – but their parents so badly wanted them to come to St Finbarr's that they said they were Christian. She had no way of checking, and anyway, she would not refuse them, not after being so adamant with the mayor.

Children with Italian, Greek, Russian and Chinese names intermingled with the O'Haras and McGoverns as they tried to figure out the rudiments of the fastest field sport in the world under the confusing but enthusiastic tutelage of Teresita. Claire winced as she saw young Eileen O'Hara swing her hurley wildly and poor Chen Li get a fine wallop on the shoulder. He seemed to recover quickly, however. Teresita could be heard roaring instructions, a whistle round her neck as she careered all over the pitch.

'Get in there, Darius, pull hard on him! That's the lad, don't be a bit afraid of hurting him – he's no relation of yours!' she bellowed at Cassia's boy, who showed incredible aptitude for the game. 'Go on, Dmitri, you'll catch her! In with the shoulder – that's it!' Dmitri Okefski was shorter than the girl he was tackling, Anna O'Mahony, but he was powerful and poor Anna lost possession. The sliotars had been posted out from Ireland, and the children were getting used to playing with the hard leather ball that really hurt if you got in the way of a blazer of a puc.

Claire knew that the children had no idea what the phrase 'blazer of a puc' meant, but if it was achieved and the sliotar was sent up the pitch at speed, Teresita cackled, 'Up the field, that was a blazer!' with delight, so they knew it was a good thing. They loved to please her, so they went at the game with gusto.

Some parents were concerned. The game seemed rough, and it was, especially for girls. But Claire overruled them and assured them the children would be fine. She hoped she was right.

The accent was a big problem in the classroom though. Poor Teresita had no idea why they couldn't understand her; she was speaking perfectly clearly as far as she was concerned. Claire would have to try to give her some elocution lessons, but the thought didn't fill her with enthusiasm.

The other issue was worse though. Gerard had not taken long to revert to type. She ignored the Catholic children who were not Irish Catholics and never asked them questions, though she did correct their work. She was violent and mean with the Russians and Greeks, and she refused to acknowledge the Chinese children at all.

The Chinese mothers in general didn't speak English and the fathers were away at work, so it was Cassia who told Claire what was going on. The Chinese children did their work diligently, but the nun wouldn't even touch their exercise books and treated them as if they were invisible.

Claire was wondering how best to handle that when she got the news that Gerard had beaten Cassia's boy, Max. The child was quiet and anxious anyway, and now he was terrified to come to school. Gerard had reinstated the leather strap and had punished the boy in front of the class. In his distress, he'd wet his trousers, and she'd made him sit in the wet clothes for the rest of the day.

Cassia and Stavros had come up to the convent the previous evening, distraught for their boy, and Claire promised she would deal with it. But how?

Reluctantly she left the window, smiling as there was great cheering for Li, who had scored a goal. She had learned that Chinese people's surnames came first, as the group of Chinese children who enrolled had explained to everyone in their classes at the first assembly how they wished to be called. The first day confirmed what she already knew, that adults were the ones who put barriers of class and colour in the way of friendships. The children of all backgrounds sat around and introduced themselves, told everyone a bit about who they were and where their families had come from, and nobody had an issue. Except Gerard. She was furious at their inclusion, though she masked it beneath an air of sanctimonious derision.

The bell rang for lunchtime, and the children would all pour into the schoolyard within minutes. There were several large trees that provided welcome shade as they sat eating their sandwiches.

Claire sighed. Now was as good a time as any, she supposed. She left the office and walked down the corridor just as children were being released for break time. She found Gerard in her classroom, deserted now of children, marking exercise books, and the nun looked up as she entered. Her small grey eyes were set close together, and there was a prominent mole on her left cheek. She was rotund, so her face could have looked jolly but it didn't, and her thin lips never seemed to smile.

'Sister Claire, what can I do for you?' she asked, her tone suggesting that Claire's needs were the furthest thing from her mind. She returned her gaze to the copious red pen marks she was putting on some unfortunate child's work.

Claire decided that straight-talking was the only way. 'You punished Max Galatas yesterday, and the child was so upset he wet his trousers, which you did not allow him to go home to change. On top of that, you are ignoring the non-Irish children in your class.'

Gerard never looked up from her marking. The silence hung between them, toxic.

Realising that the other nun didn't intend to answer, Claire spoke again. 'This is not acceptable and not how I want this school run. I want us all to get along. We have an arduous task ahead of us here, and any discord between us, or wild discrepancies in how we interact with the pupils and their parents, cannot be helpful.'

Still nothing.

'Sister Gerard, please stop your work. This is important.' Claire could hear the note of frustration in her voice despite her best efforts to remain calm. The woman was infuriating.

'To you maybe,' Gerard replied, and continued correcting, her savage red pen crossing things out furiously. Only the whites of her knuckles gripping the pen showed she was in any way put out.

'Are you saying it doesn't matter to you that a child cried himself to sleep last night, terrified to come to school today, humiliated and embarrassed in front of his peers? You don't care that children feel isolated and rejected when you refuse to even speak to them in class? How can you call yourself a teacher and be like this? I don't understand it!' Claire was desperate to get through to her, but she was hard as flint.

Slowly, the other nun took the lid of her pen and screwed it on, replacing it on the side of her blotter. 'Frankly, Sister Claire, whether or not you understand me is of no consequence or interest to me. I am a Catholic nun and a Catholic teacher, and I will teach Catholic children. That is the role I am trained for, the one I intend to continue with.' Her face was a mask. 'The other people you have allowed into this school have no business here. Their parents sent them to St Finbarr's out of laziness. They are parasites, leeching off the good nature of Mr McGrath and other good Irish Catholics who paid for this institution. They're making a fool of you, and you can't even see it. You may be willing to be taken advantage of, but I am not. I will teach those for whom this school was built – nobody else.'

'But that's ridiculous!' Claire exploded; she couldn't help herself. 'You simply cannot take that approach! I won't have it! I'll –'

'You'll what? Write to your uncle again? A long whining letter about how you can't manage me? Have me reprimanded? Dismissed?' She smirked, but it never reached her eyes. 'You forget where we are, Sister Claire. We have been landed into this place, and nobody cares how we do it, but we are expected to run this school. You don't want to go running to the bishop telling him you can't manage now, do you? You were so proud to be given this school, delighted to have a big fuss made of you, and your silly pride won't allow you to admit defeat.'

A toxic silence hung in the air.

'I don't care what you think about me, but I will not tolerate what you are doing,' Claire said slowly.

'And what is it you imagine you can do to me?' Gerard's eyes glittered with malice.

'I will have you sent home in disgrace. We all know you left under a cloud – that's why you are here. But my uncle trusts me. He knows I am not a vindictive person, nor a dishonest one. If you do not mend your ways, I will tell him the truth – that you are excessively violent, that the children are terrified of you and that you are openly discriminating against children. He'll believe it one hundred percent, because after all, this is not the first time. This is your final warning. If you do not adopt a better attitude, I will ensure that you are sent back to your convent, where you will take up another role because you will have proved time and time again that you are unfit to be around children.'

The colour drained from Gerard's face. Checkmate. She knew Claire wasn't bluffing, and the idea of being reduced to the status of a skivvy would kill her, she was such a snob. In some orders, Claire knew there was a hierarchy. Those nuns who came from wealthy backgrounds were trained as teachers and nurses, while those not so well off were given the job of serving them.

Claire could see she was seething. 'So,' she went on, 'as of this afternoon, you teach *all* of the children in this classroom, giving each one *equal* attention. You are not nasty or rude to anyone. You make no derogatory remarks about the pupils personally, their families or their race. And this' – she crossed the room and took the leather strap – 'is coming with me and will not be replaced. You are forbidden from using any form of physical punishment. Am I making myself clear?'

She could see Gerard weighing up her options and soon coming to the conclusion that she had none, at least for now. But Claire was well aware that even if she won this round, she was now at war, and Gerard was a very powerful adversary. Claire had already made an enemy of the McGraths, and Gerard would surely capitalise on that, but Claire had to do right by these children.

'Well?' she asked again.

'Fine.' Gerard spat the word, sweeping past Claire out of the room, slamming the door so hard the map of Ireland fell off the wall.

CHAPTER 6

*C*laire made no remark about Gerard not joining them for dinner, and though she'd not discussed the earlier events with the others, she knew they had heard something.

As they were about to say grace before the meal, they heard a loud knocking on the front door. Claire sighed. She was tired and hungry and longed for a meal and an early night. Mary got up to answer it, but Claire placed her hand on her arm. 'I'll go,' she said.

At the door was a very disreputable-looking man and a small dark-skinned girl. The man looked to be in his early forties, with a straggly beard and hair tied back in a ponytail. He wore rough trousers, torn and dirty, and what looked like an undershirt that might once have been white.

'G'day.' He nodded at Claire and then nudged the little girl, who was dressed in a faded blue dress and had her dark hair tied untidily in two bunches on either side of her head. She had a wide smile. 'Right-o, Miss, say what you gotta say,' the man instructed her.

'I want to go to school,' the child said confidently.

'Do you now?' Claire smiled at the little girl. 'And would you like to come to this school?'

'Yeah. They said you let in everyone, and I want to come.'

The man suppressed a smile and Claire caught his eye. 'Well, my name is Sister Claire. And you are?' She looked at the child.

'Jannali McKenzie, and this is my dad, Gordie.'

'Nice to meet you, Mr McKenzie, and you too, Jannali.' Claire thought quickly. Allowing the orthodox in was one thing, and letting in the Chinese was really pushing the boat out, but this child looked at least half Aboriginal. The McGraths, and everyone else in Jumaaroo, she suspected, would have a fit. She thought about Gerard, and made a decision. 'Please, come in.'

She led them into the drawing room and offered them a seat, but they declined. She took her notebook out. 'Why would you like your daughter to come to this school, Mr McKenzie?' she began.

A flash of doubt crossed his face, then he spoke. 'My mate Daku works here, and he reckons you're all right. The McKenzies were Catholics, but I don't hold with your church – all a load of old cobblers, if you ask me. To begin with, I thought you and Joseph McGrath were cut from the same cloth, but Jannali here – she's seven, by the way – is heart set on it. She's been watching you all every day through the fence. She reckoned it looked good, so she said she wanted to ask you.'

Claire fought the urge to have him explain himself on the subject of the mayor. This man was a stranger, and judging by his appearance, he might be a bit unreliable. But she had to admit liking him for all of that. His attitude was so different from the others, who were so anxious their children would be accepted that they were overly deferential. She found that despite his bluntness, she warmed to the man, and the girl was delightful.

'And are you a Christian, Jannali? Do you believe in Jesus?' Claire asked gently.

Jannali glanced at her father, who remained silent. 'My mum is a Bundagulgi woman and my grandfather is Woiduna, the elder of our tribe. But his family do, I reckon.' She jerked her head in the direction of her father, and both Claire and Gordie again had to suppress a smile. 'So I'm probably half Christian.'

Claire stood before her. 'Well, everyone here believes in God our saviour, and we pray often. Jesus and the Blessed Virgin are part of our lives every day. If you are happy to join us and accept that, then we'd be happy to offer you a place.'

Jannali's face cracked into a wide white-toothed grin. 'See?' She turned to her father. 'I told ya she'd let me in. You reckoned I'd have to go out to old Russell at Trouble Bay, but you don't learn nothing there, and I want to learn heaps of stuff and play that game with the sticks, so I'm gonna do it here.'

'And you are happy with that?' Claire asked Gordie quietly as Jannali looked at an onyx solitaire set resting on a mahogany side table, a gift from one of the grateful Chinese families.

He shrugged. 'She's a free spirit, that one, and she usually gets what she wants. But yeah, I heard you're all right. You stuck it to Joseph McGrath, and that's good enough for me, so I reckon, yeah, it's OK.' He spoke with his back half to Jannali, only just barely audible. 'But there's something you should understand. She's a half-caste, and they are still rounding them up – churches, the government – taking kids to missions. Her mother and me, well, we're not that keen on her being out of our sights, to be honest, but Daku was just like her – his father was a Scottish stockman and his mother Bundagulgi – and he reckons she'll be safe here.'

'Well, if you're asking me if I'd allow anyone to take her away, then I can assure you I wouldn't. But surely it isn't as you suggest?' Claire was appalled.

'It's exactly as I suggest.' He was firm. 'They reckon the ones with the whiter skin have a better chance of being assimilated into their world, not that they'd ever be really accepted of course. Daku only got the job here 'cause he's half white. He got back. It took him years, poor bugger. His mother never got over it – they dragged him from her arms. We're careful where we let her go, but he said you're all right, and my kid's like a terrier once she gets an idea in her head.' He stopped as Jannali approached them.

'Li Chen said you give out lollies.'

'Well,' Claire replied in a faintly admonishing tone – the girl would have to learn to be a little more respectful – 'if you come here, you must call me Sister Claire, and I only give out lollies on very special occasions. Now, you will be in Sister Mary's class, and she loves music, so would you like that?'

Jannali nodded. 'Are there other blackfellas here?'

Claire knew by now the language of the Aboriginals. Daku frequently used those words, whitefellas and blackfellas, which weren't derogatory terms, just how they distinguished native people from Europeans. 'No, you'll be our first one, so you'll be very special indeed.' Claire smiled at the plucky little girl and hoped she was right. White parents having their children mix with other nationalities was one thing, but she suspected they wouldn't take to having a half-Aboriginal child in the class. Claire wasn't too worried. It would be another battle, no doubt, but she'd manage. Part of her wanted to see the McGraths' faces when they got the news.

'So can I come tomorrow?' Jannali asked as they left.

'Why not?' Claire smiled.

* * *

THE FOLLOWING MORNING, Claire rang the bell at nine and gathered all the children into their places outside the classrooms. They deposited their lunches in the shade and formed an orderly line. To Claire's astonishment, Jannali was already in Mary's line and was talking animatedly with some of her classmates.

The children all filed into class, some of the older ones noting the black-skinned child but nobody mentioning it. Claire spent the day doing paperwork, and all was well until the end of the day, when she saw Gerard storming down the hill to the town.

Once again, Gerard didn't join them for vespers or dinner. It was common by now for there just to be four of them, so nobody commented. Mary was delighted with Jannali, as she was such a bright, funny little girl, and Teresita told them how she marched right up to her and asked when she could start the game with the sticks.

Once they had washed up, Claire wrote a letter home to her parents. She was about to go join the others for compline in the little chapel when, to her surprise, she saw Assumpta McGrath and three other mothers coming up the hill. Claire went to the door to greet them, dreading what was sure to be a confrontation about Jannali.

She opened the door before they could knock. 'Mrs McGrath, ladies. It's late that you are out for a stroll.' She smiled.

'We need a word,' Assumpta McGrath said, barging past Claire into the drawing room, her little sheep following her timidly. Claire recognised all of them, as they all had children attending St Finbarr's. They all very much looked like they would rather not be there.

'Certainly. What about?' Claire remained courteous despite the other woman's rudeness.

'We have put up with your antics for long enough, admitting all and sundry into our school, mixing with our children! We were trying to see it from your point of view, giving you the benefit of the doubt, but you have crossed a line now. Honestly, I... I'm actually speechless! When I discovered today that you let a native in, that half-caste belonging to Gordie McKenzie and that Abbo, well... I... Surely you can see how inappropriate that is?'

Assumpta had none of her cold haughtiness now; the woman looked fit to explode. Claire had to suppress a giggle. The others gazed at the carpet behind her, terrified this would reflect on their own children, no doubt, but helpless in the face of a McGrath decree.

'Do you mean Jannali?' Claire asked, knowing full well who she meant.

'I don't know her name, nor do I care,' Assumpta spat. 'But she is not to return to this school tomorrow, do I make myself clear?' Her nostrils flared, and her cheeks were a vivid pink; she exuded indignation from every pore. 'She can go out to the mission with the rest of them if they want her taught to read or whatever. This is supposed to be a Catholic school, and you are letting in all sorts of so-called Christians, but she's...well, she's not of our type. Either way, she can't stay here.'

'That won't be possible, I'm afraid, Mrs McGrath.' Claire kept her voice low and calm. 'Jannali's father is Catholic, and therefore so is she. She qualifies perfectly for St Finbarr's, so she will be staying.'

'I will not allow it. I'm putting my foot down for once and for all...'

'Mrs McGrath.' Claire took the other woman gently by the elbow and led her back towards the front door. 'It is not up to you to allow it or not. Enrolment in this school is solely my domain, so I'll thank you to take your leave now as I am late for my prayers. Good night to you.'

Assumpta was furious, but she knew when she was beaten.

'Ladies.' Claire nodded as the others followed her out.

* * *

THE FOLLOWING MORNING, Joseph was sitting at his desk, listening intently for once. Assumpta was apoplectic at the way the nun had treated her – practically threw her out on the street by all accounts.

'Fine, I'll deal with it,' he said as she went on and on. 'Leave it to me. Now I've things to do.' He ushered her out of his office.

'It's intolerable. I am a laughing stock, and by association, so are you, Joseph. If she'll speak to your wife like that, in front of people too, well...'

He placed his hand on the small of her back, giving her a shove. 'I *said* I would deal with it.' He shut the door, leaving her no doubt seething outside it.

He was no sooner back at his desk when he was disturbed once again, this time by several women's screams. Sighing in frustration, he went downstairs. At his front door was the old fool, Woiduna, this time with a huge dead male iguana in his arms, the creature three or four feet long, dripping blood and slime on the carpet. As he came downstairs, he could hear the old man bellowing over the screams of Assumpta, the nanny and the maid.

'You done this, the poison from your mine in our water! You are killing our fish, killing our animals, cutting off our water!' Woiduna barged in, confronting Joseph. 'I warned you! I curse you, I curse your family, your children. Don't sleep easy in your bed, McGrath. We're coming for you, as we've had enough!'

Joseph nodded to Big Bill McAllister, his handyman, and that idiot

Lockie, who had come running at all the commotion. 'Get him off my property.'

The two men wrestled Woiduna to the ground, McAllister punching the old man hard in the kidneys. They dragged him away.

'Joseph, the carpet!' Assumpta cried as she ran to him, but he shook her off and went upstairs.

He poured himself a whiskey and watched Lockie and Big Bill drag the old Abbo, still protesting, away. Big Bill looked up, and Joseph simply nodded. Between Woiduna's grandchild in the school and the old man having the audacity to come to his house and threaten him, Joseph decided he'd had enough. He was sick of that whole family.

CHAPTER 7

$\mathcal{H}$elen and Claire were walking back to the convent after morning break. Teresita and Mary had taken the entire school to the field for hurling practice ahead of a big blitz, in which it seemed every team in the school would play everyone else or something. Claire wasn't too sure, but Teresita seemed determined, so she let her at it. Claire stopped – a child was in the playground when everyone should be gone back to class. She and Helen crossed the yard to investigate.

'Jannali?' Claire said. The little girl was curled up in a ball, clearly upset. Claire's first thought was that Gerard had said or done something to hurt the child.

Jannali looked up, her normally smiling face tear-stained. 'I wasn't going to come to school, but then I couldn't stay at home either. I... I can't...' Her voice caught with emotion, and she could barely get the words out.

'What is it?' Claire asked as Helen gently helped the child up and gave her a handkerchief. 'Tell me and we'll fix it together. There are very few problems one of my special lollies can't solve.' She tried to get a smile out of the child; Jannali had quite the sweet tooth.

Jannali shook her head, refusing the colourfully wrapped sweet.

Claire caught Helen's eye. Something more than the usual was wrong. Out of the corner of her eye, she saw Daku, and he beckoned Helen over. Claire stayed with Jannali, who was still distraught. Daku and Helen had a brief conversation and then walked towards the nun and the child together.

Helen led Claire away as Daku picked Jannali up, and she buried her head in his neck. The man murmured to the child in a language Claire couldn't understand.

'Woiduna is dead,' Helen said quickly. 'The elder of the Bundagulgi. His body was found this morning in a ravine. He'd been beaten. He's Jannali's grandfather, and they are all devastated.'

'What? I can't believe it!' Claire felt for the little girl. She talked about Woiduna all the time, and she clearly adored him.

'I'm going to take her home – she needs her mum,' Daku said as they approached.

'I'll go with you,' Helen said, and Claire shot her an appreciative glance. It wasn't that she didn't trust Daku, but Jannali was in her care and she wouldn't normally give any child to anyone but their parents.

Claire nodded and rubbed the child's head. 'Jannali, Daku told me about Woiduna. I'm so sorry. I know how much you loved him and he loved you too.'

The child raised her head from Daku's neck and nodded, her little face sad. 'He's not in heaven,' she said. 'He's gone to the Dreaming ancestors.'

Claire just nodded and closed the little girl's hands over two lollies. She watched as they walked away, walking close together, Daku carrying Jannali and Helen holding the child's hand.

As Claire turned, her heart heavy, she saw Gerard, standing at her classroom window, observing the scene as well, but without a shred of compassion on her hard face.

* * *

RUSSELL GARDINER STOOD at his window at the Trouble Bay mission and watched yet another group of Bundagulgi people coming up the path. He knew it was wrong, but he cursed Joseph McGrath. The Irishman denied everything of course, but Russell knew exactly what he was doing. The land the Bundagulgi people lived on was valuable, and McGrath wanted it, either for mining, logging or farming – Russell wasn't sure which yet. The Irishman was using every trick in the book to drive the native people off their own land. Though McGrath would never get his own hands dirty – he was too clever for that – Russell had no doubt that he was behind each of the attacks.

It began with fires, which made the land uninhabitable. The Bundagulgi burned land themselves from time to time, he didn't dispute that, but the extent of the fires, and the timing of them, wasn't the work of Aboriginals. They knew when to burn and where to do it safely, protecting their shelters and water. They performed strategic and ceremonial burns, knowledge passed on through forty thousand years of habitation of this place. They burned in ever-increasing circles, allowing the wildlife time to leave those areas. These new fires were destroying everything, and killing lots of the animals the Bundagulgi needed for survival.

McGrath held a public meeting, said the fires were caused by over-enthusiastic natives and had got out of control. He expressed concern for the houses and farms of those in the hinterland, and he made all the right noises about investing in water pumps and fire hoses to ensure that such bushfires could be fought by the townspeople of Jumaaroo. But it was nothing more than empty words.

The community walked away thinking how lucky they were to have Joseph McGrath taking care of them, how they'd be lost without him, and thanking their God that nobody was hurt and property wasn't destroyed. But three Aboriginal people died in the last fire. And the camp the Bundagulgi used was burned to the ground, resulting in more people arriving to the mission. But that didn't count. Of course not.

Then, a few weeks later, McGrath dammed the river, reducing the life-giving freshwater creek to barely a trickle.

McGrath knew the Bundagulgi were superstitious, so he made sure they overheard talk of evil spirits and all of that nonsense, anything to rattle them off their own land. He planted unscrupulous vagrant natives that he'd recruited down around Undara. There were a few illegal pubs out there, frequented by natives and bush rangers, and McGrath brought them up to tell stories designed to terrorise.

And it was working. Daily, more and more people arrived at the mission. When Russell had told Woiduna that there was no more room, he was full to capacity, they turned away, and saying not a word, they trudged back the way they came. No argument, no pleading – it was what they'd come to expect from those who'd invaded their country and destroyed all they loved. Whitefellas had never done anything but let them down, and Russell's heart ached.

He felt so deeply for these gentle people and was so filled with unchristian thoughts for those that hurt and exploited them. His faith demanded he live a Christlike life, and he tried, but McGrath tested him to the limits. It was wrong to hate, and he prayed for forgiveness for his feelings, but with each new atrocity, his bitter resentment grew.

Since Captain James Cook arrived in 1770 into Cooktown with his battered *Endeavor*, it had spelled disaster for the native people. Russell's church would say that the white men were bringing the natives the word of God, that they were benefitting from his grace and being assured of a life everlasting now that they had been shown the light. And he agreed, wholeheartedly, but he didn't believe that you needed to subjugate and destroy to achieve that objective. Russell's was a loving and generous God, who cared as much for the termite and the thrush as he did for men and women. Russell longed for a day when he could gently guide these people on the right path without this endless battle on their behalf. A day without the unscrupulous greed of people like Joseph McGrath.

The people of Jumaaroo were under McGrath's influence to such an extent that they regarded the mission as something utterly separate from them. It made him so sad and angry that they were fearful of the Bundagulgi people, and with no good reason. They considered them subhuman and dangerous and as something to be avoided, just as crocodiles and snakes were.

59

To see the white community so delighted with their nuns and their school and the priest visiting all the way from Strathland, considering themselves to be such worthy Christians, made him furious, but his anger was pointless. Catholics were the worst of the worst, following corrupt papacies to the gates of hell. Dripping in gold, their priests and bishops decked out in finery, living lives of decadence and gluttony. Jesus would smash their temples just as he did with the Pharisees', appalled at such hypocrisy.

Russell needed to convert his frustration to action, and so he did all he could for the people in his care. Some of the Aboriginal practices were at odds with the Christian way, so he curbed the worst of those ideas and they seemed to accept it. Meat-eating, for example, drinking alcohol, smoking – these were not the way of God, so no killing, drinking or smoking was allowed on the mission.

The people on the horizon were almost at the mission now, so he left the group of boys he was teaching how to whittle timber. The girls were with Betty in the house, preparing the evening meal. He knew how she would take the news that there were more coming – she was the one trying to find beds and food for everyone.

Usually the Bundagulgi allowed Woiduna to communicate for them; the elder had taught himself English. He was an intelligent quick-witted man, and he commanded the respect of everyone in that community. So Russell was surprised to see some of the other younger men. He knew by their expressions the news wasn't good.

'Woiduna is dead' was all he managed to glean from the conversation. As word went round the mission, there was crying, wailing. He was having a hard time piecing the story together, they were so distraught. Some of the younger men had been raised at other missions and spoke a little English, but mostly they did not. Over the years, Russell had picked up the rudiments of the Bundagulgi language, but his grasp wasn't good enough for situations like this. He managed to speak to one of the men and put the story together. Woiduna's battered body had been found in a ravine, and the Bundagulgi thought they were cursed. Woiduna was a tribal elder and knew that territory like the back of his hand. He was surefooted as a goat despite his advancing years, and he would not have fallen foul of a plant or an animal.

Russell walked up to the house, where Betty was in the kitchen making damper. The bread was almost their staple diet these days, and though it wasn't nutritious, just flour and water, it filled empty bellies. The Bundagulgi, hearing the news one by one, were looking to him for guidance. She glanced up as he entered, his frame filling the doorway, and then looked to the clearing outside the window. She saw the new arrivals and made a pleading face. He crossed the room to stand beside her, and the women and girls retreated, their eyes never leaving him. They knew something was wrong.

'I know,' he murmured, conscious that every word and gesture were being watched. 'But what can we do? Woiduna is dead – they found his body.'

Betty's eyes registered her shock. She'd liked the elder very much, and his death would be a personal loss to her. As ever, though, she recovered quickly, and he'd never loved her more.

'He's with God. We must care for these people now.' She exhaled raggedly and began organising. 'I suppose we could put the men in the barns, but the trouble will be, how are we meant to feed everyone, Russell? I'm stretching it so much as it is. But maybe we can send them to pick some more cape plums? We have a big amount of Burdekin plums, but they only picked them two days ago, so they need at least another week in the dark before they are ripe. The Atherton oak nuts are gone. The children found a pink satinash tree, and the fruit is almost ready for picking but not yet. I'll ask Davis and the others to catch enough barramundi for a meal tonight, and we can take it from there, I suppose. And we could use the last of the flour – maybe we can try to get some more on credit from the mill if they know how dire things are...' Betty encouraged the Bundagulgi to bring as much bush tucker, as they called it, to the mission, and they did, but the volume of food required to feed so many put everyone under pressure.

'Thank you, Betty,' he said quietly. Expressing love for your wife wasn't done in his faith, but Betty was his soulmate. He knew God had sent her to him because they were the same – they loved these people, and no matter how trying the circumstances, they would do their best.

Russell knew that Pietro Gabaldi, the Italian baker, would probably allow him some time to pay if he explained, but he hated being beholden. 'I'll write to Central Council again,' he said, both of them knowing that it was a futile exercise. All over the country, Adventist missions were demanding more and more support, and the money simply wasn't there. The situation in Jumaaroo was a reflection of the situation everywhere.

As word got round, more and more people came to the mission, and they worked all night. The mission was on the edge of Black Cockatoo country, and the people felt comfortable there. At least that was something.

Russell had no doubt that Joseph McGrath was to blame. His plan of intimidation over the last few months hadn't been as successful as he'd hoped, mainly because Woiduna gave his people courage. He'd challenged McGrath publicly all the time. He wasn't afraid of the tall handsome Irishman, one of the few people in Jumaaroo who wasn't. Everyone else kowtowed to McGrath in such a sickening way. Russell recalled with distaste the day the nuns arrived and how McGrath loved all the accolades and gratitude piled on him. He was the devil, nothing less. Russell could see the evil in his eyes. And of course he had the Catholics in his pocket – they would back him to the hilt. He was even friendly with their bishop, and that nun in charge of the school was the bishop's niece. A nest of vipers.

Now that Woiduna was gone, it felt like McGrath had won.

CHAPTER 8

*C*laire woke early to the birds having their usual noisy sort-out in the peach tree outside her window. It was just after five and she was still tired, but there was no possibility of further sleep now. She'd been awake late into the night after compline, the midnight prayer, worrying about the situation with Gerard.

Though she'd won in the most recent altercation, the nun was still ignoring many of the children. Claire couldn't approach her again unless she could make good on her threat to have her sent home. Gerard could sense any weakness, and what would Claire do if she said, 'Well, fine, go ahead'? Could she actually do it? Would the bishop back her? It was far from ideal. Gerard visited Assumpta McGrath often, so that was not a good sign. Clearly they saw a kindred spirit in each other.

Of course, she could write to Rev Bill, but that would be admitting defeat before she'd even begun. No, she would have to solve this situation herself. She fought feelings of despair. Since she'd arrived in Jumaaroo, it felt like there had been nothing but battles. The McGraths, Gerard, the townspeople who followed Joseph and Assumpta's every decree... It all seemed to be a struggle. So far, she'd won each battle, but she feared for the outcome of the war.

Claire wondered if Cassia was awake. It would be nice to stroll down, have a glass of lemonade on her veranda and have a normal conversation.

The language barrier problem with Teresita was not improving either, resulting in all manner of confusion. She had asked Teresita to speak a little more slowly, and God love her, she really tried, but once she got excited about art or carpentry or hurling or anything really, she went right back to unintelligible. Some of the children were convinced she was speaking Irish, which of course she wasn't, but only Claire and the other nuns could really understand her. Claire kept reminding her to slow down, and the other nun did her best, her loud booming voice slowly annunciating what sounded, Claire had to admit, like a very complicated foreign language.

Claire had listened at Teresita's classroom door as the children recited their times tables. All the ones had become *wans*, all the threes, *trees*, sevens had become *sebmms* and the tens, *tins*. Still, the children loved her and they were finding a way to muddle through.

Mary was completely over-subscribed for music lessons, and she was working around the clock because she hated to turn anyone away, even – it had to be said – the totally tone-deaf. She taught small groups after school each day until it was time for vespers, and Claire worried she was doing too much. But Mary assured her she loved it and it gave her such joy to see children playing music. When lessons ended, there were people playing instruments everywhere – on every step of the stairs, on the balcony, in all of the classrooms. Apparently there was to be a little concert at the end of term, and judging by the current racket, it was hard to imagine anyone being able to endure it, let alone enjoy it. But she never let her doubts show to Mary, who was bursting with enthusiasm.

As she rose in her small cell and washed and dressed, she could hear movement next door. Perhaps Helen was awake as well.

Claire knocked gently on her door.

'Good morning, Sister Claire,' the other nun said as she opened the door, fully dressed and ready for the day.

'Good morning. I wondered if you might like to join me for a cup of tea since we are both awake at cockcrow?'

Helen just smiled and nodded and followed Claire down the stairs. Teresita could be heard snoring like a bear, and Claire and Helen exchanged a smile.

The two women had had very little interaction alone since they arrived, and Claire was glad of a chance to spend some time with Helen. She put the kettle on to boil and took two cups from the dresser. The kitchen was bright and sunny and had large doors that opened out to the garden. No expense had been spared, and Claire had to admit it was a pleasure to live somewhere so beautiful. There had even been ceiling fans fitted, which were operated by electricity.

More than one person had explained how it was only through the intervention and determination of Mayor McGrath that Jumaaroo had electricity at all. Several other townships in Queensland, many bigger than theirs, were still relying on pale-yellow gaslight, but Mr McGrath needed electricity for his mines and Jumaaroo benefitted as a result.

It was so hard to reconcile. Was he really as bad as Daku and Gordie McKenzie suggested he was? Was Woiduna really just a mad old man, or was there some truth in his accusations? Everyone in Jumaaroo seemed to like and admire Joseph McGrath, but then the way he came down, demanding she refuse the non-Catholics, set her on edge. He was a man used to being obeyed. Something about him unsettled her. She'd seen men like him before, her sister's husband back in Ireland being one. Tomas Kinnehane was considered a great man down at the pub, and he served the altar at Mass, raised much-needed funds for local charities and was universally loved, but what nobody knew was how he terrorised his wife and children behind closed doors. Claire longed for liberation for her darling sister Kathleen, for her to escape with her children, but Kathleen wouldn't countenance such talk. She was married and that was her lot in life. Claire wrote often and got cheery letters back, but she knew the truth.

Joseph McGrath reminded her of Tomas. He said he was from Cork, but his accent said otherwise. Cork people, country and city, had very distinct accents. To the untrained ear, it all sounded the same, a lovely lilting sing-song way of speaking, but there were distinct dialects within the accent and she was good at picking them up. Her father would laugh when she was small and could tell the difference between a farmer from Mallow compared with one from Passage West or Ballydehob. Wherever Joseph McGrath was from, she would bet it wasn't Cork. But why lie?

Claire sat opposite Helen at the table. The morning sun was already hot as it streamed through the windows. 'So how are you finding Jumaaroo?' she asked.

'I like it,' Helen answered.

'And where are you from? I can't believe we've been here so long and I don't know anything about you.' She smiled.

'Near Youghal.' Again, the minimum.

'Oh, I love Youghal! The beach there is beautiful.' Claire tried to keep the conversation going.

Helen just nodded. She wasn't a babbler like Claire, but there was a warmth and a serenity to her that Claire envied. She was how a nun was supposed to be.

Claire tried again. 'The children seem to love your class.'

'They love stories, and so do I, so we discover them together. There are some talented writers in there already, I can see.'

Claire was about to try to get some dialogue going on that subject when she saw Daku outside. He was standing, a bucket in his hand, watching a bird, a laconic smile on his face. She didn't know how long he'd been there.

The yellow-billed kingfisher was drinking from the outside tap. A white person would have shooed the bird away and filled the bucket, but not Daku. As he saw it, the bird had as much right to the water as he did. Claire learned these little aspects of Aboriginal philosophy whenever she bumped into him. He was happy to explain things, or show her things in nature she would have passed without noticing. And he was slowly telling her the story of his people – how they suffered, and continued to suffer, at the hands of white men who had no regard for their culture, for their country. Who saw them and their home as something to be exploited, used and discarded. It was a shocking and harrowing story and one that made her feel deeply ashamed of the way people of her race behaved.

His way of living, at one with the land, was fascinating to her. He even threw the nuts he used as clothes pegs back on the ground when he no longer needed them. A white person would save them for the next wash, but that was not how the Aboriginal mind worked. The earth would provide, and owning things, amassing wealth, none of that was part of their way.

He taught Mary how to use soap nuts, hard green nuts that would lather up, even in saltwater. He showed Teresita how to identify the sandpaper tree and judge the grade of abrasiveness of the leaves by their colour. He told her to use the spotted gum for her hurleys, as it was both strong and springy and the wood could be sanded until it was smooth as glass. For some reason, perhaps it was his upbringing, he took to the nuns, but on his own terms. He came and went as he pleased and took what he needed, but every day, fruits or vegetables were left at their back door and the grounds looked beautiful.

Claire went to the window and waved, beckoning him in. Slowly, he loped towards her, his movements graceful. Today he wore no paint and had a shirt on. His hair was still thick and full – she doubted a comb or a brush ever saw it – and the lines around his eyes wrinkled and deepened when he smiled at her.

'We've made some tea. Would you like some?' she called as he reached the grass.

'Sure,' he answered. He never used her title, but his tone was friendly.

He entered the kitchen, and she saw he was barefoot. His trousers were clean though ragged. Claire saw Helen smile at him.

'Hello, Daku.'

'Hello again,' he said, his voice deep and almost growling. He smiled and his face lit up.

'How are you, Daku?' Claire asked, pouring him a cup of tea and praying Gerard didn't appear. Lord knew what she would say to find an Aboriginal man sitting and having tea in their kitchen.

'Bad,' he replied, and both nuns looked at him quizzically. 'Woiduna's death is hard for us, you know? Now everyone is afraid there is a curse. They think all of this – the creek drying, the fires, and now Woiduna – is 'cause of the curse. They're going to the mission out at Trouble Bay. I tried to tell them that it's not a curse, but they won't listen.'

'Why do they think that?' Helen asked.

Daku paused, as if considering whether to go on. When he spoke, there was a bitterness to his voice Claire had never heard before. "Cause McGrath sent some fellas up to the pub out Warawoi way a few weeks back – blackfellas, but not like us – saying all sorts of lies, and they believed them. Woiduna was trying to tell them, make them listen, but…' He shrugged and sighed.

'Oh dear, that's awful.' Claire was at a loss as to how to deal with this news.

'And now Woiduna is gone, and nothing anyone can say will convince me Joseph McGrath didn't kill him.'

The clock on the wall ticked loudly as they sat in silence. Claire was shocked. She knew McGrath was not exactly as sweet as he made out, but a murderer? Surely not. Daku must have it wrong. 'I know you don't like him, Daku, and maybe with good reason, but that's a very serious accusation…'

'Woiduna went up there, to McGrath's place, and called him out, showed him what his poison did in the river, killing the fish and the animals, polluting the water. Big Bill McAllister and some other bloke dragged Woiduna away. His body was found the next day. McGrath doesn't tolerate anyone standing up to him.'

His dark eyes locked with hers, and she read a warning there, although his disconcerting stare made her feel even more uncomfortable. Something about him made her feel guilty. She had no reason to, but she did.

'Do you have any evidence of this?' Helen asked.

Daku now turned his attention to her, and she averted her eyes downwards demurely. He seemed not to feel any discomfort at staring right into a person's eyes.

'I don't need evidence. I know.' Daku was adamant. 'And now my people are rushing to the mission, thinking Russell can protect them, and it's all so pointless...' He sighed deeply, and Claire could feel his pain.

'Daku, I know you are all so upset, of course you are. But without evidence –' Claire began.

'You don't know. Joseph McGrath is just one. This is how they treat us. All over our country, they rape and beat us, they hold us in chains, they torture and steal our children – thinking they can educate or pray the blackness out of us. Don't you get it? We are not humans in their eyes, we are not people.' His eyes blazed with the injustice of it all. 'They massacred the Mardu people after they tortured them into showing the whitefellas where the water was. At Mistake Creek, they shot twelve of the Kija people and were found guilty of no crime at the inquest. Bedford Downs – at that place, Worla men were made to wear dog tags and were marched two hundred kilometres and then forced to cut down the wood they would use to burn their bodies. Down in Forest River, they made special stone ovens to burn bodies after they were shot, and again nobody was charged. I could go on and on and on, but there's no point.'

Suddenly he looked deflated, broken, and Claire felt such a wave of pity for him, for his people. He sat, his forearms resting on his knees, his head bent. She wanted to reach out, to ease his pain.

Helen leaned over and placed her hand on his back. 'I believe you,' she said quietly. 'I am shocked and horrified, but if you say these things happened, Daku, then I believe you.'

He turned and looked at her, and Claire saw a moment of connection there.

She thought quickly. If what Daku said was true, if McGrath had something to do with Woiduna's death, incredible as it sounded, she would need to do something, say something to Rev Bill at least. But she would need more than the word of the gardener. She loved her uncle, and he was a just and kind man, but he was much enamoured of the McGraths and all they'd done; he wouldn't take kindly to her firing around wild accusations. But she couldn't do nothing.

Perhaps this Russell Gardiner might know something. He was the one dealing with the Bundagulgi people all the time. She thought for a moment and then said, 'I think I'll go to the mission, speak to Mr Gardiner.'

Daku looked up, incredulous. 'Why?' he asked, as if her statement was the stupidest thing he'd ever heard.

'To talk to him, to see if he has any evidence that McGrath is somehow connected with Woiduna's death. Perhaps there are witnesses, I don't know, but we can't do nothing. And if I am to act on this, I need more than a theory.'

He shook his head. 'He won't talk to you. You mob' – he waved his hand to suggest the entire establishment – 'are Russell's enemy. You all are fighting the battle for us godless savage souls, but you all hate each other.'

Did he smirk slightly? As if the entire idea of anyone fighting for their godless souls was a source of amusement to him? Claire didn't know if he was joking or not; it was hard to tell with him.

He hadn't ever said that he resented the idea of missions – he'd been raised on one, and presumably had them to thank for his standard of education – but did he despise them all really? While he was friendly, he certainly didn't speak with any degree of deference. A community of sisters had never, she believed, been referred to as a mob before.

Claire responded robustly, despite his bluntness. 'Well, my church and his are at odds, I know, but this is too important to let that get in the way. I think I'll go up there this morning, see what I can find out.'

Daku leaned back and gazed at the ceiling. He seemed calmer now, as if the outburst of emotion had passed and he was back to his enigmatic self. He intoned in his deep voice, '"Hence loathed Melancholy, Of Cerberus and blackest Midnight born, In Stygian cave forlorn, 'Mongst horrid shapes, and shrieks, and sights unholy; Find out some uncouth cell, Where brooding Darkness spreads his jealous wings, and the night-raven sings…"' His loud laugh made both her and Helen start.

Then he faced her. 'Be careful you don't lead each other into hell, you and Russell, all saving the blackfellas.' He drained his cup and stood. His eyes rested on each of them for a moment, and just as before, without any word of thanks or goodbye, he left.

Claire looked at Helen. 'What on earth was that?' she asked.

'"L'Allegro" by John Milton.' She noted the look of confusion on Claire's face. 'The poet, you know, who wrote *Paradise Lost*?'

'No. I probably did it at school, but poetry was never my thing, to be honest. I did enough to pass but not much else. What did he mean, do you think?'

Helen's brow furrowed. 'I've no idea why he chose that poem. He's a most unusual man. He's like, well, someone from another world, isn't he?'

'I suppose he is. He's the one at home here, though, not us. Those things he said, about the way the Aboriginals are treated, do you think it's all true?' Claire asked as Daku disappeared into the dense bush that surrounded the convent.

'I think it is,' Helen replied sadly.

'Am I mad to go up there?' Claire was suddenly unsure. 'To that mission?'

Helen sighed. 'Well, the bishop wouldn't like it, and Sister Gerard will make sure everyone knows you did if she gets wind of it. But I agree with you – we have to do something. We can't just pretend we don't know, and without more evidence, we have nothing but hearsay.'

'It can't do any harm, I suppose.' Claire stood and rinsed the cups. 'The worst that can happen is he hunts me off the land. We have to try – those people do not deserve this treatment.'

Both nuns looked up as Gerard appeared in the kitchen.

'Who doesn't deserve what?' she asked imperiously.

Claire and Helen shared a glance. They would have to say something. They didn't know how long she'd been listening.

'The Aboriginals,' Helen replied. 'They're all going to the mission out at Trouble Bay because their water supply is drying up and their land has been burned and now their elder has been found dead.'

Gerard helped herself to a cup of tea and took some bread and marmalade out of the pantry. 'Look, I know that you think this is awful, Sister Helen, but please believe me, it is better for them to be institutionalised. Several of our sisters served on the African missions, and they had the same issues. These people... Look, the truth is they just do not develop the same way, to the same extent as white people. They are inferior intellectually and therefore best managed in groups.'

Claire suppressed the urge to argue. She would not have open hostilities with Gerard now after everything else; she needed to think.

The older nun went on unimpeded. 'They can be taught – to a certain extent, anyway – to do basic tasks, and if it weren't for missions, they would be roaming about naked, getting up to all sorts. The mission out there isn't Catholic, but I say let them to it. I mean, we can't be expected to deal with every heathen native on earth, so it's best for them and best for us if they are kept up there. The land is needed anyway, and they're hindering much-needed progress.'

Helen looked appalled and spoke up, much to Claire's astonishment. 'But you cannot seriously think that? That we are superior to these people simply because our skin is white and theirs isn't? Have you never read *Uncle Tom's Cabin*? Or the writings of Frederick Douglass? I don't understand this kind of thinking, I truly don't. It has no basis in fact whatsoever. People like Daku may live differently to us – they have their structures and social mores and we have ours. They are not wrong, nor inferior. They are just different. Not to mention the fact that this is their land, and they have more right to it than we do!'

If the situation were not so serious, it would have been funny. Gerard puffed up like a bullfrog, so indignant was she at being contradicted by someone she considered her junior.

'Such claptrap,' she snapped. 'They are savages that need to be civilised, for their own sakes as much as for anyone's. That naiveté is typical of someone who has never been anywhere and never seen anything. You would do well to listen to those with more experience of the world before spouting your half-baked philosophies, Sister Helen.'

She was warming to her theme. Claire wondered if she should intervene, but Helen seemed well able for the other woman. She was certainly better read, and there was a quiet confidence to her that wasn't immediately apparent but was showing itself now.

Gerard went on. 'Best let them all go to the mission, better all round.' She then tucked into her breakfast with gusto. Claire could almost hear the words coming out of Assumpta McGrath's mouth.

'And if they don't want to go?' Helen asked quietly.

'They don't know what they want, or what's good for them. They need to be directed by their betters, and anyone who thinks otherwise is frankly either very naïve or incredibly stupid.'

Her tone suggested that her fellow sisters in Christ were both of those things, and that that was all that needed to be said on the matter.

* * *

LATER THAT MORNING, as the school was a hive of industry, Claire left for the Trouble Bay mission. Despite what Daku had said about her not being welcome there, she was going to try.

She had no real knowledge about the Seventh-day Adventists except what Rev Bill said in his letter. She knew that they were very much at odds with the Catholic Church, and she did recall a priest saying something about them…or was that Mormons? The hierarchy warned about the evils of these cults, and ordinarily Claire would have given them a wide berth, but she reasoned they all believed in Jesus and wanted to serve their communities, so there was no reason not to speak to them. It wasn't the same thing, she knew, but growing up in Macroom, she and her family got on very well with their Protestant neighbours. They were all happy to live alongside each other and respect each other's beliefs. Why should this be any different?

She'd sat in their little chapel once all the children were in class and examined her conscience. She'd had to admit that a part of her knew that if she was in a more populated part of the world, with a priest to guide them, he would absolutely forbid it. But they were in the outback, and there were no higher clergy, either for her or presumably for this Russell Gardiner. They were both trying to help, and she trusted her instinct to do what was right. Her uncle, Rev Bill, a devout and profoundly decent man, often advised her and many others that in times of dilemma you should ask yourself, 'What would Jesus do?' Jesus, she felt sure, would not ignore the plight of the Bundagulgi.

It was a long walk to the mission, but there was no other form of transport available to her, so she set off in the heat, remembering to bring a bottle of water. She longed to wear something other than her black habit, but it was not an option. She'd toyed with the idea of making some lighter ones, maybe of white cotton, but she would need a dispensation from the order and she didn't like to ask.

The exercise might do her good, she decided as she walked down the main street of Jumaaroo. The canopies that extended onto the covered walkway outside the shops provided welcome shade, and she greeted everyone she met.

As she passed the Jumaaroo Hotel, a corner building with an elaborate wrought-iron balcony running around its first floor, she spotted Assumpta McGrath and some other local women having morning tea on its veranda. Claire envied them their light-coloured dresses and bare arms.

'Good morning, ladies,' she said as she passed.

'Good morning, Sister,' Assumpta answered on everyone's behalf, her tone frosty.

Assumpta had obviously not yet forgiven her for admitting Jannali to the school.

'It's unusual to see you out and about in the middle of the school day?' There was a definite note of reprimand in her voice.

The devilment in Claire, the thing that her mother always said would be her undoing, bubbled to the surface. If the white ladies of Jumaaroo were appalled at their children learning alongside Greeks,

Chinese and Aboriginals, they would be horrified entirely to think that the school principal was going to visit the mission.

'Oh, I'm just off to the mission at Trouble Bay actually. I heard they are being overrun with requests for shelter, so I thought we might be able to help.'

Their faces registered exactly what she knew they would, and she suppressed a grin.

Assumpta was the first to recover. 'Oh, there's no need for that. They manage very well out there. There is some kind of a religious leader out there, and they get money from their central organisation, I believe, so it would be best to allow them to do whatever they are doing without interfering.' She seemed, just like Gerard, to see her pronouncement as final. Her previous encounter with Claire had taught her nothing, it would seem.

'All the same, I'll go and offer anyway.' Claire gave a cheery wave. 'Enjoy your tea, ladies.' She started to walk away.

'Ah, Sister Claire!' Assumpta called her back.

'Yes?' Claire asked, a pleasant smile hiding her amusement at the other woman's dilemma. Was she going to order her back to the school?

'I don't think my husband would be happy about you going out there, so best just leave it, as I said.' There was an edge of steel to her voice – this was an order, not a suggestion.

The other women had the grace to look embarrassed. Suddenly, the patterns on their teacups became a source of intense fascination.

Claire thought for a moment. 'I'm sure a man of such generosity and civic mind as Mr McGrath would hate to see anyone in trouble, so I doubt he would object, but even if he did, I'm not sure what that would have to do with me?' Claire hoped she sounded genuinely baffled.

'Well...' Assumpta coloured now. 'It's just we understand how these things work, and since you're new here, it would be better if you didn't get involved in things that don't concern you.' She obviously was trying to redress the balance of power. Claire might win on the subject of the school, but this was outside of it, where McGrath ruled supreme.

'Oh, but the plight of the Aboriginal people *does* concern me, Mrs McGrath. It concerns me very much. Goodbye now.' She smiled and turned.

Round two to Claire.

She could feel the eyes of the town on her as she left the built-up main street and carried on to where the buildings became more sporadic and a bit more ramshackle. On she walked in the blistering heat. The earth here was so strange. A lovely reddish-brown colour, it reminded her of the red lead her father used to paint on the barns to stop them rusting. The rainbow lorikeets, kookaburras and cockatoos sat in the gum trees, and a plover had made her nest right in the road. She smiled at the memory of Jannali explaining that plovers were 'kinda dozy' and they put their nests in really stupid places. The thought of the little girl's distraught face drove her on. She and the entire Aboriginal community were devastated and had nobody to stick up for them.

Even though the landscape was so different from the lush green hills and valleys of County Cork, there was a frightening beauty to it. This harsh land was not for the faint-hearted, but if you could endure it, the rewards were multitude. Starry nights the likes of which she'd never seen, sunrises where the sky was streaked with every colour of the rainbow, deafening thunder and lightning that lit up the sky, animals, birds, insects, snakes. Twenty yards from her, a mob of kangaroos grazed lazily. A little joey peeked out from his mother's pouch, and the biggest of them, a huge grey male with bulging muscles, lounged in the sun, protecting his family.

She walked on, and after about twenty minutes, she was out of the town entirely. The road disappeared, and all that remained was a dusty unsealed track, the green mountains on the horizon and the lush rainforest almost running to the sea. The jungle seemed to almost grow before her eyes. Huge shiny leaves, incredibly vivid flowers – it was like fertility and abundance in action.

She approached a very rough version of a farmhouse, made mostly of odd bits of timber and some rusty metal. In the yard was Gordie, dressed only in a grubby undershirt and battered trousers, and he waved. He was digging a hole in the front yard. His skin was the colour of mahogany after years of exposure to the sun, and the muscles rippled on his body as he worked.

'G'day,' he called.

'G'day,' she responded, using the local expression. 'Is this your place?'

'Me castle.' He grinned and took out a pack of cigarettes, offering her one with a wink. She smiled and shook her head.

'Never before six.' She laughed, and he chuckled as he lit up.

'Where ya headed? Too flamin' hot for walkin'!' He wiped the sweat from his neck and brow with a filthy rag he took out of his pocket.

'I'm going out to Trouble Bay. And you're right, it is hot.'

'You walkin'?' He looked at her incredulously. 'It's close to six miles! You'll be dead by the time you get there in that getup!' He pointed at her habit.

'I want to go out to the mission,' she said.

'Wotcha goin' there for?' he asked, a hint of aggression in his tone.

She sighed. Yet another person with an opinion about her activities. She wondered if she should tell him the truth. Something about him made her trust him, though it was impossible to say what.

'I was talking to Daku about Woiduna. He thinks it wasn't an accident, but he has no proof. And I'm not sure, but it doesn't feel right to just do nothing, so I figured I could ask Mr Gardiner what he thought.' When she heard the words out loud, she realised how silly she sounded. She did want to help, but maybe Assumpta was right that she hadn't a clue about how things worked here. Perhaps she should keep her nose out of it.

To her surprise, he didn't say anything for a moment, just simply nodded. 'And why do you want to help them?' His tone didn't contain the incredulity she was used to.

'Well, I just think if a man *has* been murdered, then someone should notify the authorities. But the way things are, and Woiduna being who he was, well, compelling evidence would be needed before anyone would take an allegation like that seriously.'

'And you reckon you can get that?' Gordie asked with a grin.

'Well, I want to try.' She began to walk along the dusty road again.

'Old Russ Gardiner won't want your kind stickybeakin' up there, y'know?' he shouted to her back.

'So I've been told,' she called wryly in return, giving him a casual wave but walking on.

'Here, Claire!' He caught up with her. 'Can you drive?'

She turned. 'A car you mean?' she asked.

'No, a donkey and cart.' He chuckled again. 'You can take Flossie if you want, bring her back this arvo?'

She knew 'this arvo' meant 'this afternoon'.

'I think I could – would you mind? It would be so much easier.' The thought of sitting on a cart and letting a donkey do the long walk was very appealing. Her habit was stuck to her already as perspiration prickled her skin.

As a child, Claire had taken the milk to the mart in Macroom with her older brother many times, loading the churns up on the back of the cart. Her job was to catch Bob, the contrary old donkey in the field who was totally allergic to work and did all in his obstinate power to evade it.

'No worries. Hang on a tic. I'll grab her.'

He went around the back as Claire waited. Out of the corner of her eye she saw a brown-skinned woman in the window of the house. *That must be Jannali's mother,* Claire thought. She had never met her.

The woman gazed for a moment, wary. Claire waved and smiled, but the open suspicion and hostility in the woman's eyes came as a shock. She emerged from the house and gazed sullenly at Claire.

Gordie appeared again and tied the donkey – now tacked to a cart – to the gate. Taking in the scene, he said something to the woman in a language Claire couldn't understand. He then turned to Claire. 'This is my wife, Darana, Jannali's mum.'

'I'm Sister Claire.' She smiled again, offering her hand. 'Jannali is a wonderful girl, and doing so well. Sister Mary says she's as bright as a button.'

Darana's black eyes were still wary, but she shook Claire's hand. She never left Gordie's side. 'She likes it, your school.'

'I'm so glad. We love having her.' Claire smiled again, and Darana lost some of the hostility.

'Right, let's get you sorted. Up you get,' said Gordie. He helped her up onto the cart, grabbing her round the waist. No man had ever touched Claire like that before and it came as a shock, but he wasn't one to stand on ceremony. She was plonked on the cart, and he gave her the worn leather reins.

'Flossie's all right, but she don't like hills much, so you might have to lead her up the bluff by Stockton's Creek. But give her a drink there anyway. I need her back by about three.'

He gave the donkey a slap on the rump, and off she trotted.

'Thank you very much,' Claire called as she was carried away.

CHAPTER 9

*J*oseph J. McGrath ordered an Irish whiskey at the Queensland Club on the corner of Alice and George Streets in Brisbane. His membership meant that when he left Jumaaroo and came down to mix and mingle with the influential men of the city, he could enjoy fine dining and excellent company. But today he had a very specific purpose.

He was meeting his wife's brother, an insufferable fool but a man with connections. Pius James Prendergast had served without distinction in the Great War, was elevated to the rank of colonel after the Battle of Beersheba, presumably because braver men were killed, but his position in the military and his family's role in Brisbane society made him a useful ally. Luckily, he was easily flattered, and when plied with booze, he had a very loose tongue. There were rumours of what was afoot militarily speaking, but if they proved to be true, Joseph could stand to make a lot of money.

He instructed the young waiter to leave the bottle as he saw his brother-in-law sign in. He was in his uniform as usual, though in all the time Joseph had known him, he'd yet to see the man do any actual soldiering. His fair hair was carefully combed to try, unsuccessfully, to hide his receding hairline, and his pale-blue eyes were weak and watery. He was five foot eight at the most and had a slight build. Out of uniform, he would be a very unremarkable fellow indeed; in it, he fared only a little better. He was a male version of Assumpta, all pinched and pale and slightly mean-looking. They got that from their mother.

He hadn't enjoyed his trysts with the old bat, but she was useful at the time, and having her simper over him was vaguely gratifying as he worked his way into one of Brisbane's most prestigious families. But shaking off his mother-in-law was another matter. She'd outlived her usefulness once Assumpta was pregnant and with a ring on her finger, so he unceremoniously told Mrs Prendergast the affair was finished, gave her some claptrap about feeling guilty about Assumpta, that she would of course be his choice, not her silly, vain daughter, but it could never be.

She cried and all the rest of it, and he was glad to get away. In general, now that he had what he wanted from them, Joseph did all he could to avoid contact with the Prendergasts. He reckoned Assumpta's mother henpecked her husband to death, and if her daughter would have her way, she'd do the same to him. But Assumpta didn't know who she was dealing with... Nobody did.

Getting her pregnant wasn't the original plan. As far as he was concerned, she was nothing more than a passably pretty distraction. But in the end, it worked out. He needed a wife and an heir, and it gave him status in society that he'd lacked before. The Prendergasts presented as a powerful, wealthy family, but the reality was that due to the father's gambling, they were as poor as church mice, and poor people, especially those who pretended not to be, were ripe for exploitation.

Assumpta was such a snob, and he laughed at how she loved the status that being married to him gave her. He went to her bed whenever the humour took him, but while in Brisbane, he would probably seek out more exotic company in that regard. He could have had other women in Jumaaroo if he wanted to – that Cassia Galatas was very attractive actually – but he wouldn't do anything to sully his pristine reputation up there. No, he could keep his appetites under control at home, and, well, Brisbane had plenty to offer to distract a man with a fat wallet for an evening.

'Joseph!' Pius Prendergast's loud, high-pitched voice disturbed the tranquillity of the bar with its leather seats, polished mahogany and beautifully inlaid side tables.

Showtime. Joseph stood, his arms outstretched. 'Pius, it's been too long. How are you?'

Joseph embraced his brother-in-law warmly, then sat and instantly poured him a large whiskey. He tempered his accent depending on who he spoke to. Up at Jumaaroo and all around there, he was cultured but not snobbish. Out at the mines, he was able to speak perfect Occa, just like one of the blokes. It was all 'how ya goin', mate?' and 'flat out like a lizard drinkin''. But down here, he was more refined. That chameleon-like ability to adapt to his environment was one of his many skills.

'Oh, very well, old man, very well indeed. Enjoying my last weeks of freedom. I'm getting married – did Assumpta tell you? Charming girl, father made his money in opals out west somewhere but lives in Sydney, beautiful place in Botany Bay. Educated in England, so quite the lady, I can assure you.' He guffawed loudly and downed the whiskey in one gulp.

Joseph cringed inwardly. That clipped way of speaking, the removal of pronouns, was a pitiful attempt to emulate the British. It just showed how inferior these colonials felt deep down. Pius was every inch the dumbass donkey Joseph knew him to be, so he could just imagine what kind of crinoline insipidness he'd hitched his wagon to. Whoever she was, he was welcome to her. 'Congratulations. Yes, Assumpta mentioned it. She's very excited. We were starting to worry we'd never get you into the club.' Joseph laughed.

Pius grinned, which only accentuated his lack of a chin, and Joseph topped up his drink. 'Oh, you know me, Joseph, too much choice. Settling on one was tricky, but I suppose Mama is right, it's time to settle down. And Agatha really is a delight.'

'I can't wait to meet her,' Joseph lied smoothly as he summoned the waiter and handed a menu to Pius. The idea of Pius Prendergast as a ladies man was laughable. He was a balding, weedy, privately educated buffoon. But let him play the Lothario if he liked. Joseph couldn't care less. In fact, he used his brother-in-law's vanity to sweet-talk him. 'She must be something special to say she trapped you. The debutantes will be weeping into their lace handkerchiefs.' Joseph winked, and Pius lapped it up.

'Oh, there were a few tears, I heard, but even the best of us have to toe the straight and narrow eventually, I suppose.' Pius pretended to be devastated.

'Indeed we do, and I have to say I can recommend it. I got a good one in your sister.'

'Indeed you did, old man, indeed you did.' Pius drained his whiskey.

Joseph was laying it on thick, but this clown was too stupid to notice. He topped up the other man's drink once more, and they ordered food. Joseph always picked up the tab whenever they met up, and Pius never once offered to pay. Joseph only met him when he needed something, so it was an investment, but it did irk him that his brother-in-law always chose the most expensive thing on the menu, as well as the best wine. He never let his annoyance show though.

He let Pius ramble on for a while, some boring – and entirely fictitious – tale of how one particular girl was close to suicide because he'd got engaged. Joseph made the right noises at the right times, but he was miles away. He wondered how to bring the conversation around to what he really wanted to discuss.

The bottle of Château Lafite 1927 arrived, accompanied by the lobster thermidor and dauphinoise potatoes, and Pius tucked in. On and on he droned, each tale essentially illustrating the same thing: his own importance.

Joseph looked to the entrance of the beautifully appointed dining room and realised his luck might be in. Commander Alcott, a man who, unlike Pius, served his country with valour in the Royal Australian Navy, was signing in. He was a family friend of the Prendergasts and had attended Joseph and Assumpta's wedding. If Joseph could engineer his joining them, then matters would surely come round to all things military.

Pius would have to invite him though; it would be too presumptuous of Joseph. He was under no illusion as to where his lack of family left him. People liked him and he had plenty of money, so that oiled most social wheels, but he was essentially a nobody in this place obsessed with class and family. He'd never expected it of Australia – it was, as far as he was concerned, a colony of convicts and settlers – but the class system that permeated every echelon of life in London was no less pervasive here. The desire to replicate Britain was strong. The only difference was in Australia, Catholics were neck and neck with the Protestants in the snob stakes. Take the Prendergasts, for example. They were Catholics but very well connected. It was Assumpta's father's weakness for expensive women and slow horses that was his undoing, though nobody knew the reality of their finances. He'd died, and there was enough money in the estate that Pius could live a life of luxury without ever contributing anything to the world.

'Isn't that naval officer over there a friend of yours?' Joseph interjected, stopping Pius mid-flow in yet another wearying tale illustrating his own importance.

Pius turned. 'Ah, so it is.'

He stood and crossed the room. 'Archie, old man, how goes it?' Pius shook the other man's hand warmly; their families had been friends for generations.

Pius led the man over to say hello, and Joseph immediately seized the opportunity. There was a little small talk for a few minutes, Alcott asking after Assumpta and the children, Joseph replying in warm terms. But he had more important things to discuss.

'Will you join us?' Joseph asked, giving an almost imperceptible nod to the waiter, indicating he should bring another bottle of wine. Pius was as absorbent as his father when it came to booze, especially on someone else's tab.

'Well, if you're sure I'm not intruding?'

'Absolutely not, old man,' Pius responded with an expansive wave, pulling out a seat as if he were hosting. 'My brother-in-law and I were just chatting about my upcoming nuptials. I presume you've heard I'm soon to be a married man?'

Joseph knew from Alcott's face that he had no idea; the doings of the tedious Pius were of no consequence to him either. Joseph poured him a large whiskey into the cut-glass tumbler that had appeared with the next bottle of wine. Alcott drank, and Joseph filled his glass again as the idle chit-chat went on.

Alcott had the telltale red nose of a whiskey drinker. All of those who came back from the war were dependent on something – drugs, drink, gambling, women. It made them ripe for exploitation. All one needed to do was find the opponent's weak spot. Once you had that, you applied slight pressure, and click, you got what you wanted. It was a game, and Joseph loved it.

'Time enough for him to settle down, isn't it?' Joseph joked. 'Enough with the philandering and heart breaking, Pius. It's high time you joined the ranks and did your bit.' Joseph winked and the other two laughed. They were both in their late forties, though their uniforms made them look older, he thought.

'Where did you serve last time out, Joseph?' Alcott asked, and Joseph wondered if the question was as innocent as it sounded.

He answered easily, well-rehearsed. 'Munster Fusiliers. Took a bullet at the Battle of Mons.'

'That was a bad scrap I heard.'

Joseph had invented his military service, of course, but so far nobody had questioned it. He had never donned a uniform, nor would he. Fighting for someone else was a mug's game; fighting for himself was much more in his line. Luckily, the Australian theatres of war were different to his alleged experience, so he could skim over it easily. He even picked up a medal at an auction, just in case it was ever needed. Another Irishman in the British army would be a matter of no consequence to the men he mixed with now, so long as he did his bit.

He took care not to glorify his war stories. His tale was that he joined up, served as a private, got shot in the early days and came home. The end. Enough to be believable, not too much that he could trip himself up. It had worked so far. He conveniently did have an old wound – got at a different place and time, under very different circumstances – that served as evidence if necessary.

'It certainly was,' Joseph agreed, and nobody took it further. That generation had seen so much, endured such deprivation and horror, it was best just to leave it. 'Though the way the Japs are making noises now, it's looking like it might all heat up again.' He was fishing but would have to be careful. 'Between them and that Hitler in Germany, it's a worrying time.'

'It certainly is,' Archie agreed, then ordered a steak.

'Will it escalate, do you think?' Joseph asked, his tone deliberately casual.

Archie shrugged, but Pius interjected. 'Undoubtedly. Once more into the breach and all of that, eh?' He sounded delighted at the prospect.

The man was a fool. Joseph remembered seeing the Irish men come back from the war to end all wars. They were broken, mentally and physically, wishing they were coming back in boxes or not at all rather than living a pathetic half-life. And for what? He'd been a boy of fifteen when the war ended, so he was too young to serve, but that was irrelevant – he would never have gone anyway.

'The Japs are the real threat to this country, invading Manchuria. And now that the military are running the show there, we need to watch out,' Pius said.

Joseph saw the opportunity and said smoothly, 'I doubt we'll need to worry about the Japs invading us, Pius. We're too far away from anyone to be a real target surely? Besides, they are focused on China, not us...' He put his wine glass to his lips but barely sipped. He needed a clear head.

'Well, I'm not so sure about that, Joseph. Pius is right. We need to be ready,' Archie interjected as he helped himself to more wine. 'We have plans though.' The two large whiskeys and the wine were loosening his tongue.

'Really?' Pius asked, leaning in.

Joseph remained deliberately nonchalant but listened carefully.

'Strictly *entre nous*, as they say, but we are setting up a jungle warfare training centre – I'm part of the task force actually – and we are looking for locations. Actually, it's good I ran into you, Joseph. You're up in the tropics, aren't you?'

'I am. Jumaaroo – it's far north Queensland, on the Cape York Peninsula.'

'Interesting. Some of our chaps went up a while back but came back saying they needed a local to show them around. Dense, unwelcoming place up there. We need somewhere coastal of course, but also in the rainforest so our men can be trained under all conditions. A site large enough for a landing strip as well. It's proving to be a tall order, I believe.'

So the rumours were true. Joseph thought quickly. He'd been systematically clearing the natives off the land to the south and west of Jumaaroo, driving them onto the mission. He had plans to cultivate that land for sugar cane and they were a nuisance, but he'd have to recalculate. This was a much bigger prospect if he could arrange it – and he could.

'Really?' he asked, deliberately keeping his voice light and taking a mouthful of the grilled barramundi he'd ordered for lunch. He had plans for the afternoon and needed to feel fit, not bloated from heavy food and too much wine. 'And did they find anywhere?'

'There were several places, I think, along the coast there, but I'm not sure. It proved to be impossible, not sure why. Too many bloody snakes and Abbos, I assume.' He chuckled, and Joseph and Pius joined in, but Joseph's mind was whirring. He knew exactly what they needed, and he also knew exactly what he would do next.

CHAPTER 10

*C*laire tied the donkey to the fence and wearily climbed down. The cart had been a godsend, but she was wet through with perspiration and her bottle of water was long gone. The mission stretched in front of her, and she had to admit, even in her hot and thirsty state, that it was like paradise. The huge palm trees, almost dipping their fronds in the glittering turquoise sea, swayed in the gentle breeze. Beneath her feet was sand, white and so fine it was more like powder. All around the complex were huts, simple structures made from bamboo and straw, and over to the right, a little chapel. It was, like the other structures, simple, but it had a beauty to it that took her breath away. It was painted white and seemed to gleam in the bright sunlight.

A group of children, dressed in rags, had formed a circle around Flossie and were feeding her grass while two others went to get water.

'How old's yer donkey?' asked a girl of about four with matted black hair and a gap-toothed grin.

Claire smiled. 'I don't know. Her name is Flossie though. She's not mine – I just borrowed her.'

'She's Gordie's,' announced a little boy with a shaved head and two missing front teeth.

'You're one of them nuns,' a cheeky boy of about ten remarked.

'Yes, I'm Sister Claire from St Finbarr's…' she began, when she became aware of the stares of the Bundagulgi people who'd gathered in small groups around the mission.

'You there!' A tall, powerfully built man in a white shirt and dark trousers bore down on her. His iron-coloured hair was cut so close to his scalp it looked shaved, and his grey eyes were livid. 'Get off this property! Leave those children alone!' he yelled. 'Children! Go to your parents. Get away from her!'

The children were then snatched away by the adults, and everyone stood staring.

'I… I meant no harm. I…' Claire stammered.

'You have no business here. Get off this property! These children are in my care,' the man bellowed, though she was only feet away from him.

'I was only talking to them…' she tried to explain.

'I know exactly who you are and what your purpose here is. Get out!' he roared once more, and the donkey started in fright.

Claire felt her skin flush pink under his hostile stare. 'Please, Mr Gardiner, I just wanted to talk to you about Woiduna. Daku said –'

'I will not tell you again.' His voice was lower now, threatening. He stood before her, towering over her, the Aboriginal people behind him.

'Please, I just want –' she tried once more.

'I don't care what you want. Whatever you need, I'm sure Joseph McGrath can provide.' His mouth curled distastefully at even the mention of McGrath's name.

'It's Joseph McGrath I wanted to speak with you about…' she said.

He stopped and stared at her. One of the Aboriginal men said something she didn't understand, but she heard the word 'Daku'. She prayed he was vouching for her.

Gardiner thought for a moment and then abruptly barked, 'Follow me.' He nodded, turned on his heel and stalked off towards a more permanent-looking structure up ahead.

Perhaps that was the main building. It looked more like a functional structure than a house as such – a large square building with a front door and three windows. She walked behind him, feeling foolish and very vulnerable.

Gardiner approached the front door, entering and leaving it open for her.

Claire swallowed. Everyone was right. What on earth did she think she was doing, just wandering up here like some kind of misguided Sherlock Holmes?

Gardiner stood in an office to the right of the door, his arms folded across his enormous chest, his demeanour not softened even slightly. She followed him in and stood before him. There were two bare chairs and a table, but he didn't suggest they sit.

'I... I'm Sister Claire, from St Finbarr's in the town, and I...' She paused, unsure of what to say next.

'I'm aware of who you are.' He wasn't giving her an inch.

'Yes, well... I'll get right to the point...' She tried to steady her voice. 'Daku mentioned that he thought Woiduna's death was...well, not an accident, and I thought...you might...'

'Thought I might what?' he asked, that definite aggression not subsiding.

Claire steeled herself. Jesus would just tell the truth, no strings attached, and so would she. She took a deep breath. 'Have some evidence, or proof or something, that could be brought to the authorities. I know we are not of the same...well, the same church or anything. But I know you care for the Bundagulgi people, and neither of us can stand by and watch an injustice go uninvestigated, so in that sense we are the same,' she finished lamely. She longed to be anywhere but there.

The look he gave her spoke volumes, and she was left in no doubt that his sense of community would most definitely not include her. The silence hung heavily between them. Claire had no idea what to say to fill it. What should she do? Turn on her heel and leave? That would be silly.

Instead she tried again. 'I don't know what's gone on here, but I feel very strongly that if a wrong has been done, then it should be brought to the authorities, and without evidence, that would be pointless.'

His dark eyes never left hers, and it was impossible to even guess at what he was thinking. 'And Joseph McGrath doesn't know you're here?' His tone was loaded with scepticism.

Russell Gardiner clearly cared for the Bundagulgi people, and if what Daku said was true – and she had no reason to doubt it – then she could only be seen as an emissary of McGrath's. No wonder he was wary.

'Mr Gardiner.' She now held his gaze. 'I am here representing myself and my community of sisters, and with an open heart and in good faith. I do not now, nor will I ever, do the bidding of Mr McGrath. Our school is under the auspices of the diocese of Brisbane, and I am answerable to God and the bishop and nobody else. Please do not think I have any agenda other than justice, because I give you my word that I do not.'

His inscrutable face didn't show one glimmer of softness or appreciation, but wordlessly he stood back and gestured she should sit. 'Excuse me. I'll only be a moment,' he said, then left.

She sat there, unsure of what was going on now. The walls were lined with books, none of which she recognised. There was a desk, very neat, with a blotter, a pen and some clean paper, and a small wooden chair. Nothing was ornate or pretty; everything was functional.

She read the spines. *The Great Controversy Between Christ and Satan*, *The Ministry of Healing*, *Prayer*, *Steps to Christ*, *The Desire of Ages*, plus others. Most of the books seemed to have been written by the same author, a woman called Ellen G. White. Claire would have liked to take one down, see what it was all about, but she didn't dare. She was only there on sufferance as it was.

A few moments passed, then the door opened and Russell entered again, this time with a woman. She, like him, was in her fifties, short, with salt-and-pepper curly hair and a rounded figure. For every hard and angular line he had, she was soft. Her eyes were brown and kind.

'This is my wife, Betty Gardiner.'

Claire stood and extended her hand. Betty looked at it for a moment, and Claire could see the indecision there. Then she reached out and took Claire's hand, the grip surprisingly strong.

'Hello.' Betty smiled.

'Hello, Mrs Gardiner. My name is Claire.'

'It's nice to meet you, Claire,' Betty said, and her voice, though wary, held a warmth her husband's lacked.

'She's come up here to ask us about Woiduna's death, and I wanted you to be here, Betty, so there would be no misunderstanding later.' Russell stood with his back to the room, gazing out the window at the mission where people milled about in the blistering heat, seemingly unperturbed by the temperature. Both women stood behind him, beside each other in the small space.

He turned then and folded his arms across his broad chest. 'Thank you for coming. I believe it is probably in good faith, if misguided. Let me give you some advice. This entire region is run by Joseph McGrath. If you imagine for one moment otherwise, then you are foolish. My advice is to stay out of matters that don't concern you. I think it is best if you go back to your convent and your school, and we will deal with the people here. Good day to you.'

In two paces he crossed the room and opened the door of the office. Clearly that was that.

Claire was about to scuttle away, but something inside her made her stop. 'Mr Gardiner, let me tell you something that you may not know. I don't care about what Mr McGrath thinks about anything. I do, on the other hand, care about people whose homes are being systematically destroyed, whose water is being stopped and whose leaders are being hurt or worse. I don't know exactly what I can do, but I don't feel it is right to say nothing. We do not need to agree on every single thing – even within faiths there is discord – but looking at your books there, I see you are concerned with the life of Jesus Christ. I'm sure I do not need to remind you that Jesus was someone who included people, not excluded them. He was someone who gave people the benefit of the doubt, and he especially loved children. I work with children – so do you. Jesus would not have seen the differences, only the fact that we are *all* his children.'

She swept past him, but as she returned to the donkey, Betty ran after her, carrying a bottle of water. 'For the journey,' she said, pressing the bottle into Claire's hands.

'Thank you, Mrs Gardiner.' Claire smiled. She untied the reins and set off back to Jumaaroo.

CHAPTER 11

Claire found Gordie's ramshackle house deserted when she arrived, so she led Flossie around the back where an old tin bath held some water. The donkey drank greedily, and Claire envied the animal. She would have loved some water herself. She'd rationed the bottle Betty gave her, but it astonished her how much she needed to drink here.

She tethered the donkey to a gate under a large spreading tree so she had some shade, and unhitched the cart. As she set off, she noticed a twitch in the curtain.

Darana opened the door, but only a little. 'Gordie's not here,' she said. 'He's collectin' Jannali.'

'Oh, thank you, Darana. And thank him for the use of Flossie and the cart for me please.' She smiled.

'All right, fine.' Darana went to close the door.

'Could I trouble you for a glass of water? I'm so thirsty.'

Darana opened the door a tiny fraction more. She didn't look too happy at the intrusion, but she sighed and said, 'Wait here.' She returned moments later with an enamel mug of water. Claire took it gratefully and gulped it down in one go.

'More?' the woman asked.

Claire nodded. 'Please.'

Darana left the door open a little as she went to fetch the drink, and Claire could see the house was really just one room. It was tidy and clean, and the family obviously slept and cooked in the same space.

'Sister Claire!'

Claire spun around to see Jannali enter the yard. Gordie was further back, next to the track. School was over for the day.

'Hello, Jannali, how was school today?' Claire asked, glad to see the little girl had perked up a bit. She'd been so upset since hearing about her grandfather.

'Good. You wanna see me glider?' Jannali asked as she dropped her schoolbag by the front door.

'I don't know what that is?' Claire replied.

'Come in, I'll show ya.' Jannali beckoned her in, but Claire didn't want to cross the threshold without being invited by an adult.

'I think I'd better wait here.' Claire suppressed a grin at her accent, her dropped h's and her broad vowels, but the little girl was determined.

'He's shy, but he'll come out for me. Dad made a box for him. He fell outta the gum tree behind there, and a taipan nearly got him, but Dad saved him and give him to me. He says he's gotta go back in the trees, but he can't glide no more, 'cause his wing's busted.'

Claire had no idea what the child was talking about, and Darana had gone out the back door and was nowhere to be seen. 'Is he a bird?' she asked.

Jannali looked at her as if she were the stupidest person she'd ever seen. 'He's a *glider*!' She chuckled. 'Not a bird! Look, I'll get him for ya.'

She disappeared and returned a moment later with a wooden box filled with leaves and straw, and tucked inside in one corner was the cutest little creature. Claire had never seen anything like it before. He had the face of a hamster, with huge dark eyes and a long dark stripe down his head, but he had big ears that pricked up and a long furry tail. Jannali gently took him out, her fingernails filthy, and softly stroked him.

'See here?' She pointed at the creature's body. 'He's got skin between his front legs and his back legs, and they are like wings. He can fly through the trees, or at least he's s'posed to, but I reckon this one's crook. Woiduna could've fixed him.' The little girl shrugged, her dark eyes pools of sadness.

Claire stroked the little furry body as the creature picked up a leaf and began to nibble on it. It was the cutest thing Claire had ever seen.

She was interrupted by Darana's arrival with another cup, and Claire took it with a smile of thanks. She drank it all, and handed the cup back. 'Jannali was just showing me her glider. I've never seen one before. He's a beautiful little fella.'

'He's crook,' Darana said and sighed. 'Probably he'll die.'

Jannali looked stricken. 'I want Woiduna,' she said quietly, and the pain in her voice broke Claire's heart.

Darana's eyes filled with tears. She was grieving too, and Claire could see she was struggling.

Claire bent down to be eye level with the little girl. 'I know you do. You must miss him so much. And I bet he could have fixed your little glider. But how about you take him to school tomorrow and ask Daku to have a look at him? He's not as good as Woiduna, I'm sure, but he did look after a kangaroo joey last week whose mum died, so he is good with animals.'

'Can I show him to my friends?'

Claire caught Darana's eye as Gordie walked up to the house. She saw the relief there that her little girl had some friends.

'Of course you can. I'll tell Sister Mary when I go back that there is going to be a special visitor in the classroom tomorrow, and then whenever Daku comes, we can ask him to take a look. Is that all right?'

Jannali nodded and even managed a wan smile.

'Now, can you do something for me? Can you go outside and check that Flossie has enough water? It was a really hot day for her carrying me all that way, so she might need more.'

Jannali looked her up and down. 'You're a bit fat to carry, but she won't mind. She can carry really heavy loads. Once she carried two calves and a huge bag of spuds, and I reckon they were heavier than you.'

Claire chuckled. Jannali's candour was hilarious. 'Well, she might need a drink, so can you do that for me? And maybe turn her out into the field if you can do that?'

'Course I can. I always do it for Dad.' Jannali left.

By now, Darana's face was wet with tears.

'I'm so sorry about your father,' Claire said, the words sounding hollow.

'I can't...' Darana began, but words deserted her.

Gordie walked to her side and put his arm around her. She turned her face into his chest.

'How did ya go with Russ?' he asked.

'As you predicted,' Claire replied.

'Yeah, he won't want no truck with you lot, but I reckon you believe Daku. I do too.'

Claire was nonplussed. She wished she could answer him, but she couldn't. She knew Joseph McGrath was a bully and an egotist, but could he be capable of murder? Surely not?

All the way back from the mission, she'd mulled it over. She should just stay out of it. There was no evidence. McGrath was a man of good standing in the community, and he was very well connected. She couldn't wade in there throwing accusations about without proof, and Woiduna hated McGrath. She was a nun, not a detective. It wasn't her place. But now Gordie seemed convinced as well.

'I don't know what to believe,' Claire admitted.

'Nah, it was him, all right. He ordered it, but Big Bill did the job. Reckon he tried to make it look like an accident, but Woiduna wouldn't get himself into something stupid – he's a native here. McGrath was pushing the tribe to the mission and he stood up to him. You don't do that in Jumaaroo and get away with it.' Gordie shook his head, indicating the conversation was over as Jannali ran back in.

Darana moved out of his embrace, allowing the child to climb up him like a monkey.

97

'I showed her me glider. He ate a whole banana leaf today, so I reckon he's on the mend.'

Gordie's eyes softened as he gave her his full attention.

'Sister Claire says I can take him to school tomorrow and Daku might be able to do somethin' with him 'cause Woiduna can't now.'

Gordie gently tucked a strand of wild hair behind the child's ear. His unkempt appearance and the stubble on his chin made him look fierce, but there was tenderness in his eyes as he looked at Jannali. 'That's a great idea, possum.' He didn't try to explain or say anything reassuring.

By now Darana was silently weeping again, and Jannali's little face searched Gordie's for a sign that the adults could make this all better. She turned her gaze from her father to her mother and then to Claire. 'I know he died, but it don't make sense. Nothing would hurt him. Even salties or red backs, browns, nothing would hurt Woiduna. He knows them, see? And he couldn't have fallen – he could jump and run and climb better than anyone.' She was trying to find a way to understand. In her world, only snakes, spiders, crocs and the many other deadly things had to be treated with caution. The idea that a person would end another person's life was simply not within her comprehension.

'I wish I'd met him properly. He sounds like a wonderful person,' Claire said, aware of how inadequate her words were. But she had nothing to soften the sharp pain of loss and confusion in the child. There was no mention of God, or that Woiduna was in heaven now, the ideas on which her faith was based and that gave comfort to the grieving.

Gordie held her tight, his other arm around Darana.

'I'll go. Thank you for the donkey, and the water...' Claire wanted to leave this family to their grief. She turned away, and Gordie followed, walking beside her.

'I hope it wasn't too bad with Russell?' he asked, an eyebrow raised. 'He can be a bit...well, a bit full on, but he's all right mostly.'

'He thought at first that I meant harm to the children, and once he found out the reason for my visit, he told me bluntly he didn't trust me and wanted nothing to do with me.'

'I did warn ya. He sees you and McGrath as all the same. You might think different, but to him, and to them' – he nodded in the direction of the bush, and she assumed he meant the native people – 'you are all the same.'

'Are you one hundred percent convinced Joseph McGrath did it, Gordie?' Claire knew he'd said as much, but she needed to be totally sure.

'Reckon it can't be anyone else. Big Bill is a dangerous bugger, and that Lockie is strong as an ox. Though he's dozy, he's handy with his fists. Woiduna was quick and strong but no match for two of them. Woiduna went to McGrath apparently, threatened him, and not for the first time either. The old bloke reckoned he could get through to him, but nah. I reckon McGrath had enough. He knew the law wouldn't touch him. The cops don't give a monkey's about the Abbos. That mission is full to burstin' now. I reckon there can't be too many more Bundagulgi left out there. Woiduna is dead, so McGrath got what he wanted – again.'

'How is Darana bearing up? She looks crushed.'

'Yeah, she is. They were thick as thieves, them two. And they used to have blue murder too.' He chuckled. 'You should've heard them when they went at it, yelling and carryin' on. But they loved each other. Jannali too.'

'And how did he take to her marrying you?' Claire knew it was presumptuous to ask, but she was intrigued.

Gordie grinned again. 'Woiduna was mad. He didn't want her with a whitefella. Her mum died when she was a kid, but my Darana isn't one for being told what to do, even by him, and the old bloke got used to me. He was all right.'

Claire knew that was as far as Gordie was willing to go to admit his personal grief, but she could see he was as cut up as his family were.

They reached the end of the property and Claire thanked him again. 'I'm so sorry for your loss. Is there anything at all I can do?'

He shrugged. 'Nah, there's nothing anyone can do. The cops answer to McGrath, the town hall is his office, the natives mean less to him than a mozzie, somethin' annoying to swat. No one round here cares about them and that's the truth.'

He turned and left, and as Claire walked back to Jumaaroo, her mind raced. If what Gordie and Russell and Daku said was true, she felt sure her uncle would not support a man who was so blatantly a criminal. There had to be something she could do.

CHAPTER 12

*J*oseph McGrath tried to keep the skip out of his step. The meeting had gone even better than he expected.

He strode down the street in Brisbane, his head full of ideas. The land at Trouble Bay soon would be his. So much for the God-botherers being all about the next world. He laughed as he walked. He'd offered the boss of the whole Adventist church enough money, and just like that, he caved. He'd love to see Russell's face when he found out they'd sold his precious mission out from under him. All religions were the same – greedy buggers, only interested in lining their own pockets.

Of course, they'd made out like they were concerned about old Russ Gardiner and his Abbos, but he'd eased their fake worries by showing them some random land on a map he'd brought – land he didn't even own – and telling them he would relocate the mission there. Once the deal was done, neither he nor the Adventists would give a hoot where the natives went. They could walk into the sea for all he cared.

He'd not mentioned why he wanted it, and they hadn't asked. If they knew it was absolutely perfect for a jungle warfare training facility, they might have tried to do a deal with the army themselves.

Only one road in and the same one out meant it was secure. Trouble Bay had everything they needed to build the base – rainforest for jungle warfare training, the ocean for naval involvement and a long sandbar that could easily be built up to create a runway. They just needed to acquire the land, and then construction could begin immediately.

The other branches of his business would benefit too – tin, copper, logging. They would need all of that. Things were heating up in Europe and in the Far East, so men with access to minerals were the army's friend. He did very well and had more money than he could spend in a lifetime, but that wasn't the point. He loved the feeling being in control gave him.

The deeds would be in his name by the end of the week, and transferred to His Majesty's Royal Australian armed forces as soon as possible afterwards. There would be no hitches; he'd oiled the wheels in advance of the deal.

The general he'd spoken to was quite excited. The infrastructure at Trouble Bay was poor, but Joseph would supply crews to improve the road network so access wouldn't be a problem. Jumaaroo would really be put on the map. They would not just need the base, but the base would need to be fed and watered and supplied... And there was only one man who could do it all.

Joseph doffed his hat at two ladies he saw cast him an admiring glance. The new suit he'd picked up from his tailor yesterday fit like a glove, and his gold silk tie and matching handkerchief teamed with an ivory linen shirt made everyone, men and women alike, look twice. He enjoyed the admiration. He was a good-looking man – he'd known it all his life – but that wasn't enough. For true admiration, you needed money and power and status. Some people were born into these things, but he wasn't one of those people. He'd made his own luck.

Assumpta had moaned before he left about that bloody nun again; apparently she'd gone out to the mission for some unfathomable reason. The last thing he needed in the light of this new development was that curmudgeonly Gardiner joining forces with the nuns.

Though an alliance was unlikely. The Adventists were convinced the Catholics were the Antichrist or something.

The whole lot of it was a load of rubbish as far as he was concerned. If there was anything when you die, then he was sure as hell it had nothing to do with the churches, whatever colour they were. It was every man for himself, and he had no time for anyone banging on about his way being the best. His life thus far had cured him of any religious fervour. Hocus pocus, the lot of it. He went to Mass, of course, because it was expedient to do so. He even did the readings when he was asked to; it was good to be seen doing things like that. But he mostly used the time while the priest was droning on to think his thoughts, plan his next move.

An image of the determined little face of Sister Claire came to his mind. She wasn't attractive in the normal way certainly, but there was something about her, something that intrigued him, and if he were to admit it, something even alluring. He mentally shook himself. His taste in women was definitely unusual, but a nun was stretching it, even for him. Besides, he did not draw female drama into his life – he actively avoided it – and the woman was deluded on so many levels. But that said, she did need slapping down. Initially, he'd not seen her as any kind of adversary. He'd miscalculated.

His usual attack – charm, especially with ladies – seemed not to work. He was a man with a voracious appetite for the opposite sex, so the idea of living a life of celibacy was a mystery. But that small dumpy nun was impervious to his charisma, in that department anyway. He'd tried being forthright, telling her straight to back off, but that hadn't worked either. She had the bishop behind her, which was a problem. He hadn't got where he had by making enemies with powerful people. No, he'd have to box clever around Sister Claire.

He signed into the club and immediately relished the cooler air inside. Large fans that hung from the ornate ceiling made sure the patrons stayed comfortable.

He ordered a salad. He would have a visitor to his room this afternoon. Madame LeFevre, who ran the high-end agency and who was no more French than he was, assured him this new girl from Thailand or somewhere had all manner of erotic tricks up her sleeve. It was expensive, but she'd assured him he wouldn't be disappointed. He was looking forward to it.

He swirled the clear soda water in the Waterford cut-glass tumbler and smiled his thanks at the pretty waitress who delivered his food. She coloured. He'd leave her a nice tip. She might come in handy later.

As he ate his salad, he ruminated. The military were adamant – the land zoned for the new training centre would have to be secluded, with absolutely no public access. He'd guaranteed them it would be. He'd probably have to get Big Bill to round up a gang to move the Abbos and Russ out of the Trouble Bay mission, but it could be done. They wouldn't have a legal leg to stand on. They'd be trespassing.

He'd neglected to mention to the army that it was impossible to get full security with the Abbos; they were like cockroaches and could get in anywhere. He'd let the new owners discover that for themselves. But if the boys in uniform took a couple of pot-shots and did away with one or two of them, they wouldn't be long learning a lesson. The blackfellas were easily spooked, something that had worked to his advantage for some time now.

He'd had to pay Big Bill McAllister handsomely to get rid of that pest Woiduna, but it was worth it. McAllister was a brute but a handy man to have. With the elder out of the picture, the Abbos would be easier to manoeuvre.

In hindsight, though, it was a pain that they were all gathered at the mission and that he had to move them all again now. But at least he could manage what he could see. When they were all scattered over the bush, they were impossible to control. It was like minding mice at a crossroads.

He felt a sharp pang. The last time he'd heard someone use that phrase was so long ago. A different life, a different place. A face formed in his mind – Molly, the only one who'd ever cared for him.

Stop. He didn't need to go getting all nostalgic and maudlin now. Molly was dead. He'd paid for a nice headstone back in Ireland for her, anonymously of course, so he'd done right by her, as she'd done right by him.

Not any more, but in the early days, Assumpta used to press him for details of his childhood. So to shut her up, he invented a family, all conveniently dead now. But he would never tell her, or anyone, about Molly. She was the only person who'd ever got into his heart. Sometimes he wondered what she would make of him now. If she could see him, would she be impressed with his success?

Once finished with his salad, he stood and set off. He was meeting his Asian lady at two.

CHAPTER 13

*C*laire listened as Mei Wong tried to stem the tears and explain what had happened. Claire had stumbled across the small dark-haired ten-year-old outside Gerard's door, her palms red and sore, and led the child to her office.

'S-s-sister Gerard s-s-said I was to s-s-stay here,' the terrified child whispered.

But Claire turned to her and kindly said, 'It's fine, Mei. I'll explain to Sister Gerard afterwards that I wanted to speak to you.' Seeing the distress and fear on the child's face, Claire sought to reassure her further. 'You aren't in any trouble. I just want to hear what happened, all right?'

Claire deliberately kept her desk on one side of the room. She didn't like sitting behind it and making children sit on the other side; it was too intimidating. Instead, she had two chairs of equal size by the window. She sat Mei opposite her and asked, 'So can you start at the beginning and tell me what happened?'

Mei was a bright girl, and Claire knew her family had high hopes for her.

The child swallowed, wiped her eyes with the handkerchief Claire had given her, took a sip of water from the glass at her elbow and inhaled, steadying herself. 'I wrote the composition Sister Gerard gave the class to do as homework at the weekend, and she told us to place them on the desks while she went around to collect them. She didn't pick mine up at all, or some of the others' exercise books.' Mei swallowed and tried to gather her confidence.

Claire placed her hand on the girl's. 'It's all right, Mei, please go on. I promise you nothing bad will happen because you told me.'

'So I put up my hand and asked her if I should bring my exercise book up to her.'

'And what happened?' Claire asked, dreading the answer.

'She ignored me. So I stood up and brought my book up anyway.'

Claire could see the light of defiance in the little girl's face and was proud of her. 'Go on.'

'She opened my book to where I had written the composition, and then she tore out the pages, one by one, and threw them in the wastepaper basket. Then she told me to put out my hands and she… she used the strap on me.' Mei allowed the tears to fall as Claire examined the welts on her hands.

Gently Claire rubbed some ointment on them, then gave the child a barley sugar and a book about Irish folk tales and told her to stay in the office and read until she came for her.

The temper that had long since been taken under control bubbled up inside her as she strode down the corridor. Her mother, and later her superiors in the convent, had pointed out how she would have to control her temper, and she wanted so badly to be a nun, to fulfil her vocation, that she'd done it. She'd bitten her tongue and walked away, turned the other cheek so often it was second nature now, but seeing poor little Mei, and thinking of Cassia's little boy, all those frightened little faces every day, all her lessons on humility vanished.

She barged into Gerard's room, not even knocking, to find her administering the strap once more, this time to Dieter Mann, a boy whose mother had died only three months ago and whose father was not coping well. Gerard appeared shocked but said nothing.

'Children, please take an early lunch break and go outside. You too, Dieter. Quickly now, gather your lunch and off you go.'

Twenty-four students gazed at her incredulously. Dieter looked like someone reprieved from the gallows. This was unprecedented.

'Come along, before I change my mind.' She smiled and they giggled, rushing to gather their sandwiches and bottles of water. Within seconds, the classroom was deserted.

Gerard had used the time to hide her shock and return to her usual nonchalant disdain.

Claire closed the door and pulled down the blinds so they could not be seen. An altercation between two nuns would be gossip in Jumaaroo for weeks. 'I have Mei Wong in my office, with welts on her hands. You were just about to assault Dieter Mann, a child who is grieving for his mother.' Claire was seething but tried to keep her voice steady. 'As far as I can see, there are no children in your class who are not of Irish extraction that have not been beaten with that… thing, an item I expressly told you I did not want used.' Claire pointed at the leather strap, her voice low and deliberate. Gerard must have acquired another one as Claire had confiscated the first.

'And your point is?' Gerard asked, bored.

'My point, Sister Gerard, is this.' Claire stood before her, easily six inches shorter than her, but she would not be cowed. 'I am principal here. You once said I would not go running to my uncle, and though it was not an easy letter for me to write, I felt I needed support in defending these innocent children against your tyranny.'

She extracted a letter from her pocket, the Bishop's Palace notepaper clearly visible, and read aloud.

Dear Sister Claire,

I was most perturbed to read of the difficulties you are facing at St Finbarr's, and I appreciate how grave the situation must have been for you to write to me. Please convey to Sister Gerard my deep disappointment after hearing of these events. I would urge her to temper her behaviours and remember that it was Jesus who said 'suffer the little children to come unto me'.

I will visit Jumaaroo as soon as I am able with my current workload, but in the meantime, please explain to Sister Gerard how I shall expect a glowing report from you when I do come.

Yours in Christ,
Archbishop William McAuliffe

A toxic silence hung in the air, and Claire had to bite her tongue to not say more. Let Gerard respond.

'Well, well, well, the little girl went running to her uncle as I predicted she would.'

Gerard's mouth curled into a sneer.

'I knew you couldn't do this on your own, I knew from the moment I met you, and now you've proved me right.'

Gerard walked past her slowly out of the room, each footstep on the timber floor feeling like a slow mocking handclap.

Claire exhaled, placing both hands on a desk for support. Gerard was gone, she was alone. Her heart pounded and her mouth was dry. She spun around as she heard the door open behind her. It was Teresita.

'Are you all right?' the other nun asked quietly.

Claire nodded. She didn't want to draw anyone else into the conflict.

Teresita patted her on the back. 'That needed doing. Well done.' Teresita's room was next door, and Claire noticed that her students were outside as well. 'I sent mine out when I saw you were gunning.' She winked, and Claire grinned ruefully.

'I've made an enemy of her now though, haven't I?'

'Yerra, you have, I suppose, but sure, there's only one of her, and you did the right thing then.'

Claire shot her a grateful glance. It was not the way of faith to have factions and to feel ill will towards one's sister, but Gerard really did test her. 'I'm hoping I did. I had to make her stop. The children are terrified. But I don't know...' She sighed.

'Let you go into the chapel. 'Tis nice and cool in there too, fair play to whoever built it, and just rest and pray. 'Tisn't easy the job you have, girleen, but you are makin' a fine fist of it all the same.'

Claire let Teresita's words wash over her troubled mind. She, unlike almost everyone else in Jumaaroo, had no problem understanding her. She had grown up among people who spoke like Teresita, and she found the unique colloquialisms and accent soothing. She remembered her daddy telling her she was 'making a fine fist of the milking', meaning she was doing it well, and the familiar glow of pride she felt then returned now.

'Thank you, Sister Teresita. I think we are all managing, considering.'

'We are surely. Though the lads and lassies before me haven't a bull's notion what I'm going on about. But they're grand people altogether, and we're getting along some kind of way. And they're stone mad for hurling. Look at them out there now – that Li Chen lad is a topper altogether. And young Darius Galatas, look at him! He's got a wicked-fast turn so he has.' Teresita had raised the blinds to see her ragtag bunch of hurlers battling it out on the school field in the heat.

Claire smiled at her enthusiasm.

Teresita went on. 'And Sister Helen is a lovely gentle person, and the boys and girls love goin' into her with her books and stories. And sure doesn't Mary have them all thinkin' they'll be on the stage with the fiddles and pianos. Though to be truthful, there might be a biteen more enthusiasm than talent there.' Teresita chuckled, a deep sound that reminded Claire of a river gurgling over stones.

It was true. The cacophony of instruments poorly played that seemed to never end was far from melodious.

'So don't be worrying your head, girleen, 'twill all be grand. Herself will have to quieten – she's no choice in the matter. Now, I'll go out there to make sure they don't beat the heads off each other with them hurleys – they can't get enough of it. And sure 'twon't do them any harm to have a long break today, especially Gerard's gang.'

Teresita was right. Later, as Claire sat in the chapel, the muted sounds of children's happy yelling and laughter permeated the walls. There were just four pews either side of the narrow aisle, but the altar never ceased to take her breath away. It was simple, just a cross hanging by an almost invisible wire over the altar. The cloth and corporal on which lay the candles and Bible had been hand stitched at her convent at home in Ireland. Behind the altar was the tabernacle, and the sanctuary lamp was always glowing to indicate the presence of God. Despite being thousands of miles from all she knew and held dear, this little chapel felt familiar and welcoming. She could feel the presence of the Lord there, and she prayed for guidance, for forgiveness for the sin of pride, for the grace to do her job in accordance with God's laws.

She was kneeling, deep in meditative prayer, when she was startled by the church door opening. She'd heard the school bell signalling the end of the day ten minutes ago and the children's feet run past the chapel home.

She turned. It was Helen.

'I am so sorry to disturb you, Sister, but I think you should come. There are some people outside.' Helen blessed herself and genuflected before retreating.

Wearily, Claire stood, stiff from being on her knees for hours, and she too genuflected and blessed herself.

Outside in the blazing sun were Helen and Daku, with a very reluctant-looking Russell and Betty Gardiner standing behind them.

'Good afternoon, everyone,' she said, trying to sound like this was a perfectly normal occurrence. 'Shall we go inside, have a cold drink?'

Of Gerard, thankfully, there was no sign, so Claire led them, all grim-faced, into the kitchen of the convent. Helen set about preparing glasses of Cassia's lemonade, which was both delicious and thirst-quenching. The Greek woman had shared the recipe, and Mary had the drink down to a fine art now. They stored it in stone jars under the stairs, which kept it reasonably cool.

As Helen poured drinks, Claire addressed the group again. 'So I presume this isn't a social call?'

Daku spoke as soon as he realised Russell wouldn't. 'There's been a bit of trouble up at the mission. Russell and McGrath have had words – well, more than words actually.' Daku smiled despite the seriousness of the situation.

'Why?' Claire asked. 'And what does that have to do with us?'

'Apparently' – Daku shoved his hands in his trouser pockets – 'McGrath has bought Trouble Bay from the Adventist church and wants to relocate the mission inland someplace. We are Black Cockatoo people. We live out of the ocean. Going that far into the bush isn't our natural place.'

'Why does he want everyone to move?' Claire sipped her drink.

'He says he's got a better place for us, more space, some old cobber's, something like that. But he's the reason the mission is over-crowded in the first place,' Daku said.

Claire thought for a moment. 'If that is true, then I'm sure Mr McGrath has his reasons. And if Mr Gardiner doesn't want to go, then I'm sure that is that. But may I ask why you came here to tell me?'

She saw the look between Daku and Russell. Was she imagining a kind of conspiratorial frisson?

'We thought you might be able to speak to Mr McGrath,' Betty interjected, colouring once she realised all eyes were on her. 'The Aboriginal people are very upset. My husband lost his temper, and unfortunately he hit McGrath and sent him flying. And I... Well, we just thought...well, that Mr McGrath seems to listen to you. You are one of the few people here who isn't afraid to stand up to him.'

Claire struggled to figure out what was going on. 'So you thought that I would intervene?' she asked Russell, who now looked like he wanted the ground to open and swallow him.

'I understand that it is...' His voice trailed off.

'What? A bit odd? You practically accused me of trying to steal the children at the mission, you believe that the faith I have dedicated my life to is evil, and now that you've decided to knock the mayor of Jumaaroo into next week, this is suddenly my problem?' Claire knew she wasn't being very serene and holy, but honestly, the situation was ridiculous.

Russell's face burned but Betty spoke again. 'Look, I know you probably don't want to get involved, but everyone in town is talking about how you won't take the treatment he dishes out to everyone else. He's threatening to evict us, and the Bundagulgi people are terri-fied. They're so rattled after Woiduna, and now this. If anyone can get through to McGrath, get him to back down, then it's you. All we want to know is what he has in mind. Apparently there is another mission, but we never got round to discussing it. We thought, that as a Catholic nun, you could approach him and ask…'

Claire looked around at their expectant faces. 'I don't think –'

'I told you this was pointless,' Russell snarled. 'Come on, Betty.' He grabbed his wife's arm and stormed out, leaving Daku, Helen and Claire alone.

'McGrath is threatening to have Russell arrested for assault and battery,' Daku said darkly. 'And he can do it too. That bludger Seth Godfrey in the cop shop is in McGrath's pocket. I happened to be there at the mission, saw it all – the dunny was blocked, so I was up there trying to fix it. McGrath came in all swagger and flash, like he does, telling Russell they were going to have to move, the deal was done, but he had another site for them someplace. McGrath was loving it, getting one over on the Gardiners. Course old Russell refused, and that mongrel McGrath made out like it was all a done deal, reckoned nobody had a choice, everyone was gonna have to shoot through. He was goading Russell, telling him that his bosses sold him down the river, and the big man just flipped. I never saw him so mad. He accused him there and then of murdering Woiduna. Lucky there were only women and kids there or it could have turned into a massacre. He punched McGrath, a serious left hook, knocked him into next week. Flat out on his back he was, right there on the dirt, his new suit ruined and blood spurting from his spilt lip.' Daku chuckled, clearly delighted McGrath got what was coming to him.

'It was funny to see, but McGrath won't take that. Russell will pay a heavy price. I reckoned you might be the only one who could get through to him. Otherwise he'll make sure the Bundagulgi are driven off the face of the earth. He's already cleared most of us off what he sees as his land, though how he came to that conclusion is anyone's guess. Have enough bigwigs on your side and you can do anything, I s'pose, but the ones at the mission were safe at least with Russell. Now, well, who knows what will happen. Russell won't shoot through. He's decent even if he's a bit of a drongo to deal with sometimes. He'll stay and face the music, whatever it is, but even his own mob that run the show have sold him out. They probably took the money and let Russell rot and the blackfellas with him. He's all out of options, so you are his only hope – our only hope.'

Claire felt overwhelmed. The idea that she could tell Joseph McGrath what to do regarding the school was one thing; taking him to task about his private business dealings was quite another. But Daku was right. From what she knew of him, McGrath would not take a beating without there being very serious consequences for the perpetrator. And accusing him of murder in public, well, what had been rumour was now well and truly out in the open. McGrath had a reputation to maintain, and so Daku was right – Gardiner would pay a heavy penalty for his outburst, and the Bundagulgi would too.

Daku's dark eyes rested on hers for a long moment. 'You could ask him to show you the mission, the place he wants to move us, and at least then we'd know. You could be a go-between. You can say you're worried but you know he wouldn't do wrong by them, some rubbish like that. Tell him you want to reassure us that the new place is going to be great.'

Noting her look of dismay at being alone in the bush with McGrath, he continued. 'I and some of the others could track you. We'd keep an eye on you the whole time – you'd be safe. But we just need to know what he plans. I have a bad feeling about this, but we can't fight what we can't see.' He paused. 'Think about it.'

Slowly he nodded, stood up, drained his glass and left. Claire and Helen watched him retreat. Daku looked different these days; she couldn't say how exactly, except that he was wearing a shirt and his hair seemed a bit tamer or something.

CHAPTER 14

*J*oseph watched the nun waddle up his driveway. 'Assumpta!' he yelled from his office.

Within seconds, his wife was there, that familiar sour look on her face. She was still sulking about having to get that ointment from the doctor. He'd denied giving her whatever she had that was making her like a bag of cats these days, but the reality was, he knew he had.

Madame LeFevre's operation was closed down; Joseph had made sure of it. It was the last time she'd pass off one of her streetwalkers as a high-class woman to him. He'd had to get treated himself. He saw a man in Cairns, who gave him some cream and a bottle of something disgusting to take. It seemed to be working, but the itching and burning was vicious. Between that in the downstairs department and the swollen lip he'd got from that fool Gardiner, he had enough to deal with without this interfering little bee showing up.

Assumpta had ranted and raved when she got home from the local quack, screaming about being mortified and having to endure an examination for venereal disease, threatening to leave him, but he'd smirked at that. She would go nowhere because she had nowhere to go, and they both knew it.

He would, however, have to be more careful in the future. God knows what he might have picked up. Assumpta even threatened to tell Pius or her mother, but as Joseph pointed out, he had just last week settled one of Pius's accounts with a notorious Queensland family for on-track betting, so Pius was unlikely to take his sister's side. His seduction of her mother a handful of times a few years ago meant he had her in the palm of his hand too. Back then, when he and Assumpta got married, the mother was still presentable, so it wasn't a total hardship, but the encounter meant much more to his mother-in-law than to him. She'd made a total fool of herself, writing him simpering letters, begging him to continue the affair. He still had every one of those letters, of course, so he could exert that pressure any time he wanted. Elenora Prendergast was ashamed in retrospect, and he assured her that he was flattered and all the rest of it, but now he had leverage with her. Even a hint of a threat that he would expose what she really was would be enough to shut her up.

'What do you want?' his wife snapped.

He gave her a glare, one that suggested she watch her tone. He pointed out the window. 'Whatever you do, you are not to allow her into the house, right? I am not in the humour for her today.'

'Who?'

'The nun. Tell her I'm not here or something. I don't care how, but get rid of her.'

'Get rid of her yourself,' Assumpta spat.

He looked at her. This would have to stop. She was getting far too mouthy. Everything she had – the fine dresses, the china tea services, her position in the town – was all down to him. She should start showing him a bit of respect.

He stood and walked calmly towards her. He gently closed the door, then grabbed her hair at the nape of her neck, pulling her face close to his.

'You're hurting me! Let me go,' she whined, her face a mask of shock.

'Oh, I'm not hurting you, Assumpta,' he murmured in her ear.

'Believe me, if I wanted to hurt you, you would know all about it. So watch your tone when you speak to me, do you hear me?'

She didn't reply, so he tightened his grip, giving her head a shake, which caused her to yelp.

'I said, do you hear me?'

She nodded, tears of rage and pain pooling in her eyes. He released her. 'Good. Now, do as you're told and get rid of that bloody nun. And cheer up, for God's sake. You'd curdle milk with the long face.'

She backed away, only speaking when her hand was on the door handle. 'You're a monster,' she hissed. 'A dirty, cheating liar, carrying on with prostitutes. You think I don't know? You think I'm blind?'

She was almost hysterical now and he sighed. He did not need this. 'No, I do not think you're blind, and what you do or don't know is frankly of no concern to me. I just want rid of her, right?' He returned to his desk. 'And have a sandwich and a beer sent up to me – now.'

He returned to his paperwork as she left, slamming the door behind her.

Maybe the back of his hand was what was needed there. He didn't want to hit his wife – that was for less sophisticated men than he was – but if she was going to go on like this, then maybe a short sharp shock would pull her back into line. He had enough on his plate at the moment without Assumpta getting ideas above her station.

The Trouble Bay development as a large-scale military operation was finalised. Though it was not ideal, Gardiner hitting him was actually a good thing. He would get Seth to arrest him tomorrow and then move the natives while Gardiner was resting in the jailhouse.

The purchase from the Adventists had gone smoothly, and he'd had the telegram from His Majesty's Australian armed forces confirming that the money would be transferred to his account by the end of the week.

He heard the knock on the door and had an idea. He'd have to deal with the nun sometime, and now might be a good time. He'd let Assumpta tell her the lie that he was out, and then appear. He chuckled at the idea of humiliating his wife.

He walked onto the landing and glanced over the balcony.

Assumpta was haughtily telling Sister Claire that her husband was not at home and that she would have to make an appointment if she wanted to see him. He waited until Assumpta finished her little speech before bounding downstairs.

'Sister Claire!' he boomed, as if her visit was the nicest surprise he could have imagined. He glanced sideways, glad to see Assumpta's face burning having been caught out in a lie.

'Mr McGrath,' Claire said. 'I am very sorry to disturb you at home, but I wondered if I might have a word?'

'Certainly, Sister, of course.' An extravagant wave of his hand welcomed her into his home. He'd designed the house himself, and it was by far the most impressive for miles around. He'd trawled auctions for antique furniture brought out from Europe, and the curved staircase was handmade. The rugs, the vases, the paintings had all been bought by him. He allowed Assumpta to fill the home with her china and glass and things like that, but it was his house, no question. By far his favourite piece, however, was the large oak desk, with drawers either side, that he'd taken from Assumpta's father's study when he died. He'd mentioned to her mother how much he loved it, and just like that, she gave it to him. Of course he had intended to take it anyway, but it was better that she offered. It was a beautiful piece of furniture, and he loved sitting behind it.

'Please come inside. Let me get you a drink? Or a cup of tea?' He smiled though it hurt his lip. The swelling had gone down a bit, but it was still noticeable.

He wondered what Sister Claire's visit was about this time. His wife normally delivered any information via Sister Gerard, but that was before the bloody doctor told her that her problems were sexually transmitted.

'A glass of water would be lovely, thank you.' Claire smiled at Assumpta, who looked shamefacedly back at her, desperate to get away.

'Assumpta, could you see to that please, dear?' He smiled sweetly and stood back, gesturing that Claire should go ahead of him.

Once in the drawing room – a room he particularly loved, with portraits on the walls that he'd bought at auction for cheap before he met Assumpta and a beautiful gold and royal-blue Axminster rug – he invited her to sit. The sofa was a large chesterfield, but once someone sat in it, they sank down, making getting up a sort of ungainly affair. For that reason, he never sat on it, choosing instead the wingback chair, which was slightly higher and gave him a bit of an advantage. The nun perched on the edge of the sofa.

'Now, Sister Claire, what can I do for you?' he asked. Maintaining a cordial relationship with her was hard, but after the last far-less-than-satisfactory encounter, he needed to play the long game.

'I would like to talk to you about your plans for the Trouble Bay mission,' she said, quite directly.

'What about them?' He kept his tone light and mild. Inside, however, he fumed at the cheek of her. Whatever about the school, his business dealings were nobody's business, let alone this fat interfering cow's.

'Well, it has been brought to my attention that you and Mr Gardiner of the Trouble Bay mission have had some kind of dispute. I was asked by members of the community to speak to you, to find out what plans you have for the mission if it is no longer to occupy its current location. As you probably already know, the Bundagulgi people have had a lot to deal with in recent times. Their homeland has been subjected to drought because the creeks don't flow, and there were fires, and then the death of the elder Woiduna.'

Her tone gave nothing away, but her eye caught his for a split second and he felt the accusation.

'Well, it has left them feeling very vulnerable and frightened, and now the only place they feel safe is under threat as well.'

Her confidence was incredible, he'd give her that. 'Sister Claire,' he began, 'do you know the position of the Seventh-day Adventist Church on the subject of Catholics?'

She paused, taken aback a little by the question. 'I do, but either way, it's not relevant –'

'Oh, but it is. Most relevant. They don't like us, not one bit. They think we are the enemy. And that, my dear Sister Claire, is why

Russell Gardiner sent you away with a flea in your ear when you tried to speak to him a while back.'

He could tell from her face that she was surprised he'd heard about that. She'd have to learn that nothing happened in Jumaaroo without his knowledge. 'I don't see how –'

Joseph held his hand up to silence her. 'Be careful that you don't back the wrong horse here. You are a Catholic nun, and the niece of the bishop. You're doing a great job at the school, and we are all delighted to have you. But do not be foolish. The likes of Gardiner won't prove to be on your side, and if you decide to back them against your own, well, then I can safely say you won't get much support from the Church either, even from your uncle.'

He had her now. 'You came here full of ideas of how to make this place better, and I'll admit I wasn't sure your plans for the school were the right way to go about things. But it's working out and everyone in Jumaaroo is happy, and that's important to me. But trust me, this is a hornet's nest you do not want to go kicking. They will use you, and whatever perceived influence you have, but they see you as the enemy and always will. That's all there is to it.'

He knew he was patronising her. He wanted to do a lot more, but that was as far as he was willing to go for now. He watched as she processed what he said.

'I am not concerned with the position of any factions or churches. I am concerned with what is going to happen to the Bundagulgi people. They are worried, they are grieving, and as I understand it, they just want to know what alternative is proposed for them. If we could just see it. Simply that.'

God, this woman was so aggravating! She was like a terrier, never letting go. 'Well, I would have shown Gardiner. In fact, that was my intention before he decided to assault me.' Joseph smiled. He was going to play this friendly even if he felt like choking her.

'And he was wrong to do that,' Claire conceded.

'Look, I just want a peaceful life, Sister.' He sighed. 'So how about this. Let me take you to where I propose to move the mission. It's only an hour or two in my car, and we can drive most of the way. We'll go there, and you can see for yourself how much more land there would be. I would have – if Gardiner had given me the opportunity before attacking me – explained how I plan accommodation, a church, a school and anything else the Aborigines need on the new site.'

He forced himself to smile. 'Trust me, Sister Claire, it's tall poppy syndrome. I know they are saying I had something to do with that Woiduna's death, but I didn't. I had him thrown off my property for sure. The man was a pain in the neck with his mad imaginings. If the cat had kittens, he'd blame me. But I didn't *kill* him, for God's sake. Do you honestly think I'm someone who could do that?' His blue eyes locked with hers.

'Look, there are people who hate progress, hate to see anyone doing well, especially if they are not. Honestly, I'm not the devil here. I am actually trying to do right by the native people, if only they would allow me to. Come with me now – we can leave this very minute. And you'll see the place I have in mind is wonderful. It has a huge river nearby, a lake too, and a waterfall. There are acres of bush there that can be made into a really nice place, a place where they can live and grow and be happy. They are like sardines in a tin out at Trouble Bay – there is no future for them there. So what do you think? Will you come?'

He could see her weigh up what he was saying.

'And it's only two hours from here?' she asked.

'Yes. The site itself is off the track, so we might have to walk a little, but I really want you to see this place. I think you'll be impressed.'

'Very well.' As she agreed, the maid appeared with a tray of drinks and a silver ice bucket.

'Ah, some of our own orange juice. Lovely.' Joseph poured her a glass and added a tantalising number of ice cubes.

HE HANDED her a large glass full and clinked his glass with hers. 'To the future.' He smiled.

CHAPTER 15

*T*he drive in Joseph McGrath's car was pleasant.

'It's a Hudson Eight Coupe,' he explained as she sat in. She'd travelled in a few motor cars in her life but none as glamorous as this. He sat in beside her, and the overwhelming maleness of him, his proximity, his scent, all made her nervous. She was not used to being in such close quarters with men, and in particular men like him.

'It's very nice,' she said politely.

'It's a convertible, which means you can travel with the roof either up or down. It's hot today, so I think we'll leave it down and feel the wind on our faces. Are you adapting to the heat yet?' he asked as he revved the engine and gently drove off his property.

They travelled down the hill into the town, where the sight of Joseph McGrath driving the nun from the school was the most interesting thing to happen for weeks.

As they passed Wilson's Groceries and Provisions, she waved at Billy Wilson, an incorrigible eight-year-old, who was sweeping the steps. Outside the Jumaaroo Hotel, a group of working men were enjoying a cold beer, and walking on the boardwalk under the canopy protecting the shops from the searing sun was Gordie. He spotted her, and she beckoned him over as McGrath slowed down.

'I'm just going with Mr McGrath to see the proposed site for the new mission,' she said pointedly.

'Oh yeah?' was all he said.

'The ideal new location,' McGrath added as he accelerated.

Within moments, they were away from the town and driving down the coast. Claire hoped that Gordie would get word to Daku. He knew she was going up to see the McGraths today, so they were ready to track her, but keeping pace with a car was another matter.

Daku assured her that there was only one road in and out of Jumaaroo but there were several shortcuts through the jungle, so they would know where she was, but the vegetation either side of them now seemed so dense, she feared the natives would lose them.

The road was in better shape than most of the roads around the region, again thanks to McGrath, who ensured they were maintained. The azure ocean crashed mercilessly on the black rocky shore, and the abundant lush rainforest covered the mountains like a blanket. The welcome breeze buffeted her face.

'What part of Cork are you from?' she asked, the wind making her shout.

'I moved around. How about you?' he replied. Since she'd met him, his accent had snagged with her.

'Macroom.'

'Ah, the town that never reared a fool.' He grinned as he repeated the old adage.

'That's what they say all right.'

'It must feel like you are a long way from home.'

'No more for me than you, I'd imagine. How long have you been in Australia?'

'Oh, a lot longer than you, I can tell you, but the heat is still hard to endure. I dream of a nice cold winter's day.'

'So did you come with your parents as a child, or as an adult?' she persisted. He obviously didn't like to talk about himself – he batted every question back with only the most perfunctory of answers – but a part of her was fascinated by him. What you saw was not what you got, she was sure of that.

'Oh, an adult. Landed here and set about making my fortune.' He chuckled and distracted her by pointing to a mob of kangaroos lazing under a purple flowering jacaranda tree in the heat. 'Nothing like those back in Macroom.'

'No indeed. I'd seen them in picture books, koalas and possums too, but never in real life until I got here.'

They chatted cordially as the miles flew by. Sometimes they sat in silence, Claire marvelling as the diamond glints of sunshine on the waves almost blinded her. Everything – the birds, the flowers, the fish – was in such vivid hues here, it made the rest of the world pale in comparison. She could see the splendour of God's magnificent creation all around her every day, and she offered a prayer of thanks.

Though she told herself she was being silly, there was no reason to be nervous, she wished one of her sisters was with her. Teresita with her common sense and ability to see the funny side, or Mary who believed the best of everyone. Or Helen, who had taken such an interest in the fate of the Bundagulgi. Claire wondered why Helen in particular had taken the cause of the Aboriginal people to heart.

She knew very little about Helen, who was only recently professed as far as she could determine. Claire judged her to be in her late twenties, thirty at the outside. Her education in classical literature was unusual; generally, sisters were trained as teachers or nurses, earning a broader qualification. But while Helen was perfectly capable of teaching mathematics and geography, it was clear that her formal education was in literature. She was gradually opening up, a little at least, but it was a slow process.

Round and round the thoughts went in her head as McGrath deftly manoeuvred his fancy car on the now perilous roads. They had left the coast a while back and were now climbing higher and higher. The track was much rougher, and the vegetation that once had been green and inviting was now suffocating and threatening. It was so dense either side of the car, it was impossible to see further than a couple of feet into the jungle. The huge fronds, vines and plants grew well over twenty feet tall, and their abundance was oppressive.

She cast a sidelong glance at her driver. He seemed lost in his own thoughts as well.

'Not long now,' he said cheerfully as they rounded yet another bend into more of the same deep rainforest.

The cacophony of sound was deafening, ticks and croaks and screeches, rustles and creaks. She'd never imagined a jungle to be so noisy. 'It seems a long way from Trouble Bay,' she said.

'It's not as far as you think. We had to drive round the long way because of the terrain, but on foot it's much shorter.'

Well, that's good news, she thought, watching the passing dense vegetation for signs of movement.

Higher and higher they climbed, until they reached a rocky outcrop. He stopped the car and walked round to her side to open her door. Together they walked to a rock that seemed like a balcony of nature's own design. From where they stood, they could see the glistening ocean on one side, stretching as far as the horizon uninterrupted, but on the other side, a lush valley rolled away to flat bush for several miles before rising once more to another peak. It was spectacularly beautiful, like a little hidden pocket surrounded by mountains.

She followed the line of his arm as he pointed to a river that flowed through the bush.

'You can't see from up here, but further down, that river fills into a lake, maybe three or four miles square, full of fish. I intend to give them all of this, the entire piece of land, which, as you can see now, is like some kind of paradise. They'll have so much more space, and I'll fund the construction of whatever they need.' He turned and smiled. 'You see? I'm not such a big bad wolf now, am I, Sister Claire?'

Claire watched him as he told her about access roads, how they'd even bring in electricity if they wanted it, and she could hear the enthusiasm in his voice. It did look perfect – maybe she had him wrong. This site did seem a better alternative than the cramped Trouble Bay, which was on a sandbar and surrounded on three sides by water. There would never be enough space there, and expansion was impossible. She knew the Bundagulgi people didn't want to go, but people always resist change, even if it's good for them. Humans are naturally cautious.

'What do you want the land at Trouble Bay for, Mr McGrath?' she asked.

'I can't tell you that, I'm afraid. Not my story to tell, and it's a term of the sale that it stays hush-hush, but trust me, it's a very good thing.' He winked, and she had to suppress a smile.

'Well, just tell me this then. Is there no way whatever progress you have in mind could go ahead without discommoding the mission?' She suspected it was something to do with the government. Daku, who knew everything, had told her that McGrath had met with some men in Cairns recently, one of them in uniform.

'It couldn't,' was all he was willing to say. 'Look, Sister Claire, the plan I am suggesting, that the natives be moved onto what you must agree is a beautiful place and get whatever they want, is a good one. The likes of Gardiner can't – well, the truth is he won't – see that. Anything coming from me, as far as he's concerned, is bound to be terrible, but I'm trying to do right by them.'

'While lining your own pockets in the process.' Claire let the words slip out but tempered them with a smile.

He held his hands up in surrender. 'I'm a businessman, Sister. I don't expect you to understand that. Yes, I stand to make some money out of this deal. But trust me, if I don't, someone else will. Trouble Bay will be used for something else, and this is their best option.'

She looked around, ostensibly admiring the vista but in reality looking for Daku or any one of the trackers. Daku had said to stall him, give them time to catch up, so she thought quickly. 'Can we get down there?' she asked, pointing to the flat land below. Though the prospect wasn't one she relished, it would buy them some more time.

'Why? You've seen it. This is what it is. We can't drive down – the only way is to climb down that bush track, but you won't want to do that. It's too hot.'

'I'm able to if you are,' she said, setting off in the direction of the track. 'If I am to recommend this location, I have to see it properly.'

'Suit yourself.' He sighed. He went to the boot of his car and took out a handgun. She saw him slip it in his waistband and was shocked. Over his shoulder he slung a large canteen of water.

'What on earth do you need that for?' she asked, suddenly dry-mouthed, pointing at the gun.

'*Because*' – he pointed theatrically at the land below – 'that is the Australian bush, and *this*' – he waved his hand all around them – 'is the jungle, and God alone knows what lives there. If something threatens us, I think we might need something more convincing than a rosary bead to defend ourselves, Sister.' He smiled and sighed. 'Right, let's get this over with. I can't believe you are making me go down there in this heat. See the lengths I'm going to to keep you all happy, Sister?'

He'd taken off his light suit jacket and removed his tie, opening his collar, and was now only in his shirtsleeves. He'd also exchanged his polished leather shoes for rough boots. They looked incongruous with his tailored trousers and fine linen shirt, but she suspected they were more suitable for the terrain they were about to cover. Her own light lace-up brogues would have to do, she supposed. She walked behind him as they began the descent, watching the muscles ripple in his broad muscular back. As the path down became denser and darker, she found her face level with the middle of his shoulder blades. His dark hair, oiled perfectly, curled over his collar, and she caught the smell of his now-familiar cologne.

The heat was oppressive, and the humidity was thick and lay over them like a wet blanket. Within moments of starting their descent, his shirt was soaked through and she wished for the millionth time since arriving in Australia that she was wearing something else. Her habit was wet from perspiration, and the heavy fabric snagged on the sharp barbs of some of the broad green leaves. The track was only wide enough for one person and very uneven. At several points, she had to jump over rocks. Each time, McGrath held out his hand for her to take, but she so far had declined, managing on her own.

Down deeper and deeper they went, the light dappled through the canopy overhead. All around were trees and creeping plants wrapping themselves around boulders as big as cars.

'Careful,' he said, holding back a branch of a tree with a stick so she could pass. 'That's a stinging tree. The natives call it gympie gympie – means devil tree. The leaves have serrated edges that get into your skin like little syringes, and they have a kind of venom. It's excruciating.'

Claire passed the tree and tried not to shudder. So many dangerous things resided in tropical Queensland; it was hard not to feel like humans should not be there. A cone snail, which had a lovely innocent-looking shell and which she'd picked up on a stroll by the beach, could even be fatal. One of the children saw her pick it up when she and Mary had gone for a stroll and screamed at her to drop it.

'If it's a cone, leave it alone,' young Jeremy Patterson had explained, as if this was absolute common knowledge and only the most idiotic of people didn't know it.

Her knees ached from the constant downward motion. This was ridiculous, she realised. What did she think she was doing? Daku should be there by now – perhaps he was and she couldn't see him. They should turn around, go back; this was too difficult.

Something stopped her though. Pride? Not wanting to look foolish in front of this man? On and on they walked, saying nothing. At one point, he stopped and offered her a drink from his canteen, though he'd drunk from it himself first. She took it gratefully, swallowing some of the tepid water.

Her shoes proved woefully inadequate; they were caked with mud and wet through. Once or twice, McGrath had to take a penknife from his pocket and cut through vines that were blocking their path. The noise of insects, birds and goodness knew what else was deafening, and she tried not to jump at each scurrying beside her or rustle in the undergrowth. Down deeper and deeper they walked for what seemed like hours, until they finally reached the bottom of the incline. The flat bushland was before them, but to get there, they would have to cross a shallow gorge, invisible from the top.

At the edge of the gorge was a low, flat rock jutting over the edge.

She moved towards it, intending to sit down, every limb aching from the physical exertion.

'I wouldn't,' McGrath said with a smirk as he wiped his brow with a handkerchief. His hair was wet now, and he reminded her of a pirate she'd seen in a children's picture book, all dark and swarthy, with blue eyes. She mentally berated herself. She was being fanciful.

'Why not?' she asked wearily, desperate to rest.

'That's a dry creek bed, that little gorge there, and it's exactly the kind of place a saltie would love. A nice juicy human being would feed him for weeks.' He chuckled and took another drink from the canteen, once again offering it to her when he was finished.

She knew from the conversations in the schoolyard that a saltie was a saltwater crocodile, a creature so vicious and prehistoric-looking that it sent shivers down her spine. There had been one, nine feet long, basking on the creek bank near the school a few weeks back. She and the other nuns had gone to the bridge to see it, while all the parents warned their children to avoid the entire area. Jumaaroo was full of stories of people being taken by crocs and sharks, bitten by venomous snakes and spiders. It seemed to be a local pastime, trading horror stories.

As she drank, a loud bang rent the air. She jumped. McGrath had shot a bullet into the ground.

'What did you do that for?' she spluttered, choking on the water that had gone down the wrong way.

'To scare away anything that might bite us.' He shrugged and sat on the sandy bank, several feet back from the edge, the only suitable place to rest.

She longed to sit as well, so she moved towards him, plonking herself on the ground a yard away from him.

'So are you happy now?' he asked, pointing to the bushland beyond.

Claire glanced around, hoping to see a pair of eyes, or some indication that the trackers were there. 'I'd like to cross the gorge,' she said, knowing how ridiculous that sounded.

'Well, that's not happening. Why are you so determined to make my life difficult, Sister?' he asked as he lit a cigarette.

She couldn't tell if he was joking or not. 'I have no such agenda,' she replied, trying to move away from the smoke.

'Hmm.' He exhaled a long plume, and she noticed a change in his demeanour. 'Well, you may not have come out here with a plan to make an enemy of me, but you certainly are going about it the right way.' His voice was light and his eyes were focused on the other side of the creek, but she heard a note of menace.

'I don't know what you mean?' She tried to keep her tone conversational, but the mood had definitely changed.

He took another long drag on his cigarette, still looking into the middle distance. 'Well, you begin by telling me how to run the school I own, in the town I own. Then you undermine my wife, then you get into bed with my enemies, and now you are interfering in my private business.'

'As far as I am concerned, you do not own the school, nor do you own the town. And as for interfering, I was asked...and you offered.'

'Oh, you are interfering all right. I know how to handle women, you see. All of your sex, you always want something. The more straightforward ones, my favourite, want money. They give me what I want, I give them money – simple. Others, like my wife, want status, a position, so she does what I tell her and she gets to be the leader of the female pack. But you' – he turned and pointed at her with one finger – 'you have me flummoxed.'

Claire's heart was pounding now. She was in danger and she knew it.

'You don't want money, you don't want position. You've got your uncle to back you up, and only a fool would take him on. And we both know I might be a lot of things, but a fool isn't one of them.' He paused. 'So I get back to the same question – what *do* you want?'

'I assure you, I want nothing,' she said, hating the fear in her voice. 'I think we should go back. I've seen enough –'

He laughed. 'Maybe you want something you've never had, is that it? Maybe the feel of a man would dull that insatiable curiosity you have, scratch the itch that causes you to stick your beak in where it doesn't belong?'

Claire forced herself to remain calm. She would not be his plaything. Her cheeks burned. How could she have been so stupid as to allow herself to get into such a vulnerable position? She needed to get away. She stood and made for the path once more.

'You won't make it all the way up there without me, Claire, so don't try.' He never moved from where he sat, and his eyes were still trained on the opposite bank of the gorge. 'Why don't you come back here? Don't worry, I won't force you. I've never had to force a woman in my life, and under all that black rubbish, you're just a woman like any other.' He smirked.

Claire offered up a prayer, begging Jesus to help her. She stood, trembling. 'I'm going back now.'

He leapt to his feet, lithe as a panther, and bounded to her side, his face only inches from hers as he grabbed her wrist. She'd only just begun the steep climb back up, so it was easy for him to pull her back down. He shoved her hard against the bank. His hand clamped hers, vice-like, and she knew to struggle would be pointless – he was much stronger than she was.

'You are going nowhere until I say so.' His free hand pulled off her veil, revealing hair that she cut herself. She cared nothing for how it looked, so she just lopped off pieces as they became too long. Nobody had seen her head bare for years. Instinctively, she moved to cover her head with her other hand, but he grabbed that too.

'Daku!' she screamed, not caring any more if he knew he was being followed. 'Daku, help me!'

McGrath chuckled. 'So *you're* the one Daku has been getting it with up in the convent, is it? I thought it was the other one, the pretty one. Sister Gerard told Assumpta she was the one with the blackfella, but it was you all along, was it? Or maybe he's having both of you? Is that it? Lucky Daku.'

'Let me go!' she managed, but his hands held her wrists. She pulled and twisted to try to escape, but he just laughed, enjoying her struggle. It was the most horrible sound she'd ever heard. She tried to pull away, backing into the undergrowth, but he kicked a rock out of the way and gave himself a better footing.

He pushed her down, and she hit her head on the hard ground as McGrath pinned her with his body. She heard the seam of her habit rip. She screamed again, tears choking her voice.

Suddenly he released her, and his face registered pain. His hand went to his thigh, and then he screamed. He rolled off her, and as he did, she saw it, a brownish snake, slithering away. He must have disturbed the creature when he kicked the rock.

'What was it?' he gasped.

'I... I don't know, a snake...' She gathered her torn habit as she searched around to see if the creature was still there. McGrath was lying on the ground, writhing in pain, clutching his thigh, groaning pitifully.

'Show it to me,' she heard herself say, the instinct to help him over-riding her terror at what had just happened.

She knew a little of snakebites from a book she'd been given in her first week. She had no idea what had bitten McGrath, but as she raised his trouser leg, she could see the puncture marks. The leg was swelling and looked inflamed.

'Lie still,' she instructed, knowing that thrashing about allowed the poison to act faster.

'I'm going to die,' he said, gasping through the pain.

She had no idea if he was right or not. 'Don't be silly, of course you're not.' She racked her brain for an idea. There was no way she could carry him – she wasn't even sure she could get herself out, let alone a huge injured man – and maybe moving him was a mistake anyway. She tried to quell the rising panic.

'Die...can't die...' His voice was barely a whisper now.

'Look, I need to think... You're not going to die.'

The reality of what was happening dawned on her. This man, who had been about to assault her, probably *was* going to die, here in this place, so far from anyone. She had no way of summoning help, nor was she confident of her own way out. Added to that, there were all manner of things that could kill her too in the immediate vicinity. She berated herself for agreeing to come here – who did she think she was?

She forced herself to calm down so she could think. Wrap the bite – she thought that was the instruction. Wrap it but not too tightly, something to do with slowing down the rate of poison. Was it too late? She crawled over to where her discarded veil lay and, using her teeth, managed to tear the fabric. Slowly, she wrapped his leg.

'Just stay still, Joseph,' she urged as he struggled against her. 'You need to stay as still as you can.'

She tied the bandage as best she could. He was delirious now, beads of sweat gathering on his forehead, and he was drifting in and out of consciousness. The site of the bite was swelling rapidly.

'Pray...' he gasped. 'I'll die...'

'You are not going to die, you silly man. It's just a bite.' She tried to stay calm. Was he right? She had no idea.

'Please... Can't die... Can't face God...' He thrashed around, and she struggled to figure out what to do. His voice sounded different now too, his accent no longer cultured but more like working-class Dublin.

'All right,' she said. 'I can't give you extreme unction, but I'll pray with you.' She took his hand in hers, wincing as he squeezed hard. 'Almighty God, please accept into your loving kindness the soul of your child Joseph. Grant peace to those he hurt in his lifetime. Amen.'

'Not Joseph,' he murmured. 'Not Joseph. Joe...' He swallowed. Sweat soaked his shirt. 'Dead. Joe...' He was agitated again, but he was weakening.

'What?' Claire bent close to him to hear what he was saying.

'Not Joseph. Dead...'

'You're Joseph McGrath and you are not dead. Please just hold on. Daku will be here soon and –'

He opened his eyes. 'Daku, no...no... Woiduna...dead, Joe dead... I must... I... Woiduna, Joe...'

Claire felt her blood run cold. 'Did you kill Woiduna?' she asked slowly, and Joseph nodded, seemingly relieved she finally understood.

'Joe McGrath...' he gasped, and his eyes closed once more.

She held his hand as she knelt beside him, feeling helpless. There was nothing to do but wait for the inevitable. The birds, the gurgle of the creek and the hot breeze through the foliage were the only sounds. She thought of his wife, his children. Was that a confession to the murder of Woiduna? It sounded like it. And why did he keep repeating his own name?

He was perspiring profusely, and his breathing was coming in laboured gasps. He was still mumbling, but it was impossible to make out the words.

'Daku, where are you?' she called helplessly into the dense humid heat.

She was soothing McGrath, urging him to rest and assuring him that he wasn't alone, when she was startled by a strange sound. She twisted around, facing the track she and McGrath had recently descended. Out of the dense foliage came Daku.

'Oh, thank God!' She leapt up. 'He's been bitten by a snake, and I couldn't get him out of here...'

Daku cast a glance at McGrath but focused on Claire. 'Are you all right?' His face registered shock at her lack of veil and torn habit, and she blushed. 'Did he try to hurt you?'

'I'm fine,' Claire assured him. 'But I don't think he's got long.'

'Good.' Daku shrugged, not caring for the man on the ground. 'Come on, let's get you out of here.'

'But we can't just leave him.' She was appalled.

'Course we can. A croc will get him now anyway.' He held his hand out to her, to help her up the steep path.

'No, Daku. Please, can you see if you can help him?' Claire refused to budge. She had no idea if there was an Aboriginal cure for a snakebite or not, but if there was something to be done, Daku was a much better bet than she was.

'Help him?' He jerked his head incredulously in the direction where McGrath lay, now still but breathing. 'No way. We want him dead. This place' – Daku pointed across the gorge – 'is White Cockatoo country. We can't come here. Anyway, it's not his to give even if it was suitable, which it's not. He duped you.'

Claire felt so foolish. She had no idea why he was talking about cockatoos and was too tired and distraught to go into it.

He held his hand out to her. 'Come on. It's a long way back.'

Despite all McGrath's duplicity and the fact that he had attacked her, she said, 'I won't leave him here to die. No matter what, I'll stay with him, even if you won't help.' She knelt once more beside McGrath and spoke quietly to him, reassuring him he wasn't alone.

McGrath winced, even though he was only barely conscious, and Claire pleaded with Daku once more. 'Can you please at least try? He is a husband and a father, and I think he is truly sorry for his actions. Will you just try?'

Daku weighed it up, looking from her to McGrath lying on the rough ground and back again.

'Please? I'm begging you.'

Daku jumped down from the track with an exasperated sigh. Mutinously, he unwrapped her veil, opened McGrath's trousers and pulled them down roughly. Claire had never seen a man in his under-wear before, so she averted her eyes. Daku examined the puncture holes, then wordlessly left, leaving her hoping he had gone to find some plant or something and not abandoning them both.

He arrived back a moment later with an armful of leaves, which he placed on the large flat rock. Then, taking a sharp rock from the creek bed, he began to pulverise the plants, making a green paste. Once he had mashed them enough, green juice staining his fingers, he applied the mixture to the bite, massaging it onto the affected area. He then placed something from his pocket in his patient's mouth, clamping McGrath's teeth closed on whatever it was.

'What are you giving him?' she asked.

'Doesn't matter. You won't know it anyway. This will keep him sleeping so he won't move so much. He'll live, probably. Make sure he stays still, don't let the venom move around his body. I don't know what it was, but up here, it won't be harmless.'

'Oh, thank God,' Claire said with relief. 'But we can't get him out of here, can we?'

'No. Let his own people get him out. We'll pull him up there so a croc won't see him and send someone for him once we get back. Now come on.' He stood and placed both hands under the other man's armpits and dragged him. McGrath groaned.

'I won't leave him.' Claire was adamant. 'You go back, tell his men that they need to get down here and to bring something to make a stretcher.'

'You're crazy!' Daku exclaimed. 'He's the devil! He's bad, black to his heart! You have seen what he does to my people, to everyone he touches, and yet you care?'

'I do. I'm not disagreeing with you, Daku, but I will not leave him here to die. So if you can go back and get help, send them here, I would appreciate it.'

'I don't understand you. None of you. I lived with nuns just like you all of my life, and I don't understand it. You are kind. Some are not, but you and Sister Helen, you are good people. But he doesn't deserve my help.'

'That may be. But I'm asking you, do I deserve your help?'

He looked at her, his face inscrutable.

'Sister Helen would ask the same if she were here,' she said quietly, remembering the insinuation McGrath had made about Daku and a nun, watching for and dreading his reaction in equal measure. If he changed his mind in order to impress Helen, then that was a whole other problem.

'I don't think so,' he said.

'She is a Catholic nun, she loves Jesus and all of his children, so I'm quite sure she would not want you to leave this man to die, no matter what he did.'

He shook his head and sighed. 'You got water?'

'No, the canteen is empty.'

With lithe movements she'd never observed in a white person, he took the bottle, leapt to a tree, cut a piece of exposed root and amazingly extracted water.

'That's incredible,' she remarked as he handed her the full canteen. 'Do all trees hold water like that?'

'No, just the mallee eucalyptus and some others.' Then he dug his hand in his pocket, extracting what looked like several plums. 'Eat these. I'll go back to get someone.' Without another word, he left, leaving her alone once more.

As she sat beside McGrath, holding his hand and praying, her thoughts drifted to what he had revealed to her. It didn't come as a surprise – she now believed him capable of such wickedness – but what did surprise her was his need to confess. Somewhere within that black heart was a belief in God, and a fear of facing him with such sins on his conscience. There was hope for him.

She looked down at the man's handsome face. His head rested on her lap, and he was now relaxed. He seemed to no longer be in such pain and was sleeping peacefully. She hoped it was a good sign. Who was this man? A man with no regard for human life and dignity, a man determined to get what he wanted no matter the cost. Would he have violated her as he'd threatened before the bite? She didn't know.

She should feel fear or loathing or horror at his confession, and she did, but there was something else. The fact that he repented… Well, there was room for even the blackest sheep according to Jesus, and perhaps there was a way back to the path of righteousness for Joseph McGrath as well.

The sounds of dusk were all around her now as the orange sun sank in the sky, and she checked the expensive watch on McGrath's wrist. It was five o'clock. She dreaded to think how frightening it would be to have to endure hours of darkness down there, the mountains looming all around, the bush full to capacity with creatures intent on human consumption. She prayed for Jesus to stay with her and to speed Daku in bringing help.

As the shadows lengthened and the heat of the sun diminished as it sank behind the ridge of rainforest above her, she welcomed the cooler weather. It wasn't pitch dark yet, but it would be shortly. She remembered her surprise in the first few days at how quickly night fell there. She was used to long summer evenings in Ireland, where the sun didn't set in the summertime until after ten at night and rose in the small hours. Dusk seemed to last for ages there, but here it was different. You could almost watch night falling before your eyes.

She was growing stiff, so she gently moved McGrath's head onto the ground and stood to stretch. Her limbs objected to the sudden movement after such a long time kneeling, but it felt good to move about again. She walked a little but there was not much space; the creek bank was only cleared about seven or eight feet, beyond which was the dense rainforest once more. She walked to where the track came down the hill and back again, taking care to stay in the middle of the area rather than on the edges where a snake might lurk.

She took a drink from the canteen, and though she longed to take a longer draft, she decided she'd better ration it. Despite Daku's parting instruction to leave McGrath if he died, she would not do such a thing.

Sufficiently stretched, she resumed her position, placing McGrath's head on her lap once more. The motion caused him to stir, and his eyes fluttered open for a moment, then closed again. She soothed him, murmuring once more that he was not alone. A minute later, his eyes opened again, this time staying open for several seconds, struggling to focus.

'Am I dead?' he whispered.

She smiled. 'No, you're not dead. You're here in Queensland, with me, Sister Claire. We were going to see the land for the new mission, remember? You were bitten by a snake.'

'A brown?' he asked weakly.

'No, I don't think it was. Daku followed us, and he put something on the wound. He said you're going to be fine. Just lie still. He's gone to get help.'

'Not dead.' He sighed.

'No, not today.' She smiled as he drifted back to sleep. She must have dozed off herself, uncomfortable as it was in that position, because she woke to the sound of men's voices calling her name.

'Here! We're over here!' she yelled as loudly as she could, startling her patient. He was clearer now, and agitated.

'Don't move. We need to get you out of here, and Daku said to keep still so the venom doesn't travel around your body. Your men are here now. They'll have to carry you up.'

Within moments, the small clearing was filled with men, and soon they had McGrath on the stretcher and had begun the climb back up. For so many of them, Joseph McGrath was their livelihood; they needed him alive. Daku hung back, letting the white men to it, and it was only then that she noticed Helen was with him.

'Sister Helen, you didn't have to come down here,' Claire said, accepting her embrace.

'I know, but when Daku told me what had happened, I just wanted to help.'

Claire was touched by her concern.

'Teresita and Mary wanted to come too, but Daku wouldn't allow them. I promised we'd get you home in one piece. Are you all right to walk? You can lean on me if you need to.'

'I'm fine. A bit stiff and hungry, but I'll be fine. Let's get back.'

Claire followed Daku back up the steep path they'd descended hours earlier. It was dark now, and the night sounds of the rainforest were even louder than those of the day. Crickets, birds and frogs vied with the rustling branches and the sound of a waterfall off in the distance. It was the wet season, so mudslides and violent downpours were the norm. Today had been the first dry day in weeks. She was grateful for that; she could not imagine trying to navigate out of there in torrential rain.

Up and up they climbed, and it felt so much longer than the trip down. Daku offered his hand to pull them up when the terrain was nothing more than boulders, and several times they had to go on their hands and knees. High up ahead they could hear the voices of the men and then thankfully the sound of engines. Claire realised they must have made it to the top near the road.

McGrath's car was driven away, presumably with the owner stretched on the back seat, leaving the others to walk back to the town. Daku directed her and Helen up a different way, where, much to their relief, Gordie and Flossie waited with the trap.

'Up ya get,' Gordie said, helping both nuns onto the trap. He and Daku exchanged a few words in what she assumed was the Bundagulgi language, and then he turned to them.

'Flamin' sheilas always stickybeakin'.' He chuckled to show he was joking and walked in front, leading the ever-patient Flossie.

'Goodbye, Daku, and thank you,' Claire said wearily.

'I shoulda let him go. Then my people would live on country, no problems.'

Claire knew what a sacrifice it had been for him not to allow his tormentor to die. 'You did the right thing, Daku, the Christian thing. I know you are of the Bundagulgi people, but you are a Christian as well, are you not? We can be more than one thing, you know. I saw what you did, Joseph McGrath knows what you did, and more importantly, God knows what you did to save a man who has hurt your people. You are a good man, Daku.'

He shrugged.

Claire wondered if she'd imagined the look between him and Helen. The Daku she knew would have denied being a Christian; he would have said he left all of that when he left the mission. He certainly didn't practice the religion he was brought up with, and they'd discussed it on occasion.

As Daku took off in the opposite direction on foot, Gordie led them back on a dirt track, a different way to the road she'd taken with Joseph McGrath, and much sooner than she expected, they were back at the convent. Aching and exhausted, she pulled herself off the cart.

'Thank you, Gordie. I don't think I could have walked another step.' She dug in her pocket and found a barley sugar, which she gave to Flossie, who munched happily.

'Nah worries. Claire, Helen.' He tipped his hat, jumped on the cart and clicked at Flossie to walk on.

CHAPTER 16

$\mathcal{C}$laire sat in the steaming bath, scrubbing her skin. She prayed to the Blessed Virgin as she washed, longing to feel clean again. The reality of what had happened crashed over her in sickening waves. Joseph McGrath had tried to rape her. She told herself over and over he wouldn't have gone through with it, that he was only trying to frighten her, but she didn't believe it.

Had the last few hours really happened? Repeatedly, the experience played in her mind. The walk, him in his study where he seemed so reasonable, so nice. She believed him when he said it was tall poppy syndrome, that people hated progress, were resentful of those who did well. The way he made her feel, like they were on the same side, the way he lured her into his confidence, like a spider traps a fly.

She fought the panic in her chest, forcing herself to breathe through the memory. The knowledge that Daku and then the other men had seen her with her veil off, her clothes torn, made her feel so violated, so vulnerable. What if they thought she and McGrath were… Her cheeks burned at the idea. Gossip was rife in Jumaaroo – nothing else to talk about, according to Cassia – so the tiniest thing would set the rumour mill turning, and this was no tiny thing. She couldn't protest her innocence because that would be to admit there was a case to answer, so she would have to endure the whispers. She blinked back tears. What if Rev Bill heard about it? Her parents? The Reverend Mother back at home? She was alone in the jungle with a man, she went willingly, and when the men arrived, her clothes were in disarray and her veil discarded. It looked so bad.

Already there was talk – a nun and an Aboriginal having untoward relations. Claire couldn't believe that people thought there was something going on between Helen and Daku. The idea was ridiculous. They were friendly, of course; he was nice to all of them. It was just the townspeople putting two and two together and making five as usual, but it was hurtful and unfair. She sighed. There were so many areas of conflict, so many problems... The weight of it all was threatening to crush her. She longed for her life in the convent in Cork, teaching in school, the community of sisters, visits home to her family. Life was so simple then, so gentle and easy.

Her practical nature forced her to prioritise. Moping and feeling sorry for herself would get her nowhere. *Right*, she thought, remembering a joke one of the children told her last week. *How do you eat an elephant? One bite at a time.*

Listing the issues, working her way through them and making a plan was the only way. So firstly, McGrath didn't rape her. That was a fact, so she was not going to think about that again. She was fine. People would think what they wanted to and she could do nothing about it, so she tried to put that too to the back of her mind.

Secondly, Gerard was under some kind of control, based on the threat of being returned to Ireland in disgrace. It wasn't ideal, but it was better than how it had been, so she'd call that a win.

The Helen and Daku thing – if there was a thing, which she was confident there wasn't – was just more idle talk in a town where nothing ever happened. She could warn Helen, tell her what people were saying and advise her not to be seen to give them any more cause for silly speculation.

But by far the most pressing problem was McGrath's confession. If that's what it was. She knew she would have to do something, but what would be best? Her uncle? The police? Should she confront him, make him admit it again when he wasn't delirious? She would need to reflect and pray and maybe seek advice.

What was all that about? she thought as she remembered how he kept repeating his own name. And he'd admitted to killing Woiduna. No matter how hard it was to accept that a man held in such high esteem by so many was capable of murdering another human being, of actually taking a life – or at least instructing others to do so on his behalf – Claire knew that it was true. Daku, Russell Gardiner and Gordie had been right.

Joe McGrath dead. The words rang around her head as she lay there in the water. He never referred to himself as Joe. She'd never heard anyone else call him Joe either, always Joseph, and yet that's what he'd repeated over and over. He seemed agitated that she didn't under-stand him, but it was impossible to know what he meant.

The water was cold now. She dragged herself out, dried her body and put on her nightdress and dressing gown. She wanted to go right to bed but knew her sisters were still downstairs, worried about her. She should go down.

Teresita and Mary were in the kitchen. As she entered, they imme-diately rushed to ask if she was all right. They fussed over her, Mary getting her a cup of tea, into which Teresita slipped a little drop of something from a bottle she carried in her habit pocket. The consumption of alcohol was forbidden, but Claire turned a blind eye. They had few comforts, and if she knew that Teresita made some kind of concoction using sugar cane in her room, she never acknowledged it.

The tea was sweet and warming, and Mary followed it with a cheese and tomato sandwich. Claire bit into it and found to her surprise that she was hungry. It was the tastiest thing she'd ever had.

'You gave us a right fright going off like that, especially with that McGrath fella. We were worried sick, you know,' Teresita admonished her. Though Claire was technically her superior, Teresita had taken a mother's role in caring for them all.

'I know. I'm sorry. He suggested showing me the proposed new site for the mission. The Adventist church have sold him the land the current one is on, so the Bundagulgi people are worried. I was asked to speak to him about it, but he accused me of only listening to one side of the story, and I thought it couldn't do any harm.'

'And what was it like? Did you get to see it?' Mary asked. Claire knew the young nun longed for a peaceful end to the conflict and hoped the new place would be good enough.

'I did, but Daku said it wasn't suitable. It is the country of another group of Aboriginal people, so they wouldn't go onto their land.'

'Oh, that's a terrible pity,' Mary said.

Claire nodded, then sighed. 'I think I'm doing more harm than good to be honest, so from now on, I think we'll focus on St Finbarr's and what we're doing here and let the Seventh-day Adventists and the Bundagulgi figure it out themselves.'

'But that's the problem – they can't.' Helen seemed unusually aggravated. 'The Bundagulgi people are what they call the Black Cockatoo, ocean goers, and the inland people, White Cockatoo, are as different to them as Irish are to French. To an outsider, we might look the same, but we are very different with different habits and traditions. So they cannot just be shoved from pillar to post with no regard for their country or where they belong.'

'How do you know all of this, about these people?' Claire asked kindly. They were all upset, but Helen seemed particularly invested.

'Daku told me. Claire, we can't just abandon them to their fate. They've suffered so much, the Aboriginal people, not just here, but all over Australia. White men came with their guns and diseases, and these people had no answer for their brutality. Daku was stolen from his family – did you know that? Literally wrenched from his mother's arms because his father was white and they want the children who look paler. They had a colour chart they used to hold up to their skin, and the lighter they were, the more likely it was they would be taken. Daku was trained from the time he could walk to run into the bush when white people were around, to stay hidden, but he was sick the day they came – he had a fever and his mother was caring for him. They just took him, ill as he was, hundreds of miles away and forced him to stay there. And his is such a common story, it would break your heart.' Helen's voice cracked with the emotion of it all.

Claire was about to respond when all eyes turned to the kitchen door. Standing there was Gerard. Since the altercation with Claire the previous week, she'd taught her classes but had not engaged with anyone in the convent. She ate alone in her room, and apart from visits to Mrs McGrath, she spoke to nobody.

She swept into the room, her face stern as always, giving nothing away. She made no mention of the fact that Claire had been lost in the rainforest all day, though word had got out, as it always did in Jumaaroo.

Claire seized the opportunity. She wanted to offer the hand of peace. 'Sister Gerard, will you join us? There's tea in the pot, and Sister Mary made a lovely cake with the peaches from the tree.' She smiled and hoped she sounded welcoming. The current atmosphere was horrible for everyone, and it was her duty to try to resolve things, no matter what had happened.

'I don't want anything,' Gerard said, filling a glass of water. But then she turned and addressed them all. 'But I do want to tell you that I have written to the bishop, asking to be transferred. I no longer wish to stay here, so I have expressed my desire to move on in no uncertain terms. There are things going on in this convent that are, frankly' – she paused for dramatic effect – 'nothing short of immoral. And I cannot sit by and say nothing. I await his response and am hopeful, so do not include me in any plans you may have.'

'But...' Claire began, her face burning. Did Gerard know about what Joseph McGrath tried to do to her? Did he say it was something else? That she wanted it? She knew the others were shocked at how dishevelled she was when she returned, but she said her habit had been torn by brambles. She couldn't bear anyone to know the real reason, but she had a horrible image of McGrath bragging about what she and he had got up to. Salt tears stung her eyes. Gerard had been out when she got back, presumably up at the McGraths' again, so she would have heard whatever he said if he chose to blame Claire for everything.

Teresita must have sensed Claire's panic, and she discreetly placed her hand on Claire's arm, answering instead. 'We are sorry to hear that, Sister Gerard, and we all sincerely hope you change your mind.'

The two oldest nuns held each other's gaze, and eventually Gerard responded. 'I won't,' she said as she left the room.

The others sat in silence, nobody knowing what to say or do. Claire knew they were looking to her for leadership, but she just couldn't. Suddenly she felt so weary of it all, and try as she might to stop the tears, she could no longer.

'I'm so sorry. I'm making a right pig's ear of this, aren't I? Sticking my nose into things that don't concern me and allowing this awful situation to develop under our own roof. It might be better if I were the one to leave. I've done nothing but make a big mess here and now...'

Teresita snorted. 'Yerra would you wish out of that, girleen. The devil himself couldn't manage her.' She cocked her thumb in the direction of the door and the recently departed Gerard. 'She's a lighter and we all know it, so there's no point in saying otherwise. If she goes off someplace else, sure what harm? We'll manage here grand out, the four of us. You're doing your best, and that's all anyone, including God, can ask of you. You've had a terrible hard day, and what you need now is a good night's sleep. Tomorrow the whole thing will look brighter.'

Helen and Mary nodded in agreement.

'So off to bed with you. And in the morning, you have a rest, as you'll be fine and sore after all that climbing and whatever else you did today, and we'll see to opening the school.'

Claire smiled and was happy to let Teresita take the lead. She was worn out, not just physically, but mentally and emotionally as well.

* * *

SHE WOKE the following morning to the sounds of the children playing in the yard that joined the convent to the school. It was a favourite spot on account of the huge acacia, flame and peach trees that grew there. The fruit and the shade were a lure for those boys and girls not eager to rush about on the hurling field in the relentless heat. She looked for the alarm clock, but it wasn't on her locker. She smiled. Teresita must have removed it so she would sleep. It was the first morning she'd slept in in years. All of her life she'd been a daily Mass goer, but no such luxury existed here. She and her sisters got Mass once a fortnight forty miles away in the next township. She threw back the sheet – it was too warm for blankets – and stood. Her limbs ached from yesterday's exertions, and she hobbled to the bathroom, each step hurting. She saw a large purple bruise on her shoulder, from when McGrath had forced her down on the ground, and she gripped the sink to steady herself.

She washed and dressed and knelt on the floor beside her bed. She spoke to Jesus and his Blessed Mother, but not in the way of formal prayers as she normally did.

'Dearest Jesus and his Blessed Mother, I don't know what I'm doing here. I honestly don't know what to do. I am so far out of my depth. Please help me. I don't know what is going on. I'm afraid. I need you,' she whispered.

CHAPTER 17

*T*he rest of the week passed in a blur of music lessons and cut knees, and of Joseph McGrath there was no sign.

Schools, like hospitals, just go on, regardless of the turmoil around them. Claire was glad of the busyness during the day, but the nights were long. She tossed and turned, the whole mess playing out in her head over and over. Whenever she fell asleep, his face haunted her dreams, sometimes jovial and smiling, other times vicious and cruel. She woke often, her pillow wet. She couldn't confide in anyone; the thought of saying the words made her stomach churn. Daku had arrived on the scene and asked her if McGrath had hurt her, and she remembered the look he gave her when she said he hadn't, like he didn't believe her, but nobody knew what really happened out there and that was her only comfort.

She half expected McGrath to turn up, and she tried not to jump every time someone knocked on the door, but he was notable by his absence around town. She heard through the grapevine that he'd been treated for the snakebite by a specialist who'd come up from Brisbane and that he was recovering.

She would have to approach him – he'd confessed to Woiduna's murder, and she couldn't just ignore that – but the thought of confronting him was so difficult. Every night she vowed the next day she would go to his house, talk to him, but as the dawn streaked across the tropical sky and another day loomed, she knew she couldn't.

She'd started several letters to Rev Bill, but they all ended up in the wastepaper basket. No matter how she described the events, she felt it sounded sordid. She couldn't bear it.

The matter of Helen and Daku puzzled her as well. They were close, of that there was no doubt, and to hear her distress at recounting how he was taken from his mother as a child, it was clear she felt deep compassion for him and his people. But surely that was all there was to it? McGrath's remark about Daku and one of the nuns having a relationship was just nonsense; it had to be. Gerard told Assumpta, and Gerard was probably just stirring up trouble. Helen was a nun who had dedicated her life to God, and as a missionary nun she would be bound to feel strongly about native peoples. It all made sense. People like McGrath didn't understand that; he didn't know what a vocation was. For all Claire knew, he might have made it all up. Gerard might never have said those things.

Besides, there was nothing wrong with nuns having friends, and in this strange place, they needed all the support they could get. Teresita had been approached by some of the parents, fathers mostly, fascinated by their children's passion for hurling and with a view to making an adult team, and she was busy with that. Nobody thought that was odd. Claire was friends with Cassia and her husband Stavros, and that was fine. So why not Helen and Daku?

Claire looked out her office window at the children training on the field ahead of the big tournament. She smiled at the sight of Teresita yelling her head off, instructing her young charges to tackle harder, run faster. Everyone seemed to be having a wonderful time.

They were doing good in this town, despite everything. She had to remember that. Those little boys and girls got to sleep in their own beds every night, and their mothers didn't have to send them miles away any more. They were learning alongside their friends, they were learning about each other's cultures, and they were being raised to be devout Catholics. St Finbarr's was a good place, and she had to cling to that.

She took comfort in the familiar sounds: children's voices reciting poetry in chorus, little feet running in the yard, the chatter as they played and ate their lunch, the ever-present noise of instruments being played with varying degrees of competence that rang about the corridors. All of it had soothed her in the time since the event.

Amazingly, Mary seemed to be turning her ragtag bunch of musicians into something approximating a band, and there was to be a huge concert open to the entire community at Christmas. The last concert had been as Claire predicted – a cacophony of discord – though of course she was lavish in her praise. But that had just been in the school. The Christmas project was a much grander affair. There was going to be carol singing from the school choir accompanied by the orchestra. Christmas in the heat felt so strange. For all of her life, Christmas was a time of prayer and thanksgiving but also a time of fires and warm drinks and snowmen. Hot Christmas was just one more thing to try to get used to. She missed home so badly these days, but she offered up her sorrow in prayer.

To ease her sadness, she decided to go on a tour of the classrooms. She visited each group a few times a week. She wanted to make sure she knew each child personally, and they loved to hear stories of Christmas in Ireland, of the Baby Jesus being placed in the crib on Christmas Eve, the candle lit in the window of every house to welcome any passing stranger to their table to share in the abundance. She told them stories of Daidí na Nollag, Father Christmas, and how he would leave an orange or a few sweets in their stockings for them, and their eyes danced.

Growing up in a culture where everyone experienced more or less the same thing was easy, she realised. Now that they were surrounded by so many other cultures, and so many traditions, they'd decided to do a whole school project. It would be on display the night of the concert, with each child doing his or her own bit about what Christmas meant in their home. Everywhere she looked, there were children with pots of gum and scissors, crayons and crepe paper, all busy with their artwork.

On her way across the yard, she met Tony Gallori, the postman.

'One for you today, Sister,' he said, handing her a letter. She recognised Rev Bill's handwriting immediately. She took it, thanked Tony and walked back to her office with a heavy heart.

Dear Claire,

I hope this letter finds you well. I understand there are some difficulties with one of your sisters. You wrote previously explaining the issues, and I advised you as best I could. But now it seems the situation has escalated and further intervention is necessary.

Sister Gerard has requested a transfer on the following grounds: that the word of God is being obscured by the presence of godless individuals in the classroom where she is expected to teach; that she has been singled out for persecution by you because she is intent on adhering to Catholic doctrine, and it is unreasonable for her as a Catholic nun to be expected to provide a Catholic education to non-Catholics; that you have involved yourself with the Seventh-day Adventist cult and are acting as their agent in some dispute between them and the mayor of Jumaaroo, Mr McGrath, a great benefactor to our church there; and finally – and frankly I am at a loss as to what to say about this – that there are activities going on at St Finbarr's that are in contravention of God's law, in particular a nun keeping company with a man, a native man it seems.

Every fibre of my being wants to believe that these allegations are untrue. I am, of course, going to withhold judgement on these matters until we speak in person. But as you can appreciate, these charges are a serious cause for concern. If they are entirely without basis, and I sincerely hope they are, then I shall deal with Sister Gerard appropriately. But if there is even a grain of truth in them, I suggest you do your best to resolve them to the satisfaction of the Church with all haste.

Despite a heavy schedule of engagements, I am left with no choice but to travel to Jumaaroo myself and intend to be there in the coming months. I will have my secretary confirm dates.

Yours in Christ,

Rev Bill

P.S. I know this mission wasn't an easy one, and I hope you have not been given too much responsibility. If that is the case, then I must take that responsibility myself. I know you to be of pure heart, Claire, and I trust you completely, but this situation is a grave cause of concern.

Claire read and reread the letter. Her Uncle Bill's letters were always affectionate and cheery, but there was none of that in this one. He obviously thought she was losing control of the operation, and he was much vexed to have to come and sort it all out. She felt so embarrassed and such a failure. Her father's only brother had been a hero of hers all her life. His visits home to Macroom every few years were such a highlight, and the farm was scrubbed and whitewashed to within an inch of its life ahead of each visit. Collections were made by various local groups and handed over to help with his work on the missions, and he was treated like a king. Claire remembered how her heart would almost burst with pride when old Father Dineen would stand aside and let her uncle say Mass for the parish. There would be standing room only as Rev Bill endeared himself to everyone with his takes on life in darkest Africa and, later, red, burned Australia. Claire and her sisters were like film stars by association, and she loved it, but most importantly, she loved him.

He would sit by their fire at night and tell them stories of lions and elephants, of men with bones through their noses and women with so many necklaces on that it stretched their necks. He told them of the brave nuns and priests who took on African chiefs to bring the word of God to those poor ignorant black people who would never hear of the love of Jesus if it weren't for them.

She couldn't remember a time when she didn't want to go back with him, to follow him to darkest Africa or wherever he went, and when she joined the convent, she made sure it was a missionary order. The Ursulines fit that bill, and the pride on her parents' faces, but more importantly on Rev Bill's face, when she was professed would be with her forever. He trusted her, young as she was, with such a huge task, and the idea that she'd let him down and failed miserably broke her heart.

Protesting innocence was pointless. Writing back and calling

Sister Gerard a liar was so unchristian it was unthinkable, but she had to do something. She would have to put her pride in her pocket, as her mother would say, and address each issue one by one.

Firstly, the godless thing was nonsense. On that she was sure. Rev Bill himself had sanctioned the inclusion of all Christian denominations in the school, so Gerard, like Mary and Teresita and Helen, had been instructed to teach Anglicans, Presbyterians and all other denominations that sought a place. The Chinese claimed that they were Christians when they enrolled, and she'd heard from some people since that they only ticked the box to get into the school, but that wasn't her business. If they said they were Christian, then she believed them. They participated fully in all school activities, including prayers, and she had no complaints about them. The other three sisters taught everyone without complaining, and it was a Catholic school – nobody was in any doubt about that – so she felt she was on solid ground on that front at least.

Likewise on the charge of singling Gerard out for persecution. She could say hand on heart that she did not. She spoke to her in the face of her brutality towards several children. She'd asked politely first, but Gerard continued her regime of corporal punishment, so Claire put a stop to it. She remembered Rev Bill talking about one of the Christian brothers who taught him and Claire's father by using the strap to excess, and he was most adamant that it was wrong. There was no way he would defend hurting a little child, or humiliating them in front of the class. He was on very friendly terms with the Lasallian Brothers back in Macroom, and always called on them for tea when he was home. He'd commented more than once on how their ethos of Jean-Baptiste de La Salle, teaching through love, was one all teachers should live by, so she knew he would support her on that accusation too.

The matter of her and the cult, as he called it...well, she had no idea there. She was in far too deep to do nothing further, but she was at a complete loss. She would just tell him the whole truth and say she acted as she thought Jesus would. If she was wrong to get involved, then that was for him to decide. She had done what she thought was right.

The final thing, the idea that a nun was having an improper relationship with a man, was the worst of all the issues raised in the letter. Did Gerard mean her and McGrath? Or Helen and Daku? She couldn't bear the humiliation of telling her uncle what had happened, but she realised she might have to, to clear her name. If the accusation referred to Helen and Daku, then as far as Claire was concerned, it was just a friendship, nothing more. Certainly not the unthinkable that they were keeping company in any romantic sense. It wasn't fair that she could be friends with Cassia but Helen couldn't with Daku because he was male.

Sighing and dreading the conversation, she knew she would now have to raise the matter with Helen. She would have to tell her that the bishop was concerned, that he'd heard something and that he'd asked the question. She knew Helen would tell her that of course there was nothing in it, and Claire would be at pains to assure her sister that she knew as much, but the conversation would have to be had.

At least on three of the four accusations, she could set his mind at rest. The business with the Bundagulgi and the Adventists…well, she could only tell the truth.

The bell rang to indicate school was over for the day, and she rose from her desk. In the corridor she stopped Eileen O'Hara. 'Eileen, could you go to Sister Helen's room and ask her to come to my office please?'

'Yes, Sister Claire.' Young Eileen bounced off, her red pigtails bobbing along, delighted to be given a job.

Moments later there was a gentle knock. 'Come in,' Claire called.

Helen entered the room. 'You wanted to see me?'

'Yes, have a seat.' Claire smiled and moved to the seats by the window, sitting opposite Helen. She offered a quick prayer that she would find the right words.

Helen waited expectantly.

'As you no doubt heard,' Claire began, 'I had words with Sister

Gerard about her treatment of the children in her class.' Though Claire had never discussed it with anyone but Teresita, clearly Gerard had, and news of the argument, with a bias in the other nun's favour of course, had spread like wildfire.

'I did hear something. Some of the children were discussing it, but of course I stopped them.' Helen seemed perplexed as to what it had to do with her.

'Yes, well, you know how gossip works, especially here. A story starts out as one thing and gets legs, as my mother used to say.' Claire smiled ruefully.

'I suppose, for the women especially, there isn't much going on in Jumaaroo to occupy them.'

'Well, yes.' Claire paused. There was no way but to say it outright. 'Sister Gerard wrote to the bishop asking to be transferred, as she told us the other night.'

Helen nodded, her brow furrowed in confusion as to why they were having this conversation at all.

'And in that letter, she cited several reasons why she felt she could no longer stay. My treatment of her primarily, it must be said. But she also claimed – and I'll quote to make sure it is correct –' – Claire lifted the letter – '"that there are activities going on at St Finbarr's that are in contravention of God's law, in particular a nun keeping company with a man, a native man it seems".'

Claire hated to see the colour drain from Helen's face.

'She means me and Daku, I presume?' Helen's voice was choked.

'I would imagine so, yes.' Claire hid her surprise that Helen was so sure it meant her.

The silence hung heavily between them, and though Claire's instinct was to comfort Helen, rush to assure her that she was sure it was a big misunderstanding, something told her she couldn't do that.

'What will happen now?' Helen asked.

'How do you mean?' Claire didn't understand.

'Will I be asked to leave?'

'Why would I do that?' The conversation was not going as Claire imagined, but she tried to stay calm.

'Well, my friendship with Daku is a cause of concern to the bishop, so I assume you will not want me to stay,' Helen said quietly.

'Do *you* want to stay, Helen?' Something made Claire ask the question. She'd expected denial, outrage, hurt, but not this sad acceptance. Did Helen want to be dismissed? She'd assumed her sister would say it was nonsense, that she would rail against Gerard for spreading such a lie, but she had done none of that.

Helen's hazel eyes met hers, her lower lip quivering with the emotion of it all. 'I don't know,' she whispered.

Claire felt her heart sink. Surely not. This could not be happening. She'd heard of this once before, but it had been a postulant who had joined the same day as she did – not a fully professed sister – whose father had insisted she break off a romance with a lad he deemed unsuitable. The girl had joined the convent but couldn't settle, so after a time, she left the religious life and went to America with her love. That was not a tragedy, and Claire had been happy for her, as she was fulfilling her destiny. But this was different. Helen was a *nun*. A bride of Christ, not some silly girl with a fixation on a boy. And as for Daku, well, he was as far away from what she was used to as it was possible to be. Surely Helen wasn't seriously considering a future with this man?

Claire fought back the denial. She would need to judge her words carefully now. 'I am not technically your superior, Helen, so you are not obliged to tell me anything. But if you would like to speak to me as a friend, then I am here to listen.' Claire longed to help her, but a bigger part of her wished this wasn't happening at all.

Helen began to speak, sounding distant, as if describing someone else in another time. 'I… I joined the convent when my fiancé was killed in 1921. He was in the IRA and was arrested, tortured and shot by the British. They threw his body on the street, and we couldn't even recognise him. Nobody wanted me to enter the convent – my parents, his family – but I couldn't live in a world where such things could happen. I just couldn't. It was like I closed down inside. I was studying literature in Dublin, and he was doing medicine. We were both twenty years old and in love and never imagined anything bad could ever happen, despite the world we live in.'

She smiled sadly, thinking of that time, and Claire realised why she found her a little different. She had not had her education through the convent. She must have come from a wealthy and progressive family to be allowed to attend university as a woman.

'My mother was a doctor, and my father a surgeon. They were disappointed that literature was what excited me, not liver and lung function, but they supported me. And Seamus was a medical student, so that made them happy.

'I always loved the Church. I went to Mass every day, and I loved the sense of peace there. When I joined the Ursulines, I felt I'd come home. I never regretted my decision, never once in twelve years.'

'And do you regret it now?' Claire asked gently.

Helen sighed and it came from deep within her. 'I don't. But I do have feelings for Daku that I can't explain. I feel connected to him – not like I felt for Seamus all those years ago, but I feel so happy in his company.'

Claire hated to ask but she had to. 'And has the friendship progressed beyond that?'

Helen shook her head. 'No, no, it hasn't. But we talk, and he...'

'Would he like there to be more?'

'Yes. He would. I told him about Seamus, and he says I locked myself away because my heart was broken. I didn't see it like that. I wasn't locking myself away – I was living a different life, a life that brought me peace. But he says I can still have that peace, and that I can have love as well.'

'And what do you think about that?' Claire dreaded the answer.

'I honestly don't know.'

'Do you love him?'

Helen looked up and gazed into Claire's eyes. The pause was not because Helen was deliberating. She knew the answer; she was just weighing up saying it aloud. 'I do.' Her words were so simple in the end.

The silence hung between them, neither one knowing how to

proceed. Claire tried to understand. 'You are sure it is love? I don't mean to patronise you, but this is a very difficult place to be, and we are all being tested so far beyond our limits. So is there a chance that it is just an...I don't know...an infatuation? He's so exotic and different and this place is his home, so perhaps being with him makes you feel less alien here or something?' She knew instinctively she was grasping at straws. Helen was not one for flights of fancy.

'I lie in bed at night asking the same questions. He is so different from any man I've ever met, and not just because he is Aboriginal. He thinks differently. He's very well read, you know, and there is so much more to him than meets the eye. His priorities are so unlike anyone I've ever met. He's so connected to this place, like he's part of it and it is part of him. He is like a nun in lots of ways. Ownership of things is meaningless to him, and he is very still, meditative, restful to be around or something.'

'But is that love? I mean a love between a man and a woman?' Claire felt herself blush. She was uncomfortable talking of such things. Celibacy had never been a challenge for her. She knew boys growing up, of course, lads who worked on her father's farm, lads from the town who were always a bit more cheeky, trying to chat her sisters up after Mass. But she had no interest in them, nor them in her.

'I don't know. Maybe. I just know that time flies by when I am with him, and when he's gone, I miss him. Is that love? I don't know what to do. Can you help me, Claire?'

The question was so honest, so vulnerable, that Claire felt a profound sense of sympathy for her. She didn't want to cause a scandal, and Helen hadn't done anything wrong as such, but this was a complicated situation and something would have to be done. Back at home they would give her the option to be transferred, and if she took it, then they would probably monitor her for a while until they were sure it was just an infatuation that had died away. If she chose not to take that option, then they had their answer. There was no point keeping someone in a religious life who wanted something different in her heart. Claire decided to offer Helen the chance to reflect.

'I will do all I can, of course. So I must ask you something now, and the answer you give will tell us what is in your heart.'

Helen nodded slowly.

'Will you go to another convent? Staying here, with Daku around all of the time and you having these feelings for him and him for you, well, it can't go on. So if you want to continue as a nun, then it would have to be somewhere far away from him. And if you don't want that, or can't do it, then I think you have your answer.'

Helen didn't reply, and Claire saw the unshed tears in her eyes.

'I don't know,' she finally said.

'Back at home, you would have the opportunity to go on retreat, to withdraw and pray on your problem, seek clarity from God. There is nowhere here I can send you, but I can do this. I will take your class for the rest of the week. I will tell the others that you are on retreat, and you can spend your time in prayer and contemplation. You can eat separately and not speak to anyone. I am not instructing you to do this, I'm just suggesting. Sometimes we need the solitude of our own souls without the constant noise to truly examine our consciences. Will you do that?'

Helen nodded again, not trusting herself to speak. After a long pause, she asked, 'Will you explain to Daku what I'm doing?'

'Of course.' Claire nodded.

'Do people know, do you think? Parents? Mary or Teresita?'

'Nobody has mentioned anything to me, and anyway, this is between you and God, Helen, nobody else. You alone must decide. God bless you.'

Helen stood and made for the door. Hand on the handle, she turned. 'Could you tell Daku that I just need some time, that I'm not trying to get away from him? Pray for me, Sister.'

'Of course I will,' Claire replied with a forced reassuring smile.

CHAPTER 18

*A*s she suggested, Helen retreated. Daku came the following morning, as he usually did, this time bringing some fish he'd caught that had some unpronounceable name. He left the fish wrapped in banana leaves on the back step and was about to slope off when Claire called him back.

His slow, agile movements reminded her of a cat they used to have at home that seemed to slide everywhere, and no height or small space fazed her.

Claire sat on the veranda, on the bench he'd made for them, and gestured for him to join her.

'Are you all right now?' Daku asked. He'd never mentioned the dishevelled state he'd found her in, but she saw the concern in his eyes. This was their first time alone together since that day.

'I am,' she lied. 'Thank you for all you did. I don't know what would have happened if you hadn't –'

'It's fine. I wasn't far behind you. The other men were about as well, so you were never really alone. I'm just sorry I didn't get there quicker.' His gaze never met hers, fixing instead on the horizon where the hot Queensland sun was already high in the sky.

Claire chose to misinterpret his concern. She didn't want to talk about what might have happened if Joseph McGrath hadn't been bitten. 'Oh, I know, but the main thing is that you got there and were able to put something on the bite. I believe Mr McGrath is making a good recovery, thanks to you.'

Now he turned. 'I would have let him die, by snakebite or let a croc get him, whatever. That man doesn't deserve our help.'

'I understand why you are angry, I do. But in the end, you did the right thing.' She wondered how she was going to engineer the conversation around to Helen. She paused, trying to find the right words, but in the end, it just came out. 'Sister Helen is going on retreat. That means she will be withdrawing from our community here for a while, spending some time alone in contemplation. She asked me to let you know.' Claire felt so conflicted. She owed so much to this man, and he apparently loved Helen, but she found it hard to act as messenger between them.

Helen had admitted there was something going on, if not sinful or wrong by deed then certainly by thought, on his part anyway. She felt, like she seemed to feel all the time these days, very far out of her depth.

'How long?' he asked. His dark eyes glittered with some emotion, but it was hard to say what.

She couldn't make him out. He was friendly, he helped them to no end, he'd asked for her help in dealing with McGrath – but did he secretly hate all of them? It would be feasible to imagine he did; after all, he had been forcibly taken from his family and to a Catholic mission. He never spoke of those years except to say he was there and he left, so if he held a deep resentment – and he had the right to – it was hard to tell. Guilt washed over her. She had asked this man to save his mortal enemy's life, and in return he perceived that she was keeping him from the woman he loved.

'Sister Helen is the only one who can answer that.' Claire knew she sounded condescending, but she had no idea what else to say. She could feel his hurt. She'd allowed herself to be duped by McGrath, trying to pawn off land that was entirely unsuitable. She'd begged him to heal the man who was the cause of the misfortune of his family, and she wasn't even telling him about the confession McGrath had made about Woiduna's death.

'They got a notice to quit the mission this morning, and Russell has been taken in for assault, so McGrath's brush with death hasn't done anything to make him change his mind.' Daku took a handful of crumbs from his pocket and threw them on the ground, and instantly a flock of mynah birds appeared, pecking at the ground for the treat.

'Oh,' was all she could manage. So McGrath wasn't a changed man as she'd hoped.

'You spoken to him?' Daku asked, and Claire shook her head. He sighed, and the sound carried all of his frustration and disappointment in her. Just another white person letting him down. She felt wretched.

'I'll try again,' she heard herself say, though the idea of seeking McGrath out filled her with dread and shame.

He shrugged, as if her decision was of no consequence to him. Without saying another word, he stood up and left.

Bad as she felt about the whole thing, at least that was one of her issues dealt with inasmuch as she could, and she felt a profound sense of relief that the accusation pertained to Helen and Daku and not her and McGrath. Gerard could have said anything to muddy the waters and add weight to her complaints.

Immediately she berated herself for such a selfish thought, but she couldn't have borne it to explain what had happened that evening by the creek to her uncle, and it was only her word against McGrath's.

She sat for a moment, her face to the sun, and it felt good. It would get much hotter as the day wore on, but early in the morning, it was so pleasant. She thought about her predicament. She was in a position to exert some pressure – a very Joseph McGrath approach – given what she knew, but it was hardly befitting a nun. He seemed to have made a full recovery and was wielding his power once more, giving the mission notice to leave. And Russell in jail meant McGrath got a clear run at the mission without Gardiner's formidable force impeding his progress.

She needed advice. It was Saturday, so there was no school. Teresita was in her workshop; Claire could hear the sound of the plane she'd borrowed from Daku to make the hurleys. There was enough interest among the adults for two hurling teams now in Jumaaroo, and a women's camogie team as well, the female version of the sport. It was hilarious to see everyone embracing the sport, and Teresita's enthusiasm was infectious.

Claire made two cups of tea and took two slices of currant brack from the tin. Mary had been baking again.

Teresita's back was to her as she entered the workshop, a shed structure used for storing the tools of the men who built the convent, now with the floor covered in sawdust.

Leaning against the walls were several three-and-a-half-feet-long sticks – narrow and round at one end, flat and curved at the other – in various stages of production and seasoning. The nun herself was covered in sawdust, a stub pencil stuck as usual between her head and her veil.

'Good morning!' Claire called so as not to startle her. 'God bless the work.'

Teresita whipped around. 'Ah, 'tis yourself, Claire.' She beamed at the traditional Irish blessing. 'I said I'd get an early start.'

She took one of her newly made hurleys and leaned her full weight on it, it seemed flexible.

'I have thirty men signed up, enough for two teams, and I'm hoping to set up the camogie league as well. Some of the older girls here are right dingers, so they are, fine strong lassies. They'd turn on a sixpence, and speed, you never saw the like!'

Claire marvelled at her. Teresita was easily in her fifties if not more, but she had the enthusiasm of a toddler. She was a ball of energy, and the townspeople of Jumaaroo embracing her beloved game was a source of delight to her.

'I brought you tea and a slice of brack. Sister Mary got a tip from Cassia to make it with pineapple, and I have to say, it is delicious.' Claire rested the cups on a bench that Teresita had turned into a worktop. She made all manner of things for the school: stools and steps for the smaller children in the orchestra, goalposts for the school field, even some little toys and puzzles for the small children in Mary's room. Her most incredible piece, though, was a beautiful but simple cross carved from ironwood that hung over the altar in their private chapel.

'Lovely,' Teresita said as she swept the sawdust off her habit. She sipped the tea gratefully.

'A white habit would be nice, wouldn't it? Or something lighter.' Claire didn't like to complain, but their garb was so impractical. Not only did the floor-length habit brush the dusty floor when they walked, but the scapular that went over it front and back, and the belt around the middle, made flow of air difficult. The heat was oppressive day and night, but at least at night she could wear her simple linen nightdress.

'It would,' Teresita agreed. 'But we didn't sign up for an easy life. We work for God in whatever form that takes, so we just have to offer it up. But it can be hard, I'll grant you.'

They said a brief prayer that they usually said before meals.

'So, Sister Claire, is there something on your mind?' Teresita bit into the succulent brack, closing her eyes for a moment to savour the sweet deliciousness.

'There is. Would you mind if I talked it out with you? It involves our fellow sisters, so if you'd rather not, then I understand.'

Teresita thought for a moment. 'If it will help you, then I'm here to listen.'

As briefly as she could, Claire told Teresita about the contents of the letter from Rev Bill, and the gist of the conversation with Helen. When she finished, Teresita seemed remarkably calm.

'Well, on the subject of Gerard, you behaved as you should have. 'Tis your job to run the school, and we can't have the like of that going on, hurting the children and the rest of it. So I think with that anyway, you did the right thing.' She put her cup down and picked up a piece of wood, examining the grain as she spoke.

'The Sister Helen thing, well, I don't know, but I doubt 'twill amount to anything. She's lonely, the craythur. She misses home, and this is a strange place surely, so she made a friendship. You're friendly with Cassia Galatas. I have great conversations with that Canadian man, you know, Stephen Wood's father, because he used to play a game over there when he was a boy – called lacrosse – that is a bit like hurling. And sure the pair of us would be yakking about that 'til the cows come home. Mary is getting great help with the orchestra from Mr Rogers – he used to play the organ at a cathedral back in England, imagine? So we all are doing our best here. Because Daku is a young single man, it is seen as untoward, when maybe it isn't.'

Claire could hear the hope in her voice, but she knew it was misplaced. She hated to dispel Teresita's optimism but had to tell her the whole truth. 'She says she has some kind of feelings for him, and he has for her as well. Of course, nothing has happened, they just talk, but she needs time alone to think and pray and make a decision.'

Teresita sighed. 'Well, in that case, we can do no more than pray for her and support her and see what happens.'

'And on the other matter?' Claire asked. 'The Bundagulgi and Russell Gardiner and all of that?'

Teresita exhaled loudly. 'Well, that's a right conundrum surely. I know what you're at, trying to solve everything for everyone, but if the bishop is against it, and they do owe Joseph McGrath a lot for all he's done here, then maybe 'tis best to steer clear?'

'I have prayed most of the night, I've been in the chapel since before the dawn, and I honestly don't know.' Claire paused, contemplating whether she should tell her sister everything, and decided she needed some guidance.

'When the Gardiners came to me, they were desperate. They don't like or trust us, so to come asking was a big thing for them, but they genuinely care so much for the Bundagulgi, they came anyway. And then Daku asked me to have one last try. He's been so good to us, and if he hadn't turned up the other evening, I don't know what would have happened. I kind of told him I'd ask again, but I don't know. Am I making a bad situation worse?'

Claire wondered if she should tell Teresita what she knew about Joseph McGrath. She wanted to, but she didn't want to draw her sister into this mess any more than she had to.

'With the mission and McGrath and all of that,' Teresita mused, 'well, I think it might be worth one more conversation. He does seem to hold you in high regard. I mean, he took you to see the new place, so he cares what you think. And I know people say this and that about him, but he does go to Mass every week, and he built this convent and school, so he's a God-fearing man. Maybe if you try to make him understand how worried the people at the mission are, then he might change his mind?'

'And if Rev Bill sees it as me aiding and abetting a cult?' Claire gave a rueful smile.

'Look, Gerard was rightly vexed after you downfaced her, so those would have been her words. You've known your uncle all your life and you get on well with him, so you can explain that you were not working for the cult if that's what they are, but that you were trying to do right by the native people here. You were asked to intervene, and you thought it was the moral thing to do. You took him on about the non-Catholics and won, so maybe you'll win this time too. The Bundagulgi have only you now if they've locked Russell Gardiner in the jail. '

'You're right.' Claire nodded, her heart sinking. 'I'll have one more try, though he's not a man who likes to be told what to do, I can assure you.'

'Which of them does?' Teresita grinned. 'Wasn't it a lucky day we decided not to have anything to do with men and romancing?'

'It never occurred to me, and I give thanks so often for my vocation. I never felt I was missing out, did you?'

Teresita's face was hard to read, but Claire thought she saw a slight sadness.

'Do you know, Claire, I don't ever miss having a husband, but sometimes, when I'd see a child run into his mother's arms, I'd get a little pang. That love, so pure, and to feel those little arms around your neck... I loved my mammy so much, God rest her, she was a lovely person. And I never knew what it was like to be a mother. That isn't a regret – I wouldn't change a thing, and I'm happy out – but sometimes as a younger woman, that thought would come to me.'

Claire felt a profound sadness for her sister. Though her life was blessed in so many ways, it wasn't without sadness. 'Well, you have the next best thing, the love of all your pupils,' she said.

'Yerra I do then, though they don't know what I'm going on about half the time.' She chuckled, drained her cup and turned back to her hurleys.

* * *

LATER THAT MORNING, Claire set out for the McGrath house once again, feeling sick with nerves. There was no point in putting it off. She'd made a promise and would keep it. The McGrath house dominated the town, perched on the hill, overseeing everything its inhabitants did. She steeled herself for what would be a difficult conversation.

A young woman in a maid's uniform opened the door and asked her to wait in the parlour. She did, and took in the artwork and the military medals in a display case. She wondered who had been awarded them; Joseph McGrath, she assumed. She would have liked to poke around a little, get a feeling for the man. But she did not want to be caught snooping, so she resisted and stood still in the centre of the room. On and on she waited. Perhaps twenty minutes passed, and she wondered if she should remind the girl she was still there when she reappeared.

'You may go up now, Sister,' she said deferentially, allowing Claire to walk past her and up the stairs to the office once again.

McGrath was sitting at his desk, writing something, when she entered. He didn't look up for a few moments, didn't even acknowledge her presence. He finished what he was doing and then glanced up.

'Sister Claire.' He paused, and this time didn't smile. 'Again.'

He didn't offer her a seat, and she felt silly standing on the rug before him like a schoolgirl. Without being invited, she sat opposite him. A long second passed.

'Well? What can I do for you this time?' There was none of the usual warmth and charm in his voice.

'Firstly, I'm glad to see you have made a full recovery after the snakebite.'

'Yes, I'm fine.'

She could hear the impatience. Clearly a thank you wasn't going to be forthcoming, so she got straight to the point. 'I wanted to speak to you regarding the mission.'

His blue eyes glittered as he slowly inhaled then exhaled through his nose. 'Why?' One word. Cold, confrontational.

'Well, because for the native people, this move out of Trouble Bay will mean the end of life as they have lived it for thousands of years. I saw the place you had in mind, and while to you and me it looks fine, it seems it is anything but. They say that is the country of another people, and they will not set foot there.'

McGrath sat back, his head resting on his leather chair, and closed his eyes. Eventually he spoke, leaning forward, his eyes on hers. 'I have asked you politely to stay out of my business. I have provided you with all you need to do the job you came here to do. I have allowed you to have your own way on the issue of non-Catholics attending the school I built. I even took the time to show you where the natives will be placed. But none of that is enough for you.'

She opened her mouth to interrupt him, but he raised his hand and said coldly, 'If you will just allow me to finish.'

She felt colour stain her cheeks. He was speaking down to her as if she were an errant child who was being particularly exasperating.

'I have been *very* patient with you, but my patience is now wearing thin. So instead of asking you, I am now *telling* you. Stay out of my business.' He leaned over the desk, his face nearer to her, and lowered his voice. 'Are we clear? Or do I have to finish what I started?' His mouth curled into a sneer. 'But maybe that's what you want?'

A toxic combination of shame and fury rose within her. How dare he? 'What you did was a mortal sin,' she said, keeping her voice low. 'And one day you will answer to God for it. But in the meantime, I will not be dictated to by you. What you are doing to the Bundagulgi people is downright immoral and it is –'

His fist, knuckles white, slammed on the desk, causing her to jump. 'Do not underestimate me, Sister Claire. You have no idea who you are dealing with.'

Claire held his steely blue-eyed gaze. 'Oh, I think I do, Mr McGrath. I know exactly who I'm dealing with. I'm dealing with a murderer.'

'Ha!' His laugh cut through the toxic atmosphere. 'You're jumping on that bandwagon, are you? Listening to all the local gossip.'

'You told me you killed Woiduna, and you mentioned Joe McGrath too.' Claire knew she was taking a risk, but something told her to call his bluff.

He tried to maintain his composure, but his pale skin and the swallow gave him away. 'What did you just say?' His voice was barely audible.

'You don't remember, do you? You told me everything on that riverbank. So no, I would never underestimate you. I know *exactly* what you're capable of.'

His face registered his shock but he said nothing.

This was her only advantage, and she had to use it. 'And Joe McGrath – you kept saying that name, not Joseph but Joe, and saying he was dead.' Claire had no idea what, if anything, it meant, but the look on his face told her he was very shaken.

Silence hung heavily between them. Claire felt the sweat trickle down her back and tried her best not to look as rattled as she felt. Then he rose and walked around to her side of the desk. He went down on his hunkers, his powerful body close to hers, and she felt the fear she'd experienced on the riverbank once more. He was just trying to frighten her, but it was working – she was terrified.

'Listen carefully.' His breath was on her cheek as he leaned his face only inches from hers. 'You're right. You *do* know what kind of man I am, what I have done, and what I can do again. And don't think I'm above sending you the same way because you're dressed up in that.' He flicked her veil. 'I own this town and everyone in it. And I will watch you like a hawk. You won't move a muscle without me hearing about it, and even those you think are your friends, well, they know how powerful I am, what I can do. Your uncle is a long way away from Jumaaroo, and he can't help you. Nobody can. So every word out of your mouth, every line you write, every gesture, every conversation will be reported to me. And if you so much as put a toe out of line, you and the rest of the penguins will pay a very heavy price. This is a very dangerous part of the world, and I needn't remind you, awful things can happen. Am I making myself crystal clear, *Claire?*'

The mocking way he said her name chilled her. She remained still, her mouth dry, not trusting herself to speak.

When she didn't respond, he grabbed the back of her neck through the veil, clamping his fingers painfully into her skin. 'I asked you a question.'

'I understand,' she managed to whisper.

'Good. Now get out.'

He stood, straightened his immaculately cut suit and returned to his side of the desk, resuming his work. Claire stood, worried her legs wouldn't carry her, and walked out of the room. As she went onto the landing, she caught Assumpta's eye. The monster's wife was standing in a doorway. Had she heard anything? She and Gerard were forever in each other's company, so no doubt she knew about the letter to Rev Bill. Neither woman acknowledged the other, and Claire let herself out.

CHAPTER 19

*J*oseph McGrath sat looking at the door Claire had just closed on her way out. He needed to make a decision. In the course of his life, things had happened to require a change of tack suddenly. His ability to move quickly and adapt was one of his many skills. This was probably one of those times.

A wave of exhaustion washed over him. He would do what he had to do to survive, but it felt like he'd been ducking and diving since birth. Growing up in the tenements of Henrietta Street in Dublin, he used to watch the carriages of the rich pull up outside the Gresham Hotel. Ladies and gentlemen, in their fine clothes, emerged to gorge themselves on food and drink that he could only dream of. His mother got the pox and died when he was four. His father was probably one of the many men she serviced, according to the policeman who picked him up for pickpocketing when he was only six.

He'd spent his childhood in various institutions run by the Church. If that fat penguin Sister Claire thought he had any respect for her or her kind, then she was gravely mistaken. He'd happily see every last one of them rot in hell. From the age of six, no matter what punishment they meted out – and they were imaginative if nothing else in that regard – he kept trying to escape. When at fifteen he managed it once again, he presumed they got sick of bringing him back – he was free.

It was all such a long time ago.

He poured himself a whiskey, swirled his glass and took a tiny sip. If he'd had the money, he'd have had a whiskey that night, his first night of freedom spent sleeping in some farmer's shed. He'd walked back to Dublin. The place they'd sent him that last time was out west somewhere, Galway maybe. He didn't know or care; they were all the same – savage, brutal, dark places, a place where childhood dies.

Then, on O'Connell Street, Molly saw something in him, a light even the most violent, sadistic Christian brother couldn't dim. Despite his bedraggled appearance, his cheeks hollow from hunger, his wits keen from having to survive for so long, she took him in, dressed him up. She was the first one to give him nice clothes, something he'd had a penchant for since. And he worked the ladies, as she called it. Molly had a salon, a ladies' club, a nice house in Dublin out Ballsbridge way, and she engineered meetings between him and the bored wealthy wives of Dublin. They would meet there for bridge and afternoon tea, and sometimes visiting milliners would have a show of hats, things women with nothing more important on their minds needed for distraction.

She taught him the ways of manipulation and seduction, knocked the hard edges off his accent and gave him a new backstory. He sometimes appeared at the salon as Molly Delaney's nephew. Part of the cover was he was older than he was. Molly would identify a mark for him, a particularly disgruntled wife with no shortage of funds. All he needed to do was give her a bit of attention, flatter her and slowly move in for the kill. He had a one hundred percent success rate. He'd bed them and relieve them of some money – half of which he split with Molly of course – and then came the final part of the plan: He'd threaten to expose them. The scandal would destroy not just their birdcage existence but their children and husbands too. Of course they always paid up; indiscretion is an expensive business.

He and Molly would sit in her drawing room after each one with a glass of whiskey and laugh about it. It was the only place he'd ever felt happy. They could have kept going for years. They were discreet, and it was never in the interests of the clients – as they euphemistically called them – to utter a word. But he came home one night, having spent the afternoon in a hotel with a politician's wife, to find Molly collapsed on the floor. He called for help, but it was too late; she was gone. He was bereft, devastated.

He remembered the blind panic – he was alone again. He had not one person in the world who cared about him. He went to a pub, a rough one down the quays, and began drinking in earnest. Alcohol could not numb the pain, but a pretty woman might. He found one, on the corner of Amiens Street. It would cost him a few shillings, but he didn't care. However, her pimp didn't like the look of him it seemed, so refused to let her go with him. That was the last straw. He'd lashed out. He finally understood the phrase 'to see red' – all he saw was a red mist. It might have been in his mind, or it might have been the blood of the man he beat to death; he didn't know. He never heard the girl's screams, the policeman's whistle. He knew nothing but rage.

His years of escaping from borstals the length and breadth of Ireland stood to him, so when he was being moved from prison to court, where no doubt he'd have been sentenced to hang, he managed to escape again. He knew the back streets and alleyways of Dublin like the back of his hand, so once he gave the dozy prison wardens the slip, he was home free. He lay low that day, pinched some cash from a shop on Dorset Street run by two old sisters who were slow on their pins, and that night caught the boat to England. He didn't dare try to get at his bank account, so poor as a church mouse once more, he began his life again.

He looked around his luxurious office in his beautiful house. Molly's voice rang in his ears. 'You're like a cat, boy. You'll always land on your feet.' She was right, he did. The military contract was all but sealed, and what he stood to make would have him in the lap of luxury for years.

He might even throw Pius a few quid. After all, that eejit had set the ball rolling though he didn't know it. But he probably wouldn't bother. He looked around. It was time to get out of Jumaaroo; the nun was not going to stop sniffing around. She was scared of him, but he wasn't confident that fear was enough to keep her big trap shut.

It wasn't a hard decision, he was surprised to note. The town bored him now, and Assumpta and the kids did too. She was a pain in the arse, and he was fed up with her moaning. She did nothing but spend money and look presentable. He was sick of her demands. Only last week she announced she needed to go to Cairns to buy hats for the season. Nobody noticed her, so why she needed new hats was a mystery. The woman was a moron. Being a father didn't interest him in the slightest either. He'd leave her, and the businesses would be sold by the time she realised what had happened. He had a bit of organising to do, as the business was in Assumpta's name. She had no idea, of course, but his crooked solicitor in Sydney advised it, knowing that his client's credentials wouldn't withstand too much official scrutiny. He'd move everything over once he got set up someplace else, and she'd be none the wiser.

Let Pius and her mother take them in. God knows he gave that family enough over the years. The people of this backwards town would be devastated. He smiled at the thought. The adoration, the kowtowing, was entertaining enough for a while, but he was sick of that now too. All the sycophantic nonsense they went on with. They were right, the place wouldn't exist without him, but the reality was he was just smarter and more willing to get things done than they were. He was a leader; they were sheep.

It was time to go somewhere new. Find somebody new to be.

CHAPTER 20

The rest of the weekend, Claire remained alone inasmuch as she could. Teresita was busy in her workshop, and Mary taught music all day Saturday. She attended the fortnightly Sunday Mass in Strathland, travelling on the bus provided by Joseph McGrath for anyone who wanted to attend. It was more full than usual, and Claire noticed some families who were not regular attendees climbing on board, their children delighted. She felt a sense of satisfaction that even in the face of such upset, they were delivering a good message at St Finbarr's.

After returning to Jumaaroo, she declined to eat lunch, saying she needed to go to the chapel, and Mary and Teresita accepted it. They ate with Gerard, and Helen remained in her room.

All that afternoon, she wondered how on earth she was going to go on. She had a death threat hanging over her. It wasn't an exaggeration to say he'd threatened to kill her, and not just her, but poor Mary, Gerard, Teresita and Helen too...though possibly Gerard would be spared. She would have to do something; living with this terror wasn't possible. Rev Bill had said he was going to visit, but that could be months away, and anyway, McGrath was right – he had eyes and ears everywhere. She couldn't even write to her uncle – the postmaster was also McGrath's driver. The policeman in town, Seth Godfrey, was also a waste of time. His children attended the school, and they'd informed her proudly that Mr McGrath was their godfather, so Seth was obviously in McGrath's pocket as well.

She thought of Russell Gardiner, who was being held in the cell behind the police station. He must be so hot and worried. Despite his aggressive demeanour, she felt sorry for him.

All afternoon she racked her brain. She needed to get word to someone, but who? Her uncle? The police in Cooktown? Even if she did, would they believe her? Could they act on it if there was no proof? Woiduna's body was found at the bottom of a ravine, and even if the police would investigate the death of an Aboriginal, and she doubted that they would, they could find nothing but death by misadventure. He wasn't stabbed or shot or anything, so it would sound just ludicrous. Everyone here owed all they had to McGrath, so no one would ever testify against him, and she would just be represented as a crank with a grudge. As far as she understood it from Jannali, the community had placed Woiduna's body on a large flat rock, where it would remain until all that was left was his skeleton. Then his bones would be painted with ochre and buried. Bundagulgi from all over had come for the ceremony. He had been much loved.

There wasn't a telephone in the convent, and the one at the post office would certainly be monitored. She was a prisoner in this town.

She slept fitfully that night, dreaming she was alone with McGrath. He was dressed as a pirate, and he had red eyes like a painting she'd seen of Satan. He was chasing her and she couldn't get away. She woke, drenched in perspiration, and couldn't go back to sleep.

Monday at school she was distracted. Teresita asked her if she was all right as they ate lunch, but she saw Gerard glance over and so just said, 'I didn't sleep well last night, the heat I think. So I'm a little tired.'

'Have an early night tonight,' Teresita advised kindly.

She spent the day in Helen's classroom, and the children were happy to read quietly. She'd asked them to write a review of their favourite book, and they were diligently writing when there was a knock on the door. Claire opened it, and a little boy from Mary's room stood there. Harvey Ball was partially blind, and while he managed, he needed a lot of help. She went outside, almost closing the door behind her so nobody would hear what was going on.

'A lady asked me to give you this,' the boy said as he held out a folded piece of paper.

'What lady?' Claire asked him, taking the note.

'I don't know, Sister. I couldn't see her properly, but she put this note in my hand and asked me to deliver it to you.'

'Thank you, Harvey, you're a good boy.' She took a barley sugar from her pocket and handed it to him.

Sitting at Helen's desk, she unfolded the paper, glancing up to make sure all heads were on their work. She would not put it past McGrath to have the children spying on her.

Meet me in the nun's chapel at 3:30 p.m.

It wasn't signed and she didn't recognise the writing, but it was refined cursive so it was an adult and someone well educated. Was it a trap? Why though? If McGrath wanted to speak to her, he would just come to the school, and if he wanted to harm her, the chapel would not be the place he would choose, she was sure of that. A thought struck her – was it Daku? Or even one of the Gardiners? No, they would never go into a Catholic church. She was at a loss as to who it might be. The nuns' private chapel was for their use. Nobody else ever went into the beautiful, simple space, and she hated the idea of anyone being there who wasn't a member of their community.

The day dragged, and it was with a sigh of relief that she dismissed the children to go out to join Teresita's class for hurling training. She cleared the desk, marked the exercise books and prepared the classroom for the next day. When the bell rang at three to signal lessons were over, the usual ruckus filled the air.

She returned to her office, watching over the gates and playground as parents came to collect the little ones and as the older children walked down the hill to the town. She thought of Teresita's sadness as she watched the junior children run to their mothers. She'd never felt that pull to be a mother herself, but she understood how it could make someone sad. She could see the whole main street from her office, the shops, the ponies and traps, an odd car, the McGrath house on the other side of town up the hill. It was a prosperous, industrious little town, everything well-kept and painted. The canopy-covered boardwalk outside the shops was regularly swept by the proprietors. It was hard to believe that it was a town entirely under the thumb of one evil man.

3:15. She debated ignoring the note, but something told her to go. However, she would be cautious. She would watch the door from her office window, see who went in. There was only one door to the outside world. Though there was a passageway the sisters used from the hallway of the convent, no member of the public would have access to that.

She watched but the yard was clear, all the children long gone home. Mary was conducting after-school choir practice, and Teresita had crossed to her workshop a little after three. Gerard was in her room; Claire had passed her on the way there as she came back to the office. They had not exchanged many words since her announcement that she was leaving. Claire was always polite and greeted her warmly, but she got only the most perfunctory of replies.

She was loathe to leave her office, but it was 3:25 now and nobody had arrived. Someone could appear while she was in the passageway, but she would have to take that chance. She slipped out and went downstairs to the door from the hallway into the chapel passage.

The passageway was dark, lit only by a sanctuary lamp, but it was short. Claire could feel her heart beating as she turned the Bakelite handle on the heavy door leading out into the chapel to the right of the altar.

The chapel had only four pews, so the person could not hide. She sat in the back corner, head covered. It wasn't until she raised her face that Claire could identify her.

'Mrs McGrath.' Claire could not keep the astonishment out of her voice.

They had never had more than the most curt of exchanges. Since the evening she confronted Claire about Jannali's enrolment,

Assumpta made no bones about the fact that she thought Claire had notions above her station, and she never made the slightest effort to be anything more than coldly polite. Of all the people in Jumaaroo Claire had expected to find in the chapel, Assumpta was the last.

'Sister Claire, I won't stay long, but I...' Assumpta inhaled to steady herself, and Claire realised the other woman was trembling. 'I didn't overhear exactly what was said, but I heard raised voices when you came to visit my husband on Saturday. I don't know what I... Well, look, I heard you ask him why he wanted the land out at Trouble Bay, and I know he's got some big military contract. He's sold the land to the army for a base or something, but the thing is, the land he's promised to the Aboriginals isn't even his to give.'

Claire saw the tears shining in the woman's eyes but was worried it was a trap. Why would Assumpta come and tell her this?

The other woman must have read her mind. 'Look, I know we haven't been friendly. And you have no reason to trust me, but I... I'm afraid of my husband, Sister. He's a violent, dangerous man, I'm sure of it, but I can't fight him alone. He won't let me leave him – he'd kill me first – and I'm afraid for myself and for my children.'

Claire believed her. Maybe this was the help from God she'd prayed for. An ally might be just what she needed.

'I know about Woiduna as well,' Assumpta said quietly. 'I know he paid Bill McAllister. I overheard them laughing about it.'

Claire thought quickly. 'I'll trust you, Mrs McGrath.' She sat beside the other woman, who was now crying. Claire took her hand. 'With what I know – which to be honest isn't much more than you, but you're right, neither one of us alone can take him on – perhaps together we can do something. But first I must ask you, have you spoken to anyone else? Even Sister Gerard?' She hated betraying her mistrust of her sister to Assumpta despite their frosty relationship, but it was vital she knew who knew what.

'Nobody,' Assumpta confirmed.

It could be a trap. Maybe McGrath sent his wife to test her, but she didn't think so. 'Follow me.' Claire led Assumpta to the passageway and into the convent. She checked to make sure nobody was there and quickly ushered the other woman up to her office. Once inside, she locked the door and invited Assumpta to sit.

'On the night of the snakebite, your husband admitted he had killed Woiduna, but more than that, he kept repeating his own name, except he referred to himself as Joe McGrath, saying he was dead. He was delirious and there may be nothing to it, but when I brought it up when I spoke to him the other day, he paled and got very angry. He threatened me and more or less threw me out of the house, so he's hiding something. I just don't know what.'

'What should we do?' Assumpta whispered. 'I'll do whatever you ask. I need to get him out of our lives for good.'

Claire thought for a moment. She needed evidence. At least with some hard proof, she could go to the authorities or to her uncle with something concrete. At the moment, even if she could get a message to someone without McGrath knowing, it was only hearsay and conjecture, which could easily be dismissed.

'When he's out, try to get into his office, have a look around. See if there's anything you can find that we could take to the police. Without evidence, we won't get anywhere.'

'And if I can't find anything? He's not going to have a receipt book showing him paying off thugs or anything like that. He's very private, and I've never been in his office when he wasn't there.' Assumpta was nervous before she even started, but she was Claire's only hope.

'He's hiding something. He looked so shaken when I accused him. You'll never know until you look.' Claire smiled encouragingly. 'You're not alone, Mrs McGrath.'

CHAPTER 21

ow that she had confirmation that the proposed land for the new mission was not only unsuitable but not even McGrath's to give, Claire knew she needed to warn the Bundagulgi people. With Russell in jail, they would only have Betty, and she would be no match for the eviction bailiffs that McGrath would send. Claire needed to get word to them to hold their ground, but how? McGrath had spies everywhere.

Daku was the obvious person, but he had not come around since she told him about Helen withdrawing. She needed to find him. She walked as far as she dared in the direction of the bush but realised it was stupid. He could be anywhere.

Turning back, she headed instead to Gordie's house. If anyone could find Daku, it would be him. She found Gordie sitting on his porch drinking a beer and listening to Jannali as she read to him.

'G'day, Claire,' he called. 'You want a beer?' He grinned and she smiled in reply. His refusal to treat her as a nun might annoy others, but she found it refreshing.

'No thanks, but I'd love a glass of water. Could you get me one, Jannali? I need to talk to your daddy for a minute. By the way, Sister

Mary said you are learning so fast! She's so proud of you and I am too.'

The little girl beamed. 'Can I have a lolly?' she asked.

Claire raised her eyebrow.

'May I have a lolly please, Sister?' Jannali corrected herself, and Claire chuckled, digging in her pocket and producing a barley sugar. The little girl skipped inside happily.

'What can I do for ya?' Gordie asked, dragging up a misshapen stool for her to sit on.

'I need to find Daku,' she said quietly. 'It's very important.'

Even though she was out in the bush and miles from anyone working for McGrath, she was still wary. He could have had her followed – in fact, he probably had.

Gordie seemed to know by her demeanour that something was wrong. 'Everything all right?' he murmured.

'Can you find him and tell him to come to the chapel very early tomorrow, around five? I can't go into it right now, but I need to speak to him.'

Gordie glanced out the side of his eye and saluted someone passing by with a pony and trap. It was Stavros and Darius Galatas. Cassia's husband, like everyone else, worked for McGrath. Claire wondered if he was the one sent to follow her.

'G'day, Stavros!' Gordie called, falsely cheery. 'What brings you out this way, mate?'

Stavros stopped and got off, hitching the pony to Gordie's rusty old gate. 'Ah, nothin', mate, just out for a bit of exercise for the pony, y'know?' He patted the animal. Stavros worked in the McGrath logging yard outside of town, travelling to and from work by pony and cart. The animal got plenty of physical exercise every day.

'Want a cold one?' Gordie asked.

'Wouldn't say no. G'day, Sister.' He tipped his cap. 'Cassia was just saying the other day we haven't seen you for a while. You should call for a cuppa someday.' He smiled but was there something insincere about it? Maybe she was imagining it.

He approached the deck, sitting down on the timber and wiping the sweat from his face and neck with a clean handkerchief from his pocket. Darius went to fetch a bucket of water for the animal.

'Oh, I will. I've just been busy with the school. In fact, I was just up here asking Mr McKenzie if he could spare his set of chisels, as Sister Teresita is so busy making hurleys. I hear you are going to be on the team?' She forced her voice to be friendly and cheerful as if nothing at all was untoward.

'I reckon I am. My boys talk about nothing else – they love it! I went to see them play a few weeks back, reckoned I'd give it a go. Looks fair dinkum rough mind!' He chuckled. 'What about you, Gordie? You reckon you could get the hang of this mad Irish sport?' Stavros smiled his thanks as Darana appeared with two cold beers for the men and a glass of water for Claire.

'Nah, mate, not me.' Gordie took a long drink from the neck of the bottle, wiping his mouth afterwards with his sleeve. 'My missus wouldn't let me, would ya, love? In case I got hurt and ruined my handsome features.' He put his arm around Darana and gave her a squeeze, and Jannali giggled. 'Right, let me get you those chisels.' He left them and Darana and Jannali went inside.

Stavros chatted about how well Max was getting on in school now that he was in the same class as his brother. He never mentioned that it was the absence of Sister Gerard rather than the presence of Darius that made him so happy. Claire made idle chit-chat for a few minutes. She was frustrated that she couldn't say more to Gordie, but she wouldn't risk it in front of anyone else.

Stavros drained his beer and placed the bottle on the ground by the door. 'Well, I'll best be off. Cassia warned me not to be late. But if you're ready, I'll give you a ride back? Darius can walk, he's young and able.'

Claire held his gaze for a second longer than was necessary. Was he spying on her or was he genuinely out for a spin with his son? 'Ah, no, that wouldn't be fair...' she began. She wanted to talk to Gordie, but it wasn't going to be possible with the Galatas family around.

'I don't mind, Sister,' said Darius, who'd come to join them.

'Thank you, Darius, that's very kind of you.'

Gordie arrived with a box of chisels and handed them to Claire.

'Thanks so much. Sister Teresita really appreciates it,' Claire said.

'No worries. No rush back with them – I'll call in someday whenever I need them back.'

Claire sat up on Stavros's trap, and they left to go back to Jumaaroo. He kept up a steady stream of chatter all the way, about hurling, the fact that his younger son was really enjoying the music classes, the best way to treat mosquito bites. He told her that Cassia hadn't been feeling so good recently and missed her friend calling for a cold drink. It was true Claire hadn't called to Cassia for a while, but since everything had blown up, she didn't trust confiding in anyone. Sometimes she felt so isolated and alone, she feared she would weaken in Cassia's kind presence and reveal some of her concerns.

'Darius tells me Sister Helen isn't teaching at the moment? I hope she's not sick?'

'No, not sick at all. She's fine, thank God. I'm just standing in for her for a while, as she has some things she needs to do.' Claire remained non-committal and chatted easily, but in the back of her mind, she wondered. Maybe she was becoming paranoid. Was Stavros encouraging her to visit his wife so she would confide in her and they could both report back to McGrath? Surely not.

They brought her to the door of the convent, and Darius handed her the box of chisels from the cart.

'Sister Teresita will be pleased. She's been working so hard to have a hurley for everyone who wants to play.' Claire smiled her thanks.

'She's an incredible person.' Stavros was sincere. 'So much energy! All of you sisters have. You've all made life so much better for everyone here, Sister Claire, really. Our children can stay at home, and with all of the music and the sport and all the reading, it was a good day the day you all came.' He took off his hat and wiped his brow. 'It's hard for the women out here. Us men work all the time, so that's fine, but there's not much for the girls to do, no picture house or even nice shops. You and the other sisters are a breath of fresh air, fair dinkum. Have a nice evening.'

He tipped his hat and shook the reins, and the pony trotted back down the hill. Claire watched his back as he went, one hand holding the reins, the other on his son's thin shoulder. She knew from Cassia how much Stavros loved having Darius and Max at home. He loved his boys with all his heart, and he was so grateful when she arranged to have Max removed from Sister Gerard's classroom. Was he that duplicitous that he would say such things but at the same time spy on her for McGrath?

CHAPTER 22

Claire found him at 5 a.m. in the chapel as she'd asked, which was the first surprise. To say Daku was unpredictable was not true, but he lived by an entirely different set of rules, and though she liked him, she didn't really understand him.

If he hadn't turned up, she was willing to use Helen to summon him. Something told her that once Helen came out of retreat, no matter what she decided, Daku would be around again. How he would discover Helen had rejoined the community was anyone's guess, but he seemed to just know things.

He was an Aboriginal man, proud and deeply protective of his people, but being raised on a Catholic mission and all that entailed made him different to the other Bundagulgi people she'd encountered. The others, the ones she saw at the mission, or Darana, or occasionally Aboriginal people she saw in town, were wary and actively avoided contact with white people. They were inherently mistrustful, she supposed, and who could blame them? There was no good aspect of European colonisation of Australia for the native people.

She'd read the occasional newspaper article about the missions. The tone was always the same, that the indigenous people were a problem to be dealt with. The political attitude seemed to be that they needed to be managed. A special minister of state was responsible for them, and he had the final word. Claire was horrified at the lack of autonomy the first Australians had over their own destiny; it was tantamount to slavery really. But then her deep faith told her that bringing the word of God to these gentle people was a good thing. It was why she had become a nun, to be the voice of Jesus and his Blessed Mother and to bring his grace to those who had not been as fortunate. The longer she was in Australia, though, the more she questioned it.

Not her vocation – she believed completely in that – nor did she think that telling people about the Lord was anything but a joyous thing. But the manner in which it was done wasn't right. Surely the people could embrace the Christian message without having their culture annihilated at the same time?

Daku had told her of the pagan belief systems of the Bundagulgi people, how they believed their ancestors walked among them, how in the time before memory, the Dreamtime as they called it, the creatures of the earth were formed. Over the months that she'd known him, he'd explained how they were all connected – people, the land, the oceans, the animals, the plants. He told her about burning, how Australia was a land that needed fire, but how there were designated ignition points – the same ones used for thousands of years – where fires could be lit safely. But the white men didn't care about their ways, they ignored their knowledge, and they were destroying the land in the process.

As he stood at the back of the chapel, she noticed how much more presentable he looked these days. His hair, while still long, was cut and seemed a little tamer. He wore a shirt and trousers now, though he was still barefoot. He was tall and powerfully built while being as lithe as a tiger. His skin was dark but not as black as some of the others. His white father's genes saw to that.

'Thank you for coming, Daku.'

He looked at her, and she saw the pain of loss in his eyes. 'Gordie said you wanted to see me. Is it about Helen?'

He said Helen's name in a proprietorial way. He probably saw Claire as the barrier between them.

'No. As I said, Sister Helen has chosen to retreat, to pray and to be alone.' Claire hoped she managed to keep the emphasis off the word 'sister'. She needed him on her side, and if he saw her as the enemy, then her plan would fail.

'You locked her up, you mean.' His almost-black eyes were inscrutable.

'Look, Daku, I know you think that I have interfered in some way with your friendship with Sister Helen, but I give you my word that I have not. She came and spoke to me in confidence, and said she needed some time to think. Of course I granted her request for time off from school, but that is all I have done. Sister Helen will, I am sure, when she's ready, talk to you, but please be assured nobody is locking her anywhere. She is as free as you are.'

Daku shoved his hands in his trouser pockets. 'Doesn't matter anyway. I'm moving on.'

This information was the last thing she needed to hear. She knew from others that it was common practice within the Aboriginal community for the men to just wander off. They might be back in a few days, but often it was months or maybe even years. They didn't give any notice, or tell anyone. Jannali had explained it one day when she was talking about one of her uncles, that it was called 'going walkabout'.

'When do you plan to go?' she asked, fearing his answer. He was in no way answerable to her. McGrath employed him, and that contract meant nothing to Daku, but she knew that Helen would not want him to go without a conversation at least. Besides, Claire needed him.

He shrugged.

She knew she should not use their feelings for each other as a reason for him to stay around Jumaaroo, but she had no choice. 'And you'd go without saying goodbye to Sister Helen?' Claire asked, praying she was playing this right.

'She doesn't want to see me.'

It was a statement, but Claire heard the glimmer of hope there. He must have believed her when she said she wasn't keeping Helen from him, so the only other possibility was that she didn't want to see him. It was hurting him, she could tell. Claire burned with feelings of guilt once more. Daku had been so good to them, and the way he saw it, she was ruining his chance of happiness.

'I don't think that's the case.' Claire had to tread very carefully. Whatever went on between them was private, and she couldn't get involved. At home – and Claire doubted Helen was the first nun to develop feelings for a man – it would be dismissed as foolish fanciful notions and she would be reprimanded and sent far away, the man to never cross her path again. Sisters did leave – not often, but she'd heard of it – but those were very rare cases. Perhaps she should have been firmer with Helen, reminded her she was a bride of Christ, not an ordinary woman, and that she should remember her relationship with Jesus and forsake all others. But Claire didn't feel she had the right to, nor was it the moral thing to do. Helen would have to come to her own conclusions, without influence.

'What is it then? She has not come out for days, she left without even telling me...' He sat on the back pew and put his head in his hands.

Claire felt so sorry for this kind, decent man. He was nothing like her, but in that moment, they were both just people, struggling to deal with what life had thrown at them. 'I think she felt confused. She needed time alone, to think and pray, but I don't think she wanted to hurt you, or that she was trying to get away from you. Daku, she is a Catholic nun, and she takes that very seriously, so please try to understand.'

He turned to face her, his eyes searching her face for a hint of a lie. He must have known how impossible the situation was. But the ways of the heart... Well, she had no idea about the ways of the heart herself, but it certainly seemed to be complicated.

'I love her.' The words hung there, heavy and poignant.

Claire had no idea how to respond. Should she acknowledge his feelings? Should she tell him he was misguided? Or that it would be best for him to find a woman from the Bundagulgi people?

'And I think Sister Helen knows that, but as I said, she has a lot to consider.' It was as far as she was willing to go. She couldn't contemplate what the outcome would be if Helen decided she reciprocated his feelings, as that was for her to decide. Claire would neither dash his hopes nor give him reason to be optimistic.

'So why did you bring me here?' he asked.

'Because I need your help. I've found out that the proposed new mission site isn't just unsuitable as you told me, but McGrath doesn't even own it. So if the Bundagulgi people are driven off the Trouble Bay site, there will be nowhere for them to go. Russell is in jail thanks to his assault on McGrath, so Betty is all they have up there. You need to go up and refuse to leave. Lead the men, hide the women and children, and make sure they do not force you off that land.'

Daku's mouth twitched in a hint of a smile. 'Are you advocating revolution?'

'Well, I'm just saying you need to stand your ground, that's all.'

They sat in silence for a moment.

'Will you do it?' she asked quietly.

He looked at her, his face inscrutable, and then, without saying a word, he left.

CHAPTER 23

*C*laire sat in the chapel, everything going round and round in her head. She hoped he would do as she'd asked, but he had been non-committal. Surely he would go and defend his people though. He wouldn't be doing it for her; he would be doing it for them. Or would he just walk off into the bush, leaving the whole disappointing mess behind? It was impossible to know.

Meanwhile, she knew she had to do something about McGrath. If Daku and the others could buy a bit of time, refuse to leave the mission, then she would need to make sure that by the time the police got involved, it would be as an investigation into the wrongdoing of Joseph McGrath rather than as backup for the bailiffs.

And time wasn't on her side. If only Assumpta could come up with some evidence, even something small, enough to get the police to consider the possibility that he was not as he seemed, then that would be enough. She felt sure that if they just found one loose thread, then the whole mysterious story would come undone. McGrath's face when she mentioned his repetition of the name Joe McGrath gave him away. She was convinced he was hiding something.

Later that morning, when Cassia brought up a jar of honey from her hive and a delicious cake she baked called baklava, they had a cup of tea together in the kitchen. Cassia looked awful. She'd lost weight and seemed so tired, and Claire asked her if everything was all right.

She sighed. 'Yes. Well, not really. I discovered a lump, here...' She pointed to the side of her breast. 'Stavros said I should go to the doctor, but the only surgery is in Strathland and it's so difficult to get there. Last week, he asked for a day off to take me. We were going to take the pony and cart, but once he heard why, Joseph McGrath offered Stavros his car.'

Claire fought to keep her expression neutral.

Cassia went on. 'Stavros was so worried about me. I'm tired all the time. He didn't ask McGrath himself for the day off, but his foreman must have told the boss, so Mr McGrath called Stavros in. He was so nice, offering the car, and telling him that if I needed to go to the hospital or anything, there was no problem, that he would help in every way he could. He even offered to pay for a specialist in Cairns.'

Claire fought the urge to tell Cassia why her husband's employer was suddenly being so considerate. She was sure he was trying to get in with the Galatas family because he knew Cassia was her friend.

'And did you go?' Claire asked.

Cassia nodded. 'It's not good news, the doc thinks. I have to go to the hospital next week. There is someone there who will look at it and decide. I...' Tears filled her eyes. 'I can't die, Sister Claire. I can't leave Stavros and my boys...'

Claire placed her hand on Cassia's, feeling bad for neglecting her recently while she was going through all of this. Claire normally called to see her at least once a week, but she had been so consumed with everything and was wary of everyone now, so she'd stopped. But Cassia had been the first person to treat her like a normal person, and had offered the hand of friendship. Claire could reciprocate now.

'Would you like me to come with you to the hospital?' Claire offered, and her friend smiled.

'Thank you, but it's all right. Stavros will come. We might be late getting back. I'll have some food ready for the boys, but perhaps you would just check in on them? I've never left them at home on their own before.'

'Of course. How about I arrange for the boys to have their dinner here at the convent? They can do their homework and maybe help Sister Teresita with the hurleys in the workshop – they'd love that, I'm sure. Then after dinner, I'll bring them home and wait in your house until you get back. Would that help?'

Cassia smiled and sighed. 'It really would. I know Darius is twelve now, and maybe I mollycoddle them, but I hate the idea of them there on their own. I've had to tell them that I'm a bit sick, so they're worried and...' She sighed again, a shuddering sound that came from deep within her. 'Back in Greece, I would have family around now, parents, aunts, so many people to help. Over here, we are so alone, just Stavros and me. He was born here, but his mother is dead and his father, well, we never see him, no idea where he even is. Sometimes I wish we could just go back to Santorini.'

Claire nodded. She knew exactly how Cassia felt. She too felt so far from home and more alone than she'd ever been.

They chatted for a while, Cassia changing the subject. She explained she didn't want to dwell on her illness until she knew the whole story, so they talked about this and that, nothing of any consequence, and Claire tried to focus on her friend.

If Cassia had heard the rumours about Helen and Daku, or the argument with Gerard, she never mentioned it. It was hard to believe she didn't know that Claire had gone to the mission, or that the Gardiners had visited her. And Cassia's silence on the subject made Claire suspicious. She longed for it not to be true, but was Cassia cultivating their friendship all along to spy on her? She was so worried about her health, and dedicated to her family... If McGrath offered her a way through, help with medical things and so on, would it be enough to turn her friend against her?

Claire realised in that moment that McGrath was turning her into someone she didn't recognise. Her friend was ill and worried about the future, and all Claire could do was be suspicious. She decided that no, that was not how she was. She would not allow one evil man to change her world view.

As Cassia stood to leave, Claire gave her a hug. 'It's going to be all right. I'll pray very hard that it turns out to be nothing serious, and I'll ask the other sisters and the children to say a prayer for a very special intention. Prayers can move mountains, you know.' She smiled.

'Thanks, Sister Claire. I'll take all the help I can get.'

She let Cassia out and saw Helen walking in the garden. It was dusk, a time Claire usually avoided the outdoors because the mosquitos were out in full force – and they found her pale Irish skin particularly delicious – but she'd not seen Helen for days and wanted to check on her.

She took some of the citronella ointment Cassia had made for her weeks ago that was supposed to repel the biting insects. She was about to rub it on her face and hands before crossing the garden, but then she noticed Helen talking to someone. She couldn't see who it was, but she could guess. Helen was earnestly explaining something, gesticulating in a manner most unlike her. She seemed very het up, whatever it was about. Then, just as Claire was about to go out, or at least make a noise to indicate she was there, Helen disappeared behind the huge bougainvillea.

Claire stood at the kitchen door, unsure what she should do. Helen had seemed distressed – perhaps she was in trouble. Maybe it wasn't Daku, or maybe it was and he was upset or angry. However mortifying it would be to intrude on their private conversation, Claire had to check on her. She let herself out, slamming the door loudly. Within seconds Helen reappeared in the garden. As Claire walked towards her, she saw her face was tear-stained.

'Come inside,' Claire urged gently, placing her hand on Helen's elbow.

'I... Oh, Claire, I don't know what to do...' Helen's voice was choked with emotion.

'Come inside, we can talk. Please...'

She led Helen to her office, as the kitchen was too public. Claire sat her down and sat opposite her, waiting for her to speak.

'Daku is leaving. He won't say where or for how long, and he gave me one more opportunity to be with him. I said I needed more time, I wasn't sure, and so now he's gone.' Shuddering sobs racked her body, and Claire had no idea how to respond. If Daku left now, Helen would not be the only one who would be in trouble.

'And he said he was going today?' Claire hoped she didn't sound callous, but she needed to know.

Helen nodded, but then said, 'Well, he didn't say when exactly, but he won't see me again, that's the thing. He told me how he feels, he gave me the opportunity, and I didn't take it. That's the end of the story as far as he's concerned.'

'And is it the end for you?' Claire asked gently.

'I...' Helen looked wretched. 'I suppose it has to be. I mean, if he's gone...'

'But that is not you making a decision, is it?' Claire knew she was pressing the issue. She longed for her sister to say it was all a big mistake, a misplaced infatuation, a friendship that got out of hand, some explanation, but deep down she knew the truth even if Helen didn't yet. Claire would be doing Helen, Daku and their entire community a disservice by simply brushing her concerns under the carpet and pretending everything was fine now that Daku was gone.

Helen looked at her, distraught and terrified.

Slowly Claire shook her head. 'So you must ask yourself, if you were to be given the option to go to another convent – and I'm not saying that is an option, but if it were – to leave here, go somewhere else, continue in the order and never see him again, would you take it?'

'I don't know.' Helen's voice was barely a whisper now. 'I love my life, I love being a nun, a teacher. I love God and my life consecrated to him, but...' She fixed Claire with a gaze, the dawning realisation coming as a shock as she said the words aloud for the first time. 'I love him too.'

'Well, there is your answer.' Claire smiled and laid her hand on Helen's.

'But I can't betray my vocation, the promises I made... It would be a sin so grievous –'

'No, it isn't. You can't help how you feel, Helen.' Claire tried to find the right words. 'You have not sinned – you fell in love. Love is a gift from God, so how could that be a sin?' She smiled. 'I never felt that, never once in all of my life have I looked at a man and wondered what if. I know some other sisters have, or yearned to be mothers, but that was never for me. So I'm not saying I understand, but I believe we are all children of God, and love, the purest of all the emotions, comes from him. He would not have ordained that you and Daku meet, have feelings for each other, if it were not part of his plan for you.'

'Do you really think that?'

Claire could hear the longing for understanding in her voice. 'I do. You didn't set out to have this happen, and neither, I must assume, did he. But, Helen, please...' She searched for a way to say it without being condescending or bigoted. 'Be very careful. Daku is not just an ordinary man. He's unlike anyone we would have known back at home. He is so far removed from what we understand that life with him, if that is what you choose, may be very difficult indeed.'

'He told me about Gordie and Darana,' Helen said quietly, and Claire just let her talk, as it seemed to soothe her. 'Gordie's first wife died in childbirth. The baby was lost as well, and he was heartbroken. He left their house and his business and everything he had down south, around Victoria somewhere, and came up here.

'He had money, it seemed. Someone recognised him a few years ago, some bigwig up from Melbourne, and told everyone in the hotel one evening how apparently the McKenzies were a very wealthy family. But Gordie refused to talk about it. He wanted to be left alone, to remove himself from the world. He became friendly with Woiduna – the elder was impressed with his woodworking apparently – who took him under his wing. Gordie wasn't like other white men. He wanted to learn from the tribal people, he wanted to understand about bush tucker and bush medicines, about how they burned the land, how they cared for their country. And Woiduna saw he was serious, that he didn't want anything from them except to learn, and so he welcomed Gordie in. That's why Gordie is so connected to the Bundagulgi people.

'Anyway, Darana was only seventeen, two decades his junior, but she set her heart on him. Her mother was dead, and Woiduna, her father, raised her. She was promised to another man from a neighbouring tribe, but she went to her father and said she didn't want that man, she wanted Gordie. Of course, Gordie refused, said she was too young, and anyway he was torn apart with grief for his wife, but Darana was not one to be dissuaded. She pursued him, refused to give in, and eventually Gordie fell in love with her. Woiduna wasn't happy, not just because of the arrangement with the other tribe, though this man she was to marry had been supporting her since she was a baby apparently, but also because he knew society would never accept them, either of them. Hers would reject the whitefella, and European society would be appalled that one of their number would have a black woman.'

Claire was fascinated, and though she thought she probably should not be listening to such a personal story, she let Helen go on.

'Woiduna was right of course. Both groups shunned them. And when she became pregnant, well, it was the talk of the region. But Daku's point was that they loved each other, they still do, so they made it work. Of course some people still won't accept them, but they don't care.'

'And would you care?' Claire asked. 'Could you disregard the opinions of your family, friends, the people here, and just be with Daku? Does he mean that much to you?'

Helen sighed, but there was a note of defiance when she spoke. 'We wouldn't have stayed here. He's highly educated and capable, so he could get work somewhere, and I can teach. We'd have survived.'

'It sounds like you've made your mind up,' Claire said with a sad smile.

Helen wrung her hands in her lap; her usual stillness and composure had deserted her. 'But he's gone,' she said.

Claire said a swift prayer that she was wrong.

CHAPTER 24

*A*ssumpta made sure the nanny had taken the children for a walk, and Joseph had gone out somewhere in his car. She had no idea when he'd be back. They'd barely communicated since the day he pulled her hair and threatened to hurt her.

She crept upstairs, making sure the windows were open so she'd hear his tyres on the gravel should he return. They were. His office was unlocked. He never locked it because he thought she wouldn't have the audacity to invade his private space. And up until last week, he would have been right. Her heart was thumping in her throat, and sweat prickled her back. If he caught her, or if Big Bill or Lockie or any of the staff saw her and told him, she knew she would pay a very heavy price.

But she had no choice. Surely if he could be prosecuted for lying regarding the sale of the mission and the murder of Woiduna, he would go to prison and she would be free. She was grasping at straws, she knew, but she had to try, if not for herself, then for her babies.

She turned the handle and entered. The room smelled of him, of his spicy, woody cologne, his cigarettes, the leather of his shoes. It was a completely male room, and it was, she realised, nothing like the rest of the house, which was airy and decorated in chintz and light fabrics. It had dark expensive furniture and heavy oil paintings, and a royal-blue Axminster rug covered the dark floorboards.

She crossed to the desk, opening the window behind it that over-looked the avenue up to the house to listen for anyone arriving. With trembling hands, she sat at the beautiful oak desk that had once belonged to her father. How she missed him. Her mother always accused him of spoiling his only daughter, and Assumpta knew she was right, but she worshipped her papa and he adored her in return. His desk was all she had of him now, and she was hardly ever near it. She could count on one hand the number of times she'd been in her husband's study.

The desk was neat, as was the room. Joseph was meticulous in everything, and so nothing of any interest was on the surface. But she knew what to do. She reached down by the desk's right front leg and felt around. She found the button and pressed it, and just as she remembered, a secret drawer popped open. It was behind another shallower drawer, and only someone who knew it was there would ever find it. Her papa used to keep lollies in it for her when she was little – her mother disapproved of treats – and Assumpta knew if she managed to evade the nanny and get to her papa, he would let her press the button and choose a lollipop or a lemon sherbet.

She peered inside the hidden space. There was a buff envelope lying there and nothing else. Assumpta reached in and took it out, slipping it inside the waistband of her skirt without opening it. She smoothed her ivory cashmere cardigan over it and closed the drawer once more. She had no idea what the envelope might contain, but she was sure it was something that Joseph would not want the world to know, and therefore, it might hold the key to her freedom.

There was only one place in Jumaaroo she could go to be safe, so she closed the window and left the office, walked out her front door and set off towards the convent.

A hum of little voices singing in preparation for the Christmas concert greeted her as she climbed the hill on the opposite end of town. It was after morning tea and before lunch, so hopefully she would find Sister Claire in her office, though she'd heard from the other mothers that the principal was taking Sister Helen's class these days.

She entered the school grounds and noted with relief that Sister Helen was in her classroom, sitting on the desk and reading to the children, who were all enraptured by whatever story she was telling them. Nobody noticed Assumpta pass the window. She walked in the back door and began to climb the stairs towards Sister Claire's office when she stopped. A male voice was coming from the landing above. Could it be Joseph? Suddenly her mouth was dry. She was sure whoever was up there could hear her heart beating in her chest and would see the envelope through her clothes. The urge to flee was strong, but where could she go? She needed to get to Sister Claire. She crept back down the stairs, squeezed herself into an alcove beside a full-sized statue of some saint on a wooden plinth and tried to steady her mind. There were two staircases at either end of the school, one leading to the front door, the other to the back of the building.

She heard heavy footsteps on the bare floorboards above; it was definitely a man. She swallowed and pressed her body to the wall behind her. If he turned left and went out the front door, he would definitely see her, and she prayed he'd turn right towards the back of the school.

'Thank you, Gordie. I'll see Jannali gets her lunch.'

It was Claire's voice. Assumpta relaxed. It was just that Gordie McKenzie.

'She's in such a rush to get here in the mornings, she'd forget her flamin' head if it weren't screwed on.' Gordie chuckled and then hurried down the other staircase.

Assumpta exhaled, realising she'd been holding her breath. As the nun turned, Assumpta stepped out of the shadows.

Claire jumped. 'Mrs McGrath!'

'I'm sorry if I frightened you,' Assumpta whispered, lightly tripping up the stairs to the landing. 'We need to talk. Can we go to your office?'

200

'Of course.' Claire gestured she should enter the office and closed the door behind them.

'Lock it, please,' Assumpta said.

'Very well.' Claire turned the key in the lock and looked expectantly at Assumpta, who reached under her cardigan and extracted the envelope.

'There's a secret compartment in my father's desk, the one Joseph took from our house, and I knew how to unlock it. I found this, but I haven't opened it yet. I wanted us to do it together.'

She handed Claire the small parcel, and Claire used a letter opener from her desk to slit the seal. Inside were several documents, and Claire opened them one by one, her brow furrowed. 'These are identity papers, a passport issued by the Irish Free State and British Commonwealth of Nations, a birth certificate, a photograph of a woman, and a letter.' One by one, she passed the documents to Assumpta for her to examine.

The passport was issued in the name of Joseph McGrath, in Cork City. But the photograph inside was not of the man they knew. The Joseph McGrath in the picture was slight, with sandy hair, and looked to be only in his mid to late twenties.

Claire opened the letter and read aloud.

My darling Joe,

I'm writing this the night before you sail. I know why you are going, and I know all about the new opportunities and everything. But now that it's happening, I'm so worried that something might happen to you, or that you'll get out there and forget all about me. I know if you were beside me, you'd laugh and say I'm being silly, but it's how I feel.

Please write the moment you dock in Sydney and let me know you are all right. I'm going to be like an old hen, mithering everyone until I hear you're safe. And, Joe, please, don't be holding out for the perfect job or the perfect house – anything will do. I'll come the moment you tell me to, and we'll have a wonderful life together out there in the sun. The rain is relentless here all the week, and I can't wait to marry you under blue skies.

I wish you'd let me come with you now, but I know you're right about that, and Mammy and Daddy would have a fit. They're going to have a fit anyway when I tell them my plan is to go and join you in Australia, but at least by then you'll have a home and a job, so they can't object too much or say we are so irresponsible.

So travel safe, my lovely fiancée Joe, and know that I miss you and love you so much and that I'm counting the days until we're together again. I'm going to slip this letter in your bag in the morning, and I know I'm going to cry like a baby on the quayside, but it's just because I love you so much.

Your Rose xxx

P.S. I love you.

Assumpta didn't recognise her own voice. 'I don't understand. What's going on? She calls herself Joseph's fiancée, this Rose, and she calls him Joe, which is something I never heard anyone call him.'

Claire handed her the passport, open to the photograph page.

'But that's not Joseph.' Assumpta scanned the page. 'And the handwriting is nothing like Joseph's and the address... You see where he signed his name here?'

Claire took back the hardbacked green passport. '*Saorstát Éireann*, Irish Free State' was written around a gold harp, and the name Joseph J McGrath appeared beneath.

The black and white photo of the woman beside the passport in the envelope was a studio photograph. She was pretty, with dark hair and a gentle smile. Written on the back was 'Your Rose x'. The birth certificate was issued in Cork also and dated 1910. The Joseph McGrath they knew was older than twenty-four years.

'What does it all mean, Sister Claire? Who are these people...'

Claire led her to the window and sat her down. 'I think, for some reason, your husband has assumed the identity of this man Joe McGrath. The evening he was bitten by the snake, he kept saying Joe McGrath is dead, as well as Woiduna. It was as if he were admitting to the murder, or maybe murders, but as I told you, he was delirious so I didn't know. But I think he may have killed this young man and used his identity.' The gentle delivery did nothing to detract from the enormity of what she was saying.

'So if my husband isn't Joseph McGrath, then who is he?' Tears pooled in Assumpta's china-blue eyes.

'I've no idea,' Claire said quietly. 'But he is someone very, very, dangerous, so we must be extremely careful.'

CHAPTER 25

*T*he following morning dawned like every other – clear, hot and without even a puff of a breeze. Claire dressed, feeling immediately the familiar hot and sweaty restrictions of her habit. She'd not slept a wink; instead, she spent all night tossing and turning, trying to decide what to do. Assumpta had gone home, leaving the evidence with Claire, though if Joseph appeared and went looking for it, Claire dreaded to think what he'd do. She needed to act fast. The bailiffs would be at the mission any day. Russell Gardiner was still in jail, and Joseph was not around but nobody knew his whereabouts. Silently she offered up her suffering, beseeching the Blessed Virgin to be by her side that day.

She prayed and breakfasted with the community as normal, and once it was nine o'clock, she rang the bell. The children streamed into the school, their cheery voices failing, for the first time, to lift her spirits. She wished she could tell how the day was going to go. Where was Joseph McGrath? Had he come home last night? He was a criminal, a murderer, and as far as she could see, a man entirely without remorse. His coldness chilled her. The only saving grace, and it was slight, was that despite his protestations to the contrary, she knew he had faith. It didn't inform his actions in this life, clearly, but she saw for herself how he was when in the throes of pain and delirium. He believed in God and did not want to meet him without confessing his sins. Somewhere deep inside, he was a God-fearing man. She clung to that belief; it was all she had.

She decided to write a letter home. If the worst happened, then at least her last letter could be a cheery news-filled one that would give her parents comfort. She pulled a paper and pen towards her and began.

Dear Daddy and Mammy,

Greetings from Queensland. I hope you are both well and all the family too. Life here is –

She paused, sucking on the pen, a habit from childhood.

– wonderful. St Finbarr's is shaping up nicely, and as I write, the children are all working hard in their classrooms. Sister Mary is making great strides with the music. Honestly, she is a gifted teacher, and under her gentle instruction, the sounds coming from the entire building are becoming more harmonious with every passing day. Sister Teresita is up with the lark making hurleys, of all things. She's got the whole place mad for the game. Everywhere you look these days, there are people from all over the world wielding hurleys and yelling at each other to pull hard or proclaiming things to be a mighty puc altogether. It's so funny to hear all the Cork-isms out of their mouths, but it makes it feel a little like home.

Sister Helen continues to inspire little minds with her huge library, and the children of St Finbarr's are well on the way to being the best-read bunch in the southern hemisphere. And Sister Gerard is doing a fine job preparing the older boys and girls either for further study or to join the workforce.

She knew her account of Gerard sounded less enthusiastic than her descriptions of the others, but it was the best she could manage.

I'm planning a visit to Cooktown today that will take the entire day. You can't imagine how remote this place is. There is only one bus each week.

She had thought she might post the letter in Cooktown to ensure it got to them, but what if she didn't make it to Cooktown? She'd post it in Jumaaroo, and hope Postmaster Robert Baxter didn't pass it on to McGrath.

It is extraordinarily hot and humid every single day, and we pray for a breeze. The wildlife, the birds and the trees and plants are like nothing we've ever seen, but sometimes I long for the cool lush green hills of home.

Give everyone my love and tell them they are in my prayers all the time.

She blinked back tears. She would give anything to have her father here now; he would protect her as he'd always done. But he was thousands of miles away, oblivious to the peril she was in.

Please pray for me.

Your loving daughter,

Claire

She folded and sealed the letter before she could go on. Hers were not a family that gushed their love for each other, but not one member of the family ever doubted it. She wiped her eyes. This was no time for sentimentality. She needed to be clear-headed and strong, but she did allow herself to imagine her parents' pleasure at seeing Dinny Welsh, the postman, cycling up the rutted lane to the farmhouse in Macroom with the letter all the way from Australia. It would be read over and over, shown to all the family and any neighbours that called. Her mother would cut the stamps off and give them to her friend Sheila Condon. Sheila's daughter Mary taught at the primary school, and she'd show the boys and girls the Australian stamps. Mammy would write in her Christmas cards a bit about the family, but Claire knew the fact that they'd had a letter from Australia would feature, so great mileage would be had by that one sheet of paper. She prayed they got it.

She addressed it, disguising her handwriting, and rapped on the window as Bart Jones, a tall athletic boy, crossed the yard. He looked up and she beckoned him in.

'Yes, Sister Claire?'

'Could you post this for me on your way home?' she asked with a smile.

He looked a bit confused as to why she couldn't do it herself but nodded cheerfully. 'No worries, Sister. You got a stamp and everything?'

She smiled at his broad Australian accent. 'I do. I just need it popped in the post.'

'No worries,' he repeated, taking the letter.

It was ten thirty, almost time for the children to break for morning tea. No child actually had tea – they usually just drank some water and had a piece of fruit or a sandwich – but some of the Australian phrases were deliciously quaint and reminiscent of a time that none of those children remembered.

The bus to Cooktown was at eleven. The police officers there were not in the control of McGrath; she'd checked with Gordie who seemed to know these things. If she could get there and show them the evidence, along with what she knew, surely it would be enough to arrest McGrath. She was about to check her bag once again, make sure she had everything, when Teresita knocked.

'I came to say goodbye. Have a nice day.' She smiled kindly. If she thought the school principal tearing off in the middle of the week to visit Cooktown was odd, she never said it.

'Thank you.' Claire felt herself welling up again. *Stop it*, she admonished herself. She longed to tell Teresita, to feel less alone, but it would put her and the rest of the community in very grave danger. She'd been warned not to interfere with his business again, and she was about to defy him. Best it was her alone who felt his wrath if anyone had to.

Teresita was fiery and might just confront McGrath. She would not believe someone could be so far above the law as he was. If Claire had not seen his venomous fury for herself, she wouldn't have believed it either.

In his eyes, she saw pure evil, nothing short of it, and it terrified her. He had behaved so ruthlessly. He'd created an empire, a persona, a family, all based on lies and deceit, and despite her belief in the fundamental goodness of people, she knew that if she threatened to bring it all down around his ears, he would not hesitate to eliminate her, habit or no habit.

'Claire, it's not my business, but is everything all right?' Teresita asked.

'Fine.' She managed a weak smile. 'I just have some things I need to do in Cooktown.'

'Tell me to mind my own business if you like, but are you meeting your uncle there by any chance?'

Claire hated lying, but in this case it was necessary. 'I am. He hasn't got much time, so he asked that I come as far as Cooktown to meet him.'

'I thought it must be that. Look, I know you must be worried about everything, but either way, Gerard has made her decision. She's just waiting to hear where she's to be sent. You did your best, you did what was the right thing – what more could he expect?'

Poor Teresita believed her need to see her uncle was about the Gerard debacle, and it was for the best that she thought that. But then she spoke again. ''Tisn't that though, is it? Look, I know this is all very upsetting, but Helen is back in her classroom, there's no sign of himself, so maybe 'tis all going to blow over?'

Again, the kind nun was wide of the mark, and Claire inwardly sighed with relief. Teresita had no idea of the real reason Claire needed to get away from Jumaaroo and the ring of steel that surrounded the town. 'I know, but I feel out of my depth. I just need his advice, and I'd like to see him anyway.' Claire was quietly adamant. Her reasons could not withstand a cross-examination, and despite her bluster and funny mannerisms, Teresita was astute.

'Well, you know best, but mind yourself. I'll take care of everything here while you're gone,' Teresita said, and her kindness tugged at Claire's heart. What if this was the last time she ever saw her?

'I couldn't go at all if you weren't here. In fact, you've been such a support, such a help to me, I thank the Lord for you every day.' Claire swallowed. 'God bless you, Sister Teresita. You really are a gift from God.'

The nun coloured. Like Claire's family at home, Teresita was unaccustomed to such emotion, but she looked pleased despite her embarrassment. 'Go on outta that, and mind yourself, do you hear me? This place is crawling with yokes that can bite you and sting you, and do you know that there's even a fish that looks like a stone but is poisonous? Now, who are we to question the good Lord's creations, but what was he thinking with that one, eh?' She chuckled, and Claire joined in. 'Right. I'll get back before they have the place torn asunder. God bless.' She turned to leave, and Claire fought the urge to hug her.

Claire was once again alone. She'd said a quick goodbye at breakfast to the others, Gerard barely registering her as usual.

Ten forty-five. She could see the hotel where the bus stopped from her office window. People were beginning to mill about, waiting for the weekly way out of Jumaaroo. The town was its usual bustling self: deliveries to the hotel from the local farmers, beer to the pub, the housewives buying the makings of the evening family meal, babies in prams, men at work.

She saw Mr Baxter in the post office exchange the time of day with Sal Deterro, the blacksmith. Some women were having morning tea on the hotel veranda. Did they know that this was all a façade? That Jumaaroo was a prison, a dictatorship every bit as awful as any in the history books? To what extent did they understand that one man ruled it all with an iron fist and that one step out of line and he would exact revenge?

She sighed. Ten fifty. The bus would be there at eleven. It was time.

CHAPTER 26

*C*laire waited under the canopy that ran the length of the main street. To her right stood a young woman she recognised as one of the maids at the McGrath house.

'Good morning, Daisy.' She smiled.

Daisy coloured a deep puce and mumbled a greeting, and Claire wondered what was wrong with her.

Also waiting for the bus was a couple she didn't recognise, middle-aged, down at heel. Beside them stood Mr Dolan, who worked for McGrath Industries. He'd installed the hand-operated washing machine in the convent when they first arrived, back when McGrath was anxious that the nuns be given every convenience. She remembered that day and how they'd all marvelled at his generosity. The kitchen was kitted out with a lovely china dinner service and all manner of appliances to ease the burden of household tasks. Little did she know then.

She greeted him as well.

He nodded respectfully. 'Good morning, Sister.'

Eventually, the bus rounded into the square, the driver exited, and everyone lined up to climb aboard. As she was about to board, the barrel-chested Big Bill McAllister, who'd lit up a cigarette, made no effort to help her up the step. She refused to catch his eye. This was the man who'd beaten Woiduna to death on McGrath's orders. A moment of panic threatened. What was she doing? Defying McGrath's threat by getting on a bus driven by one of his thugs?

Stop it, she admonished herself. He had no reason to be suspicious. People went to Cooktown all the time. She could be getting school supplies or something.

She forced herself to climb up into the bus. She settled in a window seat and spotted Stavros Galatas across the street. He gave her a cheery wave, which she returned. Why was Stavros around the town in the middle of the working day? He should surely be at work, unless McGrath had sent him to watch her?

Sitting on the veranda of the hotel was Assumpta, surrounded by several women Claire recognised as mothers of children in the school. Assumpta looked exquisite in a dove-grey floor-length day dress, overlaid with a lace skirt. Assumpta was so slim, her waist was no wider than a handspan, and her blonde hair was coiffed perfectly. Claire had seen her but crossed the street before she got to the hotel. She didn't want to acknowledge her, nor did Assumpta react to her. Neither of them trusted themselves not to give something away. Assumpta was the only person in the town who knew her plan.

McAllister had some words with a man passing on the street, finished his cigarette and then climbed into the driver's seat. The bus lurched to one side under his enormous weight. Claire got a waft of the cigarette smoke on the hot air, and it made her a little nauseous. *But it could be nerves too*, she thought. She had a small bag, which she held on her lap. Intertwined between her fingers were the rosary beads her mother had given her the day she got her first Holy Communion.

Big Bill turned the key, and the bus sprang to life. She caught a waft of his body odour as he stretched to turn the wheel, and she swallowed as her stomach churned. Slowly they drove back out of the square, the town its usual hum of activity, just like any other day.

They were soon away from the town, passing Darana and Gordie's place. There was no sign of life, and Jannali was at school. Once they left the environs of Jumaaroo, the sealed road, courtesy of the ever-benevolent Joseph J McGrath, ended abruptly, and was replaced by the dusty rutted track. The noise of the engine combined with the heat and the endless bouncing made conversation impossible even if she had been so inclined. She sweated in her habit, the bottom and back of which stuck to the leather seat as she fought the nausea caused by a combination of fear, travel sickness and heat. There was a window but she dared not open it for fear of what might fly in. Behind them, the bus left a cloud of red dust. The very soil of this land was so different to what she was used to. That rich terracotta red, not the loamy dark brown of her homeland. Would she ever see Macroom again?

After twenty minutes, the bus stopped. There was no building or sign to indicate a bus stop, but the maid from McGrath's house got up and exited. Claire was reminded of the Mossgrove crossroads at home; there was no house there, but it was the convergence of several country roads, up which were farms. The weekly bus from Macroom to Bandon stopped there, and to the uninitiated it would look like the middle of nowhere as well, but several people would get on and off.

Perhaps the girl was visiting her family; it was probably her day off. Claire watched as she crossed the road in front of the bus, and soon they were off again. There was a township further on, just a ramshackle collection of outbuildings and a pub, but the couple got out there, leaving just her and Mr Dolan. He was on the back seat and she second from the front on the right.

Big Bill drove the bus on, its engine labouring in the heat, the road now just a strip between the ocean and the rainforest. Every so often they passed a cliff face, where the track had been hacked out of sheer rock. At several places there was only room for one vehicle, so at intervals there were roughly created lay-bys where a car could pull in to allow another to pass. There were so few vehicles on the road, they were not needed to any great extent.

To her left, the turquoise Coral Sea crashed mercilessly against the white sand. She'd thought Ireland had white sand – her parents had taken them to Inchydoney outside Clonakilty as children to play on the beach and swim in the cold Atlantic – but Irish beaches were nothing like Queensland ones. The sand at home was fine, but it wasn't the brilliant white of the tropics. Sand in Australia was made up of silica, which squeaked when you walked on it in bare feet. It was impossibly beautiful, with blue sea beyond that was filled with fish of every colour, size and shape.

The road was bordered on the right by the Daintree rainforest, its dense jungle of twisted roots and huge leaves a humming, living presence. It was almost dark in there, so dense was the canopy, and the children were warned not to wander in the rainforest as it held all manner of snakes and creatures that could kill them. Claire smiled at the memory of Teresita's reaction when one of the students listed off in gory detail all of the things one needed to be wary of in tropical Queensland: 'I was never anywhere so beautiful but also where Mother Nature is saying in a loud voice that she doesn't want us here.'

It was true. Such beauty, but such danger to the uninitiated. Daku spoke of his country with such passion and pride, but he understood it; all the Bundagulgi people did. To them it was benign and bounteous; it was home. But not for her. She'd take Macroom and its harmless wildlife and gentle rolling hills any day.

On and on they bounced. Several times, she was catapulted upwards, only to land back in the seat with a thud. She kept her rosary beads in her hand, praying all the time. Soon, Big Bill pulled the bus into a lay-by. Perhaps there was another vehicle oncoming? But Mr Dolan got up, nodded as a goodbye and got off. He was followed by the driver, leaving her alone on the bus. She sat there as the minutes ticked by. She assumed he was having a smoko, a ritual, she had learned, never to be tampered with here. It was the divine right of every Australian man to take his smoko – a break for a cigarette – and woe betide any employer, even the mighty Joseph McGrath, who tried to curtail it.

She waited – five minutes, ten, fifteen – but of Big Bill there was no sign. She wondered if she should get off and check. She hesitated, reluctant to engage him in even the most perfunctory of conversation, but realising waiting longer was ridiculous, she stood, her body as it separated from the seat making a very unflattering sound. She was relieved nobody could hear it.

Gripping her bag containing the passport and other incriminating documents, she got off the bus and looked around. Big Bill was nowhere to be seen. She walked around the back, hoping to find him there, but there was nobody. The cacophony produced by her surroundings was, as usual, loud. Day and night, the noise was relentless: the crashing surf, the squawking birds, the rustle at ground level of God knew what – snakes and rats probably – and the creak of the coconut and banana trees as they swayed in the tropical breeze.

She stood there, wondering what to do and fighting the feelings of panic. A rustle to her right made her jump. Out from the jungle walked a cassowary. She'd seen one before, but not this close. The huge bird, taller than her, calmly passed by in front of her, its sleek black feathers almost brushing her. She froze, barely breathing, her heart thumping wildly. She now knew the red horn on its head was made of a kind of cartilage or bone and was very hard. If the creature attacked her, there would be nothing she could do. Thankfully, it seemed totally disinterested in the arrival of a small Irish nun, and she exhaled as it disappeared into the undergrowth once more.

She'd just have to walk, she supposed. It was about ten miles back to Jumaaroo, she guessed. Maybe this was McGrath's idea of a joke; it would be funny to let her think she could leave but then dump her out here, meaning she'd have a long hot walk back. At least she hoped that was all it was. She could imagine him sitting in his office, chuckling at her.

The ocean on her left was so inviting as she felt the beads of perspiration slide down her face. Her thighs chafed as well, rubbing together as she walked. Of course it wasn't the done thing for nuns to swim, but even if she flouted the rule, she'd probably be stung by a box jellyfish and die.

Johnny Blackstone, one of the ten-year-olds in the gang she called the highwaymen, much to their delight, explained about a fellow he heard of who got stung by a box jellyfish, and who was still screaming from the pain even after Doc Marseilles pronounced him dead. While she was certain Johnny was exaggerating, she'd heard enough horror stories to keep her out of the deceptively inviting water.

On she trudged, watching the edge of the rainforest the whole time. She might well be being observed – the Bundagulgi people still inhabited that place though in much smaller numbers now – but there was no way of knowing.

She prayed as she walked. The Five Glorious Mysteries, starting with the Resurrection. An Our Father, ten Hail Marys, a Glory Be. The next one, the Ascension. The hypnotic effect of the beautiful prayer calmed her frayed nerves as on and on she walked.

She was lost in prayer, so the arrival of the car behind her startled her. She stopped and turned. Big Bill McAllister was at the wheel of a beautiful maroon and cream car. She had no idea what the make was, but she knew she'd never seen it before. She stood aside, unsure of what to say.

There was no need for her to say anything, because McAllister got out and promptly pinned her hands behind her back, tying them with a length of rope. Claire was so shocked, it took a moment for her to react.

'What… What do you think you're doing?' she began, but McAllister shoved a gag into her mouth, tying it tightly at the back of her head. Then he pushed her in the direction of the back door, shoving her in. Sitting on the back seat was Joseph McGrath.

She landed awkwardly, half falling across him. With extreme difficulty, she righted herself, gasping as a searing pain shot from her shoulder down her arm. She struggled to breathe – her nose was blocked and the gag made breathing through her mouth difficult. Tears stung her eyes as she leaned on her arms pinned tightly behind her. She looked at McGrath, unable to speak, and he said nothing, his mouth set in a determined line.

McAllister threw her bag in the boot of the car and sat in. Wordlessly, he drove a couple of hundred yards, pulling into a gap in the rainforest. Immediately the sunlight was obscured by the canopy of trees. Although she made noises of protest, the gag prevented her from forming words. Her shoulder was in agony; she thought it might be dislocated.

McAllister turned the engine off, got out and walked away, leaving her alone in the car with her tormentor.

CHAPTER 27

*A*ssumpta wasn't listening to Doreen's endless tale of how her Christmas cake was so much more moist now that she'd changed the recipe. The meaningless prattle of the other wives bored her at the best of times, but today she couldn't concentrate. It struck her how they were all prisoners there, like birds in cages. Her cage was gilded, but it was no less a prison than anyone else's.

She'd done as she was asked, despite all her misgivings. She hoped it would work now for all their sakes. If it didn't, the consequences didn't bear thinking about. She had to prioritise, and that was all there was to it. She'd missed another period. She was sure now she was pregnant again. She sighed. She didn't want another child, but she'd love it, she supposed, and anyway there were no options. She just hoped the disease Joseph had given her wasn't going to affect the baby. The symptoms had cleared up by now, thank goodness – she'd nearly gone out of her mind – but one heard terrible stories of women who gave birth to all sorts of handicapped children because of those dirty illnesses they picked up from men.

She'd heard Joseph with that slutty maid Daisy. It had been the final straw that made her go to Sister Claire. The humiliation of it, in her own house. She'd lain there, tears leaking onto the linen pillowcase, her heart breaking. She was sure he chose the bedroom beside theirs on purpose. He wanted her to hear it all, to make her face a maid who had slept with her husband.

The cheeky madam told her that she was to have the day off today. No explanation, just that she wasn't going to be around the house. Mr McGrath's orders apparently.

What had she done to make him hate her so? More to the point, who was he?

He'd come home late last night, and never spoke to her. She was in bed when she heard him come in. He mustn't have checked his desk, because he left this morning, again without a word. She swallowed a sip of tea, her stomach churning.

When she met him, he was so charming, such a funny man, and oh, how he flattered and flirted. He told her how beautiful she was, how lucky he was to have her, how he wished he could contain his ardour until they married but it was impossible in the face of her beauty. And she'd fallen for it hook, line and sinker. Of course she'd slept with him, every opportunity they got, so it was no surprise she fell pregnant. But even though it wasn't ideal, she didn't care as much as she should have when the doctor confirmed it. They were in love and they were engaged. It was just all a bit sooner than usual. Joseph had been wonderful, telling her that while he hated that she had to face any gossip, he was secretly thrilled, how he longed to have a baby with her, how they would be such a happy family. She loved the looks of pure envy on the faces of her girlfriends the day she married Joseph McGrath. He was like a film star, and men and women alike were putty in his hands.

They'd found a seamstress who was a genius, and the wedding dress was a vision in lace, all soft and flowing. But the slip was rigid and unforgiving and held her little bump in place so nobody could confirm the reason for the rush. They suspected, of course, but she was so deliriously happy, she didn't give a hoot.

Their honeymoon was spent in Jumaaroo. And she instantly detested the place – the heat, the dust, the flies, the lack of anything interesting to do or anywhere nice to go. There were no concerts or parties, nothing to divert a young woman used to such things. Joseph was, to her bewildered astonishment, utterly unsympathetic to her distress. There was a ring on her finger and a baby in her belly, and as far as he was concerned, that was his debt paid.

He worked all the time. He'd recently bought some businesses and they needed his attention, he explained to her once, but not in the sweet cajoling voice of their courtship. Now he snapped and dismissed her complaints. He told her to decorate the house properly, to keep herself in shape and to hire staff. She hardly saw him.

She had no idea what she'd done wrong. She tried everything. Cooking his favourite meals, or at least instructing the cook to do it, being the perfect hostess, reporting information to him she gleaned from the wives, she did it all. The ardour and excitement of the bedroom dimmed the moment the ring was on her finger too. Before, he would gaze at her, his eyes soft with love and longing. But now their coupling was a perfunctory affair, no eye contact, no soft words of love. He was rough, and it felt like it was only for his gratification. She hated it, but it was the only time she had him to herself. It was pathetic, she knew, but she couldn't help herself. She'd loved him.

She tried everything – being more seductive, even wearing lacy underwear she'd bought in a specialist shop in Brisbane – but nothing worked. He barely touched her once the pregnancy began to show; it was as if he found the growing baby somehow distasteful. She had prayed that once the baby was born, he would change, that he would love her and the child, but that too was a vain hope. He barely looked at her or the baby. The twins were no different – it was as if they were someone else's children.

Eventually, in desperation, she wrote home, telling her mother how horrendous married life was, hinting at how Joseph had changed. But she got nothing back except a curt note to the effect that she'd made her bed and could now lie in it. Her father died after the wedding but before the baby was born, and the way her mother went on, you would think that the pregnancy was entirely Assumpta's doing.

Her mother was strange about Joseph. She almost simpered when around him, but she had turned on her only daughter for some reason, blaming her for everything. It hurt Assumpta, used to being her parents' pride and joy.

She tried to tune into the conversation once more. Staying out in public today was the safest thing, she and Claire had decided. He couldn't do anything if she was on public view.

CHAPTER 28

'So you just couldn't do this the easy way, could you?' McGrath smiled sadly as they sat in the back of the stationary car. He spoke as if kidnapping her caused him a deep personal sadness but could not be avoided.

Claire tried to scream, but only a muffled whimper came out.

'Don't bother. Nobody will hear you.' He patted her knee kindly. 'Let's go for a walk.'

He opened his door and went around to hers, opening it and standing back chivalrously.

She got out, though it was difficult with her hands tied and her shoulder hurting so much. She was so hot now, perspiration dripping down her face, but she couldn't wipe it. She tried to push the gag out with her tongue, but it was tied too tightly.

He took her by the elbow, and she howled, the pain shooting through her body. 'Oh, I'm sorry, Sister. That oaf McAllister doesn't know his own strength. Here' – he went around to the other side and took her other arm – 'is that better?'

Claire had no option but to walk as he propelled her along beside him. He was dressed impeccably as usual, today in cream trousers and a tan linen jacket. On his head he wore a fawn-coloured trilby, and as usual, his tie and pocket square matched, red paisley today. The sandalwood smell of his cologne filled her nostrils. She thought she might vomit.

They followed a path through the jungle for several hundred yards, until they came to what looked like a pond. Its surface was covered in greenery, lily pads and weeds, rushes growing tall along the edges. Flies and mosquitos buzzed around her face, and she couldn't swat them away. Then he stopped, bent down and tied her feet with a wire. It dug into her ankles as he twisted it to make it secure.

'A mangrove swamp. Full of crocs,' he said conversationally. 'You know they don't eat their catch right away? No, they get their victim, clamp them in their powerful jaws and roll them in the water until they drown. But then they hide the carcass in a den or a cave or something, let it rot, and only then do they eat it. Now some people are disgusted by that, but as I always point out, what is wine but rotted grapes? We love old mouldy cheese, meat that's been hung for weeks, so we're no different. A bit of time adds to the flavour.'

Claire couldn't respond. A mosquito stung her several times around the eye. She felt sick. She was entirely at his mercy.

'Now, as I said' – he folded his arms and observed her – 'I asked you to just do your work at the school and stay out of my business, but you refused. I warned you, so don't say I didn't. I gave you a fighting chance, but you are a stubborn little woman, aren't you? Stupid too, as it turns out, but then females tend to be. So the fact remains that I told you to do something, you did the opposite, so now here we are.'

He plunged his hands into his trouser pockets, his demeanour suggesting he was weighing up a particularly vexing conundrum. 'Now, you are a woman of God, a bride of Christ and all that, and anyway, as a fellow Irish person, I won't let the croc drown you. That would be a horrible way to go. And there's one in there.' He jerked at the pond with his thumb. 'They say he's thirty feet long, and sure you, fat as you are, would only be a snack. He might not be bothered with you – lazy buggers they are. So I'm going to do the humane thing. The croc will eat you, because I'll somehow get you in that pond, and the bishop will never know what happened to you because Big Bill will swear on a stack of Holy Bibles that he let you off in Cooktown. Several people will testify that they saw you, so unfortunately for you, I'll get away with murder.' He chuckled. 'Again.'

He reached into his pocket and pulled out a small revolver. 'Hop over there to the edge like a good woman. I don't want to have to drag you.' He winked, clearly enjoying the moment.

Claire prayed as hard as she could. She closed her eyes, seeing her parents' sweet faces before her, her sisters, their farm at home. She would soon see the faces of Jesus and his Blessed Mother. It would be fine. She refused to allow the idea of a crocodile in. It would not matter what became of her earthly remains; she would be in heaven with God.

'Come on, Sister Claire, I don't have all day.' He sounded bored.

She stood, incapable of movement even if she wanted to. Then she heard it, a whirring, and she wasn't sure if the sound was coming from inside her head or outside. Then a dull thud. She opened her eyes, and to her astonishment, McGrath was on the ground, bleeding profusely from a deep wound over his eye. Beside him was a large L-shaped boomerang.

Daku had shown her his boomerangs before. The smaller returning type was used to entice birds out of the swamps, where they could then be caught in a net. But the larger L-shaped ones were used for disabling prey. He told her how the Bundagulgi would throw them at the leg of an emu, for example, to knock it to the ground, where-upon it would be killed and eaten. Daku's was made of dark wood and was beautifully decorated. She thought she recognised it now, but of him there was no sign.

McGrath seemed confused, concussed probably, but he recovered and managed to get onto his hands and knees. His gun had fallen from his hand, and he scrambled across the ground to retrieve it. Claire was immobile. She tried to wriggle free again, but the pain in her shoulder was agonising and she couldn't.

A gun then exploded with a loud bang. Her eyes left Joseph McGrath, and she saw him. Russell Gardiner again shot his rifle into the ground just where the mayor of Jumaaroo was crawling. Russell had come out of the jungle, and his gun was trained on his prey.

The Irishman wiped his bleeding head with his sleeve and blinked, apparently unsure if what he was seeing was real. Then from the other side came Daku, who bounded towards them, retrieved his boomerang and wiped the blood from it on his trousers. He smiled at Claire before removing the gag and the rope from her hands. She cried out as her arm was released. Daku then stooped to untie her feet. From behind Russell came several Bundagulgi men, also armed with boomerangs and spears. Daku picked up McGrath's gun and pocketed it, while Russell Gardiner kept his weapon trained on McGrath.

'All right, on your feet,' Russell said, dragging the man to a standing position. 'The police will have a few questions for you.' He said something to the men in the Bundagulgi language, and immediately they responded, using the ropes and wire that had bound Claire to do the same to McGrath now. They were strong, and Claire saw the sinews in their arms tighten as they twisted the wire, causing their victim to yelp in pain.

'Get off me! I swear you'll all hang for this! You don't know who you're messin' with. I'll kill you... You have nothin' on me, nothin' at all! You will be laughed out of the station. I swear I'll... Jesus...' Claire was surprised to hear that working-class Dublin accent again, just like when he was delirious from the snakebite.

'Do not blaspheme the name of the Lord!' Russell bellowed, taking a step closer, his rifle now pressed to McGrath's chest, still cocked and ready.

Claire was speechless, but Daku's eyes glittered with satisfaction. He hated McGrath for what he'd done to his people, and unlike Christian philosophy, he didn't believe in turning the other cheek. His was a world of cause and effect. Retribution and revenge were part of Aboriginal life, and he'd often argued with her on the subject. He was a gentle soul with a kind heart, but he could never subscribe to her ideas.

'You came,' she managed to say.

'I thought you needed looking after,' he responded, stuffing the balled-up fabric of the gag unceremoniously into McGrath's mouth. The mayor was still protesting, but like with her just moments ago, now his speech was unintelligible.

'And Mr Gardiner, I thought he was in jail...' The emotion of it all threatened to overwhelm her.

'Well, he was, but when I told those fellas about the land and how it wasn't even his to give if we would have taken it, they got a bit mad. Reckoned it was time to fight back. But they needed Russell, so they went down there and busted him out. There's only old Seth there, and those blackfellas are hard to dissuade once they set their minds to something.' Daku grinned as he kicked McGrath behind his knees, causing him to collapse on the ground. He then searched McGrath's pockets for the car key, finding it and tossing it to Russell.

Russell stood before Claire. 'Are you all right?'

She looked into his eyes and felt such profound relief. These men had saved her life. She didn't trust herself to speak, so she just nodded.

'Russell and this mob here'll deliver this mongrel to Cooktown. The chief of police from Cairns will have to be called, but the blokes in Cooktown are good enough for now. They don't answer to McGrath,' Daku said. 'And I'll bring you home, though I reckon the cops will want to talk to you soon too.'

Claire nodded. 'One minute. There's something you'll need in the car.'

They all walked back along the track, spears and a shotgun trained on McGrath. The Aboriginal men shoved McGrath into the car, two sitting either side of him, daggers drawn, while the others stood guard outside. Claire extracted her bag from the boot of the car and handed the envelope of information to Russell. She briefly and quietly explained to him what the papers were and how she came by them, and she saw the look of relief on his face. This was going to be enough.

'Thank you,' Russell replied, and Claire knew he meant it. 'You've been very brave.'

'I'm just glad it's over. Now can I please go home?' She fought back tears. Her shoulder was in agony, and the bites on her face were swelling and itchy.

'Of course.'

Daku came back and looked at her shoulder. 'You'll need someone to attend to that…'

'I'll call Doc Marseilles when I –' she began, wincing as she spoke.

'Nah, one of our women will do it. You'll be all right.' He winked and grinned, then went to the car door and opened it, addressing McGrath. 'Right. Russell's gonna drive and these fellas are beside you, and so if you move a toe, they'll stick one of those poisoned spears in you. And believe me, that's not the death you want, you get it?' Daku seemed to be enjoying himself. 'See you back in Jumaaroo.' He waved cheerily at the back of McGrath's car as Gardiner started the engine.

Within moments they were gone. It was only then that Claire spotted Flossie waiting patiently, Gordie's cart shacked to her. 'How did you know where to find me?' she asked weakly, wincing with pain as she climbed on the cart.

'We saw you on the bus. I've had our fellas watching you for days, so they saw you leave and let me know. You can't see us, but we never let you out of our sights. I reckoned I knew where McGrath would stop. Couple of my mates saw him here yesterday, just walking round – they've been following him too. We watch him all the time, a bunch of us, waiting for a chance. It's why I took the job at the convent. So we followed the bus. The road goes right round, but it's only a couple miles as the crow flies.'

'Incredible.' She allowed him to place some blankets behind her to rest against. 'You all saved my life.'

'Well, as whitefellas go, you're not so bad, we reckon. It was the council at the mission that made the decision to help you, not me or Russell. You tried to help us, so that's how our way works.'

He helped her get settled, although each movement was agony. Then he jumped up on the other side and clicked the reins, and Flossie set off at a trot.

'Reckon we just got to hope the cops down in Cooktown will believe Russell now. We saw him about to shoot you. They'll probably need to talk to you, but we don't think his influence goes all the way to Cairns. Hope not anyway.'

Claire smiled through the pain. 'They'll believe him.'

'You seem very sure,' Daku remarked, his eyebrow raised questioningly.

'I am and it's a long story. I will tell you, but for now I need to get home.'

'Fair enough.'

Daku turned to face her. For the first time, Claire saw what Helen did. There was something intriguing about him. He was a contradiction – gentle yet ferocious, intelligent yet primeval. His dark eyes were expressive, and his connection to all forms of life around him was intriguing. There was something so raw about him, so honest, and he exuded integrity.

If he told Helen he loved her and that they would be all right, then that was the truth. He was not a liar. Claire would miss her, but she would not want her to stay in the convent if it wasn't the right life for her. Daku and Helen would face problems, bigotry and all the rest of it, but she would be loved and cared for, and that gave Claire comfort.

'You and Helen will be all right,' she said as Flossie walked on, each step jolting her shoulder. Despite her pain, she spoke through gritted teeth. 'She's made her decision and she's choosing you.'

'How are you so sure?' he asked, not taking his eyes off the road ahead. She felt a rush of affection for him. He didn't dare hope, but she could hear the longing in his words.

'The Lord works in mysterious ways, Daku.'

CHAPTER 29

*C*laire sat in her office, her shoulder smelling of tea tree oil and something else. Despite the injury now being an old one, she did the exercises the Bundagulgi woman had told her to do, and it was so much better. Darana's cousin Kirra from the mission had come the afternoon Daku brought her home and had for a couple of excruciating minutes manipulated her shoulder back into place. She'd screamed in agony, but when it clicked back, it was better. Kirra gave her an ointment to use every day. It was so pungent but seemed to be doing the trick. She was almost completely healed.

'Come in,' she called as a gentle knock on the door interrupted her train of thought.

'A letter for you, Sister.' Mei Wong held an official-looking envelope, with Claire's name and address typed neatly.

'Thank you, Mei.' Claire took the letter, then asked, 'How are you getting on in Sister Helen's class?'

'Oh, it's lovely, Sister Claire. She is so nice.' The dark-haired little girl smiled shyly. She didn't need to say she too was glad to not have anything more to do with Sister Gerard. 'She's reading us *Little Women* and even the boys like it. She says there are no such things as girls' books or boys' books, just good stories.'

Claire warmed at the girl's enthusiasm. 'Good. I'm glad. I wasn't much of a reader myself, between you and me, but I loved *Little Women* as well.'

May grinned and left.

It had been a bit of a job to manage Gerard's class now that she had gone back to Ireland. Claire had received a very apologetic letter from the Reverend Mother of Gerard's convent, assuring her that Gerard would no longer be teaching once she got back. The Reverend Mother said how sorry she was to hear about Gerard's behaviour, and she wished Claire every success at St Finbarr's.

Some new sisters were being sent out, and Helen was staying on until they arrived, though Claire hoped she would stay in a lay capacity once she married Daku. There was a lot of paperwork – releasing a nun from her vows took time – so Helen was being patient, and in the meantime, they were all managing as best they could. Helen was determined to be laicised properly, and that involved not just the mother house of the order but the Vatican as well, and it was a sign of how much Daku loved her that he understood and was willing to wait for as long as it took.

Nobody knew what had really happened between Claire and Assumpta, but rumours were rife, and as was usual in Jumaaroo, theories abounded in the wake of the arrest and trial of their beloved Mr McGrath. The case was covered in all the papers as he was tried for the murders of Woiduna and Joseph McGrath. Some papers reported that his real name was Francis Madigan and that he was wanted for another murder back in Ireland as well as a fatal assault on somebody at a race meeting near Brisbane. Initially people didn't believe it, but as more and more salacious details emerged of how he'd stolen someone's identity and how he'd left Ireland one step ahead of the law, even his most ardent supporters had to admit they'd been duped.

Gerard had taken the bus to Cooktown a few days after the arrest, and despite Claire making an effort to wish her well, she rebuffed all overtures of friendship. She didn't visit Assumpta either before she left, obviously thinking that Assumpta had taken sides and chosen Claire over her.

Mary made her a lovely packed lunch to take on the journey and had crocheted a blanket as Gerard complained of the cold constantly on the voyage out, but both were left on the kitchen table. Teresita didn't make such an effort. She allowed Gerard to take the lead, and when Gerard issued a curt farewell, Teresita reciprocated in kind.

So much had happened in the months since that day when she'd come so close to death. The sale of the mission out at Trouble Bay had fallen through, the government not wishing to be seen doing business with someone as nefarious as Madigan. They found another site closer to Brisbane, which was better apparently anyway.

To everyone's astonishment, Gordie bought the mission from the Adventists. It seemed the rumours that despite outward appearances he was actually quite wealthy were true. The original sale was deemed null and void by the courts, and all of McGrath's assets were frozen, so Gordie had his lawyers approach the Adventist church and make an offer, which they accepted.

Gordie claimed he wouldn't trust the Adventist church not to sell it again to the highest bidder, so he bought it for what McGrath was going to pay. It had been renamed in honour of Woiduna. Jannali and Darana were thrilled, and Gordie even made a sign that was driven into the sand at the entrance. It simply said 'Woiduna's.'

It seemed he was happy to let the Gardiners continue what they were doing. He had no interest in being involved. He liked a simple life, and seeing the big smile on his little girl's face was enough.

There had been an official renaming, and though the Bundagulgi celebrated that they were now the owners of their own little patch of land, the poignancy was not lost on Claire. The entire country was theirs, but that was an argument for another day.

She and the other nuns watched in fascination as the Aboriginal men performed a smoke ceremony and some traditional dances while the women cooked on open fires. The nuns were invited to sit in the circle, and the natives told stories, which Daku translated for them. They ate some bush tucker, foraged from the land. Claire realised early on it was best not to ask what anything was and just try it.

Jannali took great delight in informing her as she bit into what she thought was a piece of meat that it was in fact a grub.

Rev Bill had visited as soon as he could, horrified to learn what had been going on and worried for his niece's safety. Once she assured him that they were all fine, he had been most sympathetic to the plight of the Bundagulgi people. And while he would never have any dealings with Russell Gardiner, he said that she had his blessing in establishing cordial relationships with the native Australians.

He met Daku and Helen when he visited and also gave them his blessing. To see their beaming smiles after the meeting was such a joy. Helen and Daku were so in love, it was plain for anyone to see.

On the last evening of his visit, he and Claire walked in the garden together and talked about it all. He commended her on her bravery as her bishop, but admonished her for taking such risks as her uncle, and they'd laughed at the irony of that.

'What would I say to my brother if something happened to you, Claire?' he'd asked sincerely. 'Please do not put yourself in danger like that again.'

'I doubt I'll have the opportunity now that Joseph McGrath – or should I say Francis Madigan – is out of our lives for good.' She smiled. 'I'm looking forward to a nice peaceful life.'

Just then, Teresita's voice cut through the serenity from over the hedge. 'In with the shoulder! That's right, good and hard! It won't kill him – he's a fine lump of a lad!'

'Or as peaceful as it ever gets here.' Claire chuckled.

Rev Bill returned to Brisbane, and life slipped into a kind of pattern. Assumpta had shown gumption nobody thought her capable of by applying to the court to run McGrath Industries. For tax purposes, and unbeknownst to her, the business was in her name all along, and she made an impassioned speech in court about how so many people in Jumaaroo relied on McGrath Industries for their employment and that it would hurt the entire town if she was refused. So the court approved it. To everyone's relief, it was business as usual.

Big Bill McAllister was arrested, and Lockie told the whole truth of how he and Big Bill beat Woiduna to death, leaving his body to the animals. Both were now in prison, but for everyone else, life carried on. Mrs McGrath was the new boss, and she was slowly learning the ropes. Her brother, Pius, and his new wife had arrived to help, and between them they were managing fine.

Claire didn't think she was imagining it – the Aboriginals seemed to be in town more these days. And though there was a long history of mistrust on both sides, she sensed a slight thaw.

Claire opened the letter Mai had delivered. It was printed on official government paper.

Majesty's Penal Establishment
Long Bay
Sydney
New South Wales

Date: 14 June 1935
Inmate: Francis James Madigan
Visiting Order Ref: 574946384
Order in the name of: Sister Claire McAuliffe
Address: St Finbarr's Ursuline Convent, Jumaaroo, Queensland
Date of Visit: 1 July 1935
Time of Visit: 08:00—09:30
The inmate named above has requested a visit through the governor's office. This request has been granted.
If you will not attend, please fill out the attached form and return.
John Brittas
On behalf of Governor M Moreton

CHAPTER 30

She'd carried the visiting order around in her pocket for a few days before consulting anyone. Apart from anything else, Sydney was days away, the journey would be gruelling and uncomfortable, and she didn't even know what he wanted to see her about. It might be to laugh at her, to mock her that she secretly had feelings for him and was willing even at that late stage to make a fool of herself for him. She could just see him smirking at her, goading her. Was he right, she wondered? She went to the chapel and examined her conscience fully in that regard, and emerged fully confident that she didn't harbour any silly affection for him. There was a possibility that he was asking to see her just to prove a point, to have the last word, but she didn't think so.

Rev Bill had warned her against it once she told him about it. He was livid that Madigan would treat people as he had. He'd put Claire's life in danger, so Rev Bill was totally against her visiting him. Everything her uncle said was true. She'd confided to him about the attempted rape and the manner in which she was convinced she would die. He was so deeply upset, on such a personal level, that she almost felt more sorry for him than for herself. Rev Bill wrote saying that Madigan was undeserving of her mercy, that he'd never even apologised and was still a dangerous man. But he didn't forbid her to go; he had too much respect for her to do that.

She'd held an informal meeting in the convent when she got the visiting order, seeking her sisters' advice. They were surprised he was put on trial and held so far away, but since the primary crime he had to answer to – the murder of Joseph McGrath and the assumption of his identity – happened there, it was deemed the appropriate location. The murder of a man back in Dublin was taken into consideration – the assault of the man at the races who died as a result of his injuries – as well as his role in the killing of Woiduna. The result was a short trial and a sentence to hang. Apparently he never contested any of it and admitted his guilt.

The news had shocked her despite everything. She knew she was right all along about his accent, that he wasn't from Cork, but everything else had been so convincing. He really was a master of deception, and he'd fooled everyone. Assumpta, her family, his business associates, the entire town of Jumaaroo, and even the army had been taken in by him.

Something niggled at Claire though. She couldn't hate him. The night he was bitten by the snake, she saw something in him, a vulnerability, a faith in God. She wasn't sure exactly what it was, but she was sure that under all of his lies and sins, despite all he'd put her through, there was a shred of decency. She tried to voice this to Rev Bill and to her sisters, and they looked at her like she was insane. How could she feel compassion for him? She knew that it sounded deluded, but she couldn't shake the feeling.

Helen thought it was best to ignore the visitation order, fearing that Madigan would only try to manipulate her. But as Teresita pointed out, if he was capable of that, he wouldn't be sitting in Sydney now facing the noose.

'I think you should do whatever you want. 'Twas you he nearly killed. He's going to hang – the court case is over and done with, the verdict handed down – but he might want to apologise. Everyone should get a chance to do that, shouldn't they?' Teresita looked around. 'He can't raise a hand to you in there, sure he can't, so what's the harm?'

Claire smiled her thanks and turned to Mary. The young nun blushed to be the centre of attention, but she said quietly, 'I think Jesus would go.'

Claire thought for a moment and realised Mary was right. 'I'll go.'

CHAPTER 31

July 1935

Claire tried not to flinch when he was brought into the visiting room. She'd arrived early after an arduous five-day journey, and the forbidding building almost made her turn on her heel and run. She forced herself to stand and look up at the prison, the glass in the windows glinting in the bright winter's sunshine. The endless travel had worn her out, but the coolness of the breeze in Sydney in July was wonderful. She was staying at the convent in Ashbury on the outskirts of the city, and only the Reverend Mother knew the purpose of her visit. She'd been welcoming and understanding and insisted Claire stay for a while and have a break before making the trek back to Queensland. Claire thanked her but knew that Jumaaroo was where she needed to be. She had come for a reason, and she would see it through. And once she had, she'd go home.

The prison was a dingy place, and it smelled awful. There was no furniture, nowhere to sit, so she stood and waited until Madigan shuffled in, manacled to two prison guards.

He looked old. She'd not seen him since the day he tried to kill her. His dark hair wasn't the lustrous mane it once was – now it was lank

236

and greasy and streaked with grey – and his fine tailored clothes were replaced by a dun-coloured shirt and trousers.

'Thank you for coming, Sister.' His voice was low, his Dublin accent strong.

'You're welcome.' She smiled and he returned it.

An awkward silence hung between them. She was determined not to make it easy for him. After all, he was the one who'd summoned her.

Eventually he spoke. 'I… I'm…sorry for draggin' you all this way. It's a long trek. I really didn't think you'd come.'

'Assumpta insisted I come in her car as far as Cairns, and then I got the train.'

'Assumpta's car?' He seemed bemused.

'Yes, your old car actually. She's learning to drive. Stavros Galatas is teaching her.'

'Good for her.' He nodded.

'Yes. She's managing everything. Her brother and his wife have arrived in Jumaaroo and are helping her, and everyone is relieved they still have a job. At least having everything in her name meant the entire town wasn't decimated.'

'I didn't do that out of the goodness of my heart, Sister.' He gave a wry smile. 'It suited me, but I'm glad it's working out.'

His candour was surprising and refreshing. The old Joseph McGrath would have taken the credit.

'How's everything else going?' he asked.

The guards stood either side of him as they talked, and it felt so awkward. Had he really brought her down there to talk about Jumaaroo?

'Well, Gordie McKenzie bought the mission and renamed it in honour of Woiduna.' She said the elder's name with no trace of apology.

To her surprise, Madigan burst out laughing. 'Well, that beats all. Gordie McKenzie, and he going around with his arse hangin' out of his trousers, fooling everyone. Who'd have thought, eh?'

'Indeed.'

Another silence.

'Why did you want me here?' Claire asked.

He sighed, his sapphire-blue eyes resting on hers. He was different, and not just his dishevelled appearance. The arrogance was gone, as was the condescending attitude. Despite everything that had happened between them, there was something compelling about him, something deep. She couldn't explain it, but somehow she felt they were connected souls. She couldn't even say she liked him – what she knew of him horrified her – but there was a force binding them together. She could see he was planning what to say before speaking.

'I wanted to say sorry for everything I put you through. And I s'pose I wanted the last face I see to be a friendly one. Nobody else would consider it, and I wasn't sure you would, but you're a much better person than most, Sister Claire, so I thought it was worth a shot.'

She was confused. 'Nobody else would consider visiting? Is that what you mean?'

'Well, that. I wrote to Assumpta, said I was sorry, but it's too little, too late there, I think. I can't blame her. Anyway, I wouldn't want her here, and I'm sure she's no interest in lookin' at my ugly mug one last time. Her brother wrote back to me, saying I was never to contact them again, that he wouldn't give my letter to her. There's no chance of me ever seeing any of them again anyway, so the Prendergasts are safe enough. But you're allowed to have a priest with you at the end, so I asked whether you could come instead.'

Her face must have registered her shock.

'Did they not tell you?' he asked, genuinely stricken.

She shook her head and swallowed. 'So it's today? Now?'

'Now… Well, in less than an hour.' He smiled again. 'You'll soon be rid of me for once and for all. I'm to be hung at nine, but –' Seeing her face, he added, 'If you don't want to, I understand. It's probably not a nice thing to watch.'

She saw him properly now, without the fine clothes, the cologne, the hair oil. He was just a man, a vulnerable child of God, no matter what he'd done. She made a decision.

238

She walked to the corner of the dark, musty room and sat on the floor, leaning her back to the wall. She patted the space beside her, and the officer nodded. He released the metal cuffs binding Madigan to the officers and shackled both Madigan's hands and feet instead. Hands before him, his feet able to move forward only a few inches at a time, he shuffled towards her and lowered himself awkwardly to sit on the floor beside her.

'Tell me your story, Francis,' she said quietly. 'Who are you?'

He sat there for a long moment, his hands joined between his knees. Then he spoke.

The story emerged of a child abandoned and abused, a handsome young man loved but exploited, who eventually became a hardened criminal without remorse. It was told without self-pity or blame for anyone but himself, and it struck Claire that Molly was the only person he'd ever loved or who had loved him for who he was.

'You'll soon be reunited with Molly,' she said.

Madigan smiled. 'Ah, I don't know. Depends where I end up. Mol was no saint, I can tell you, but she...' He sighed. 'She was good to me.'

'Tell me about Joe McGrath.'

Madigan stared at the floor between his feet and spoke quietly. 'Once I battered your man in Dublin, I knew I'd done for him. I had to get away or face the noose there, so I nicked a few bob and got on the boat to Liverpool. I bought a ticket off a fella in a pub, in his name of course. He was going to Cork on a ship that was going ultimately to Australia. Of course I'd no intention of getting off the boat in Cork.'

'Go on,' she urged.

'So in Cork, we were docked in Cobh for a day and a night, and I kept my head down. Never disembarked. Then one evening out on the deck, I overheard the pursers through the window allocating cabins. There was a fella who was supposed to be sharing with some- one, but there was an odd number of single men, so they allocated him a twin cabin on his own. Seeing my chance, I went down to the cabin number they mentioned and bagged one of the beds. The man was Joe McGrath, and he was none the wiser, just thought I was his cabin mate for the trip. Poor lad was sick as a dog all the way over, chucking his guts up day and night, so I looked after him, brought him bread and gave him water and all of that. He told me he was going out to get a start. He was a carpenter and heard there was loads of work in Australia. He told me all about his girl, how he was going to get set up and bring her out and they were going to live happily ever after.'

He looked at her, knowing he had to tell her the full story, but he was reluctant to go on. She waited.

'So the night before we were due to dock in Sydney – we'd stayed in the cabin pretty much all the time – I told him he should go up on deck, get some fresh air, that he looked like death warmed up. He agreed and up we went. It was easy, pitch dark and nobody about. It was blowing a bit of a squall, so he leaned on the railing, gulping in the fresh air, and I just grabbed him and threw him overboard.'

Claire tried not to react. He'd been judged and sentenced.

Francis now seemed lost in the memory as he went on. 'He was light. He hadn't eaten a bite really, and he was a skinny little lad to begin with. I went back down, took his papers and what bit of money he had and got off the ship as Joseph McGrath.'

'God rest his soul,' Claire said quietly.

'Ah, there's no fear for him, Sister. He's gone straight up. He was a good lad, said his rosary every night, loved his parents and his girl. He was welcomed into the pearly gates.'

'And you?' she asked. 'What will become of your soul, do you think?'

'I think we both know the answer to that, Sister, don't we?' His voice held no trace of fear, just resignation.

'Are you afraid?'

He shrugged. 'I'm tired, that's what I am. Been ducking and diving all my life, and part of me is glad it's over.'

'I can understand that. Do you want to say anything to anyone? I could pass on a message?'

He shook his head. 'There's no point in telling any more lies. I don't have anything to say.'

'Not to Assumpta, your children, to Rose even?'

'Would it help?' He seemed younger, more vulnerable than she'd ever seen him. 'They won't want to hear from me.'

'Assumpta might, in time. She loved you, you know. And your children will now grow up without their father, so they should have something from you to at least let them know you loved them.'

He turned his head to look at her. 'I didn't though. I saw Assumpta and the kids as a chain around my neck. I was leaving them once I'd sorted you out.'

'They don't need to know that.'

'Tell them I'm sorry then. That I was a bad man, that I did wrong and if I could turn the clock back, I would. That their mother is a good woman who tried to do right by me, but... Look, I'm past help. She didn't deserve what I put her through, none of you did.'

They sat, her body touching his, and she took his hand in hers. 'So you truly repent?' she asked gently.

He nodded. 'I... I... Maybe I was born bad or something, I don't know. I've had a lot of time to think in here. I see faces at night in my dreams. Your man Woiduna, Joe McGrath, the fella I robbed to give Assumpta's father a dowry, you, Assumpta...so many people hurt who didn't deserve it. And now I'll pay for my crimes, I suppose.'

She felt the pressure of his hand on hers.

'I'm afraid of hell.' His voice was barely audible.

'Will we say a prayer?' she whispered.

He shook his head. 'No good to me where I'm going.'

She returned the pressure of his hand. 'Do you know the story of the Prodigal Son?' she asked, and he nodded. 'Let's say an act of contrition together.' She began the words of the prayer all Catholic children learned at seven years of age. 'Oh my God, I am heartily sorry...'

He joined in, his voice low and filled with pain. 'For having offended thee, and I detest all my sins, because I dread the loss of heaven and the pains of hell, but most of all because they offended thee, my God, who art all good and deserving of my love. I firmly resolve with the help of thy grace to confess my sins, to do penance and to amend my life. Amen.'

They sat in silence for a moment.

'I haven't much time to do penance or amend my life now, do I?' He smiled ruefully, and she saw a flash of the old charm.

'No, but I truly believe you will be forgiven.' Claire blessed herself.

'Do you forgive me?' he asked, and for the first time since she'd known him, his eyes were bright with unshed tears.

'I do, Francis,' she whispered. 'I forgive you.'

Together they sat in silence for a few moments, his hand in hers, until the governor's assistant appeared and nodded at the officers, who helped first Claire to her feet and then Madigan.

'This is it,' Madigan said. 'Wasn't it Ned Kelly whose last words were "such is life"?'

'I believe so,' Claire agreed, giving him a smile.

'You can follow behind Sister,' the officer said as they walked, the governor and his assistant in front. They travelled the length of the stone corridor in silence. Claire prayed as she walked, begging God to allow the soul of Francis Madigan a place in heaven.

Her heart was thumping as she entered the room. It was whitewashed, and the only window was high on the wall. There was a trapdoor in the middle of the room with a 'T' marked on it. Madigan's feet were placed on the T, and the shackles were removed from his feet and replaced with a leather binding above the ankles. At the same time, a white hood was placed over his head and the noose looped around his neck. Claire's eyes were drawn to the rope stretching through another trapdoor in the ceiling.

Everyone was silent.

'God bless you, Francis. May Jesus and his Blessed Mother welcome you into the kingdom of heaven,' Claire said in a loud voice as the executioner pulled the lever. The trap door opened, and Francis Madigan fell through to his death.

EPILOGUE

*T*he newly constructed chapel in Jumaaroo glistened in the winter sun. It was August, and there was a welcome breeze as the guests made their way to the first wedding in the town.

Claire, Teresita, Mary and the two new arrivals, Sisters Dympna and Bonaventure, sat in the side chapel with the children of the St Finbarr's choir and orchestra.

The Bundagulgi had to be convinced to attend, but several were there despite looking wary of their surroundings. Daku was someone they looked up to, and they knew how instrumental the sisters were in securing their future, so they agreed. Assumpta had been approached by Claire, at the request of the Bundagulgi, and asked to release the dam that was curtailing the water supply, and the rivers and creeks flowed once more.

Slowly, relations between the natives and the whitefellas were improving, but Daku warned Claire not to expect miracles. The Aboriginals had every reason to feel as they did about Europeans. But it was a start.

The mission was thriving, and Russell and Betty were still there, but Daku explained there was a subtle but important change. It was owned by the Bundagulgi now, and though the concept of ownership of land was alien to them, they felt more secure knowing that nobody could remove them or harm them. They came and went on their own terms, and Russell and Betty were having to adapt accordingly.

Despite the joint objective of the mission and St. Finbarr's, there had been no communication with the Gardiners apart from on the renaming day, and Claire didn't expect there to be.

Daku relayed that Russell seemed to have forgiven his church for selling the land from under them, and though Daku couldn't understand that, Claire could. She and Russell were more alike than he – or the Catholic Church for that matter – would like to admit: both slow to change, both ruled from on high, where those on the ground followed orders and obeyed their superiors.

So often people suggested that she and her sisters wear a lighter habit, but that was not permitted, and therefore, she wouldn't consider it. Perhaps one day a decision to allow it would be made, and she would welcome it, but until then, she would abide by the rules.

She scanned the church and was pleased to see so many happy faces. Mary had insisted on catering the wedding breakfast and had been working day and night with the help of many of the mothers in the town to prepare a feast that was to be served in the school hall after the Mass.

Assumpta had lent them all the china and glassware for the wedding breakfast, and when she delivered it to the school the previous night, she confided to Claire that she'd had a letter back from Rose. Assumpta had sent a note to Rose once she discovered the truth about her husband. The authorities had informed Rose and Joe McGrath's family back in Ireland of what had happened, but Assumpta felt she should write as well. She'd asked Claire to help her compose the letter, and it was one of deep condolence.

Assumpta knew Claire was with him at the end, and somehow it brought them closer. Claire had passed on Francis's thoughts to her and the children, embellishing his love for them a little, and it seemed to bring some comfort.

'What did Rose say?' Claire had asked as they carried boxes of teacups and saucers to the hall.

'She was grateful that I wrote. She explained how she'd spent all these years imagining that he had just forgotten about her. The shipping company assured her he did disembark in Sydney, so it was the only reasonable conclusion.'

'God love her.' Claire felt such pity for her.

'She talked about coming out to Australia anyway. She never married and feels like she never will – this Joe was the only man she ever loved. But she wants to at least visit the place they had intended to live. So I think I'm going to welcome her and offer her a stake in the business or a lump sum or something. She may not want to come all the way to Jumaaroo, but she deserves some compensation. Joseph's company – or should I say my company – is worth rather a lot of money, so it only seems fair that Rose get something.'

'That would be a kind thing to do, Assumpta.' Claire smiled and the other woman returned it. They were friends now.

Jannali was the flower girl, and Helen's sister Margaret was the matron of honour. Helen's family had come out from Ireland for the occasion and were genuinely pleased she'd found happiness once again, though they were as bemused by the Bundagulgi as Claire had been at first.

Daku, on the other hand, charmed them with his warm gentle ways, and Helen's father, a doctor, was fascinated by all of the bush medicine Daku told him about. Her mother worried for her, as was natural, and Claire reassured her that Helen would always have family at St Finbarr's and that Daku was a good man who loved her daughter deeply.

Daku stood, not in a suit, of course, but in clean trousers and an open-necked shirt, as formal as he was willing to go. He'd joked that he drew the line at shoes. True to his word, he was barefoot. Helen said she didn't mind what he wore.

The bridal dress, on the other hand, was simple but exquisite, made by Cassia who was recovering slowly. She and Stavros were managing to keep going, and Claire realised with relief that he was never spying on her for Madigan. She'd asked Francis that day in the jail. He admitted he'd tried to recruit the Galatas family, bribed them with care for Cassia, but they refused. She would have forgiven Stavros if he had been working for Madigan, but it was nice to know that the Galatases were her genuine friends.

As she gazed at the packed church, she realised that at long last, Jumaaroo no longer felt alien and strange. To her, now, it was home.

Mary moved to the organ, a beautiful one donated by Rev Bill, and began the bridal march. All eyes turned as Helen, looking radiant, walked up the aisle.

Daku turned, and the look on his face left Claire in no doubt – this was a match made in heaven. As Rev Bill said the Mass – his appearance in Jumaaroo the night before the wedding had come as a surprise to everyone but Claire – she prayed for the couple's future happiness.

It wasn't an easy path they had chosen. There was tremendous prejudice in the world, and they would face more hardship than most. But they were devoted to each other and both strong, resilient people. If anyone could make it, Helen and Daku could. Gordie was best man, looking much tidier than usual – though that wouldn't be hard, she conceded with a smile – and Darana sat proudly beside him.

She prayed for the Bundagulgi people, that they could now live a life of peace, as they chose to live. Though there was a long way to go, slowly the world was coming to realise the wrongs done to these gentle people and efforts were being made to put at least some of these right. It heartened her to see tentative friendships growing between some of the Bundagulgi children and the white ones, facilitated mainly by Jannali. She was a force to be reckoned with even at eight years old. She refused to allow anyone to treat her differently. She spoke the language of her people and English fluently, easily slipping from one to the other. She'd managed to gather enough Bundagulgi children from the mission and beyond for a hurling team, and once a week they now came to St Finbarr's for training.

She prayed for her community, her school, her family at home, who'd been given a very sanitised version of events by Rev Bill when he went home for Christmas. Her mother had written a long letter all full of concern, and she'd pleaded with Claire to take more care. Claire smiled as she read it and could hear her mother's gentle admonishment. Rev Bill offered for her to go home, either for good or for a break, but she'd declined. She would go home maybe in a year or two, when the whole place was running smoothly, but for now she needed to be in Jumaaroo.

And finally, as she did each night, Sister Claire prayed for the repose of the soul of Francis Madigan.

THE END

I sincerely hope you enjoyed this book and if you did I would be delighted if you would leave a review.

Just click this link:

Amazon.com/review/create-review?&asin=B087QJXF4C

To hear about special offers, new books, or to download a FREE full length novel, just join my readers group. Its 100% free and always will be.

www.jeangrainger.com

This story landed into my lap. It doesn't often happen that way but for me, the stars aligned beautifully with this book.

In the year 2019/2020, my husband, my two youngest children and I set off on the adventure of a lifetime. We bought a caravan and a 4WD and drove all over Australia.

It was the year of the bush fires that devastated that most remarkable of countries, and it was also the year of the Corona virus. The fires didn't stop us, but the virus did. It sent us home to Ireland three months early, but not before we'd spend an unforgettable nine months there.

This is how this story came to be.

One fabulously hot tropical day last year, (very few Irish stories start like that) my family and I were knocking about in Cooktown, in Far North Queensland, Australia.

A wild, dangerous, and breathtakingly beautiful place, steeped in Australian history, for it was there that a very worried chap called Captain James Cook realised he had a massive hole in his boat, the HMS Endeavour, in the year 1770. Luckily for Cook, unluckily for the native Australians, they welcomed him ashore and helped him repair it.

First contact was cordial and relatively successful. However as you probably know, the white man's occupation of Australia after Cook is a sad and brutal story of the destruction of the Aboriginal people's way of life. 40,000 years of living as they did, deeply connected to country, (their phrase) annihilated.

If you haven't read about it, I suggest you do. We all should know.

So, there we are, The Graingers in Cooktown, and my husband takes the kids off to the museum while I caught up on some writing. A couple of hours later, himself arrives back and says to me, 'you have to go there, it's an intriguing place. It's in an old convent and they have all kinds of things that you'd find fascinating.' - he knows the kind of things I find fascinating after sixteen years together - not what most people find fascinating admittedly, but anyway - I digress.

So off I go down to this old (for Australia) building. It's on a hill in the town and instantly recognisable as a convent. The ground floor is dedicated to the Captain Cook story, and the first contact and so on, but as a visitor to Australia for twenty years, I'm fairly familiar with that. so I wander upstairs where one of the curators has directed me, to the 'nun's section.'

Upstairs in this building it is absolutely roasting hot. Now, they have added air con to the building but still, wow. Hot. So I said to one of the staff, as I perused the many perplexing items the sisters thought necessary to bring from County Waterford in the early 1900s, and saw the photos of the nuns with their long black habits and starched veils, 'What on earth was going through their heads I wonder?'

Now, it was hot for me, with air conditioning and wearing shorts and a t-shirt, so what it must have been like for the nuns, without air-con, and in that heavy, black habit, I just could not imagine.

'Well,' says the wonderful lady running the whole show, 'I can take you upstairs to the third floor to show you where they slept if you like? It's a bit of a store room, but you can see it?'

She didn't need to offer twice. So together, we climb a narrow stairs and soon we're under a tin roof. The air con isn't getting as far as here, the humidity is so bad my shirt is stuck to me and my hair is wet, and this is the dry season.

During the wet season, when the temperature is just as hot but the humidity is so much worse, well, the mind boggles.

I can see in my mind's eye the little iron beds, each nun with her own tiny space, a curtain separating one from the other. All manner of intriguing things are just stored up there, I'm like a kid in a sweet shop. By looking at their possessions, I get a sense of them, who they were, but it was nebulous, fleeting, like someone you see for a second out of the corner of your eye.

And then she tells me.

In the 80s, a man met these very nuns, in a nursing home in Brisbane and he interviewed them. They were all over ninety by now. The interviews were recorded on cassette tape, and were in a box, beautifully stored and I suspect, never listened to, in the storeroom of the museum.

The curator bemoaned the fact that they weren't digitalised, of course, it was all to do with funding and red tape, and the slow moving wheels of government administration of museums.

'Could I listen to them?' I ask, holding my breath, waiting for her to say it wouldn't be possible. But in that wonderful 'can do' spirit that is so much part of the Aussie psyche she said,

"we don't have a tape player but if you can get one...I don't see why not!'

I contacted my brother-in-law's sister Karen, a lovely person who lives in Cooktown, who dug out an old tape player her daughter had used for distance learning, and delivered it to the museum for me.

I spent the rest of the day, sitting in the curator's office, blissfully engaged in the stories of the Irish nuns. What it was like, seeing snakes and crocodiles, dealing with the heat, learning to live in the tropics, the children who attended the school, the families who lived there.

I was mesmerised, and after several hours of testimony, (they all sounded like they left Ireland last Tuesday - not seventy years earlier by the way) a story came to me.

I absolutely loved writing this. I wrote it in our caravan, and so much of the story is informed by those I met in the nine months I spent travelling in that wonderful country.

I spoke to an Aboriginal man called Russ, who showed us the bush, opening our eyes to a landscape so diverse and incredible, we just bumped into him one day in the outback, a place with red dirt as far as the eye could see. His love and deep understanding of his country was such a special thing to experience and definitely one of many high points of my time there.

For my children, and for us too, the wildlife was another. I met more animals in nine months than I did in the previous forty eight years.

Kangaroos, wallabies, koalas, echidnas, quolls, Tassie devils, possums, wombats, snakes, crocs, spiders, so many birds, became the characters of my daily life.

I spoke to toughened farmers, trying to survive the drought, firemen and women battling the bush blazes that ravaged New South Wales and Victoria in those long weeks of 2019/2020. I met with the descendants of settlers and convicts and universally, to a man and woman, it was a fantastic, never to be forgotten experience.

Thank you Australia, I will never ever forget it, this book is my love letter to you.

Jean Grainger,
   Cork, Ireland. May 2020.

If you would like to read more of my books, perhaps you might like to try something a little bit different.

The Star and the Shamrock, tells the story of two German Jewish children who managed to escape Nazi Germany on the Kindertransport, an evacuation programme for Jewish children. Like all of my stories, it is loosely based on facts, fictionalised of course. Liesl and Erich end up in Northern Ireland.

You can read it here
https://geni.us/TheStarandtheShamrocAL
Here are the first chapters to get you started,
The Star and the Shamrock

Liverpool, England, 1939
   Elizabeth put the envelope down and took off her glasses. The thin

paper and the Irish stamps irritated her. Probably that estate agent wanting to sell her mother's house again. She'd told him twice she wasn't selling, though she had no idea why. It wasn't as if she were ever going back to Ireland, her father long dead, her mother gone last year – she was probably up in heaven tormenting the poor saints with her extensive religious knowledge. The letter drew her back to the little Northern Irish village she'd called home...that big old lonely house...her mother.

Margaret Bannon was a pillar of the community back in Bally-cregggan, County Down, a devout Catholic in a deeply divided place, but she had a heart of stone.

Elizabeth sighed. She tried not to think about her mother, as it only upset her. Not a word had passed between them in twenty-one years, and then Margaret died alone. She popped the letter behind the clock; she needed to get to school. She'd open it later, or next week... or never.

Rudi smiled down at her from the dresser. 'Don't get bitter, don't be like her.' She imagined she heard him admonish her, his boyish face frozen in an old sepia photograph, in his King's Regiment uniform, so proud, so full of excitement, so bloody young. What did he know of the horrors that awaited him out there in Flanders? What did any of them know?

She mentally shook herself. This line of thought wasn't helping. Rudi was dead, and she wasn't her mother. She was her own person. Hadn't she proved that by defying her mother and marrying Rudi? It all seemed so long ago now, but the intensity of the emotions lingered. She'd met, loved and married young Rudi Klein as a girl of eighteen. Margaret Bannon was horrified at the thought of her Catholic daughter marrying a Jew, but Elizabeth could still remember that heady feeling of being young and in love. Rudi could have been a Martian for all she cared. He was young and handsome and funny, and he made her feel loved.

She wondered, if he were to somehow come back from the dead and just walk up the street and into the kitchen of their little terraced house, would he recognise the woman who stood there? Her chestnut hair that used to fall over her shoulders was always now pulled back in a bun, and the girl who loved dresses was now a woman whose clothes were functional and modest. She was thirty-nine, but she knew she could pass for older. She had been pretty once, or at least not too horrifically ugly anyway. Rudi had said he loved her; he'd told her she was beautiful.

She snapped on the wireless, but the talk was of the goings-on in Europe again. She unplugged it; it was too hard to hear first thing in the morning. Surely they wouldn't let it all happen again, not after the last time?

All anyone talked about was the threat of war, what Hitler was going to do. Would there really be peace as Mr Chamberlain promised? It was going to get worse before it got better if the papers were to be believed.

Though she was almost late, she took the photo from the shelf. A smudge of soot obscured his smooth forehead, and she wiped it with the sleeve of her cardigan. She looked into his eyes.

'Goodbye, Rudi darling. See you later.' She kissed the glass, as she did every day.

How different her life could have been...a husband, a family. Instead, she had received a generic telegram just like so many others in that war that was supposed to end all wars. She carried in her heart for twenty years that feeling of despair. She'd taken the telegram from the boy who refused to meet her eyes. He was only a few years younger than she. She opened it there, on the doorstep of that very house, the words expressing regret swimming before her eyes. She remembered the lurch in her abdomen, the baby's reaction mirroring her own. 'My daddy is dead.'

She must have been led inside, comforted – the neighbours were good that way. They knew when the telegram lad turned his bike down their street that someone would need holding up. That day it was her...tomorrow, someone else. She remembered the blood, the sense of dragging downwards, that ended up in a miscarriage at five months. All these years later, the pain had dulled to an ever-present ache.

She placed the photo lovingly on the shelf once more. It was the only one she had. In lots of ways, it wasn't really representative of Rudi; he was not that sleek and well presented. 'The British Army smartened me up,' he used to say. But out of uniform is how she remembered him. Her most powerful memory was of them sitting in that very kitchen the day they got the key. His uncle Saul had lent them the money to buy the house, and they were going to pay him back.

They'd gotten married in the registry office in the summer of 1918, when he was home on brief leave because of a broken arm. She could almost hear her mother's wails all the way across the Irish Sea, but she didn't care. It didn't matter that her mother was horrified at her marrying a *Jewman*, as she insisted on calling him, or that she was cut off from all she ever knew – none of it mattered. She loved Rudi and he loved her. That was all there was to it.

She'd worn her only good dress and cardigan – the miniscule pay of a teaching assistant didn't allow for new clothes, but she didn't care. Rudi had picked a bunch of flowers on the way to the registry office, and his cousin Benjamin and Benjamin's wife, Nina, were the witnesses. Ben was killed at the Somme, and Nina went to London, back to her family. They'd lost touch.

Elizabeth swallowed. The lump of grief never left her throat. It was a part of her now. A lump of loss and pain and anger. The grief had given way to fury, if she were honest. Rudi was killed on the morning of the 11th of November, 1918, in Belgium. The armistice had been signed, but the order to end hostilities would not come into effect until eleven p.m. The eleventh hour of the eleventh month. She imagined the generals saw some glorious symmetry in that. But there wasn't. Just more people left in mourning than there had to be. She lost him, her Rudi, because someone wanted the culmination of four long years of slaughter to look nice on a piece of paper.

She shivered. It was cold these mornings, though spring was supposed to be in the air. The children in her class were constantly sniffling and coughing. She remembered the big old fireplace in the national school in Ballycregggan, where each child was expected to bring a sod of turf or a block of timber as fuel for the fire. Master O'Reilly's wife would put the big jug of milk beside the hearth in the mornings so the children could have a warm drink by lunchtime. Elizabeth would have loved to have a fire in her classroom, but the British education system would never countenance such luxuries.

She glanced at the clock. Seven thirty. She should go. Fetching her coat and hat, and her heavy bag of exercise books that she'd marked last night, she let herself out.

The street was quiet. Apart from the postman, doing deliveries on the other side of the street, she was the only person out. She liked it, the sense of solitude, the calm before the storm.

The mile-long walk to Bridge End Primary was her exercise and thinking time. Usually, she mulled over what she would teach that day or how to deal with a problem child – or more frequently, a problem parent. She had been a primary schoolteacher for so long, there was little she had not seen. Coming over to England as a bright sixteen-year-old to a position as a teacher's assistant in a Catholic school was the beginning of a trajectory that had taken her far from Bally-creggan, from her mother, from everything she knew.

She had very little recollection of the studies that transformed her from a lowly teaching assistant to a fully qualified teacher. After Rudi was killed and she'd lost the baby, a kind nun at her school suggested she do the exams to become a teacher, not just an assistant, and because it gave her something to do with her troubled mind, she agreed. She got top marks, so she must have thrown herself into her studies, but she couldn't remember much about those years. They were shrouded in a fog of grief and pain.

Chapter 2

Berlin, Germany, 1939

Ariella Bannon waited behind the door, her heart thumping. She'd covered her hair with a headscarf and wore her only remaining coat, a grey one that had been smart once. Though she didn't look at all Jewish with her green eyes and curly red hair – and being married to Peter Bannon, a Catholic, meant she was in a slightly more privileged position than other Jews – people knew what she was. She took her children to temple, kept a kosher house. She never in her wildest nightmares imagined that the quiet following of her faith would have led to this.

One of the postmen, Herr Krupp, had joined the Brownshirts. She didn't trust him to deliver the post properly, so she had to hope it was Frau Braun that day. She wasn't friendly exactly, but at least she gave you your letters. She was surprised at Krupp; he'd been nice before, but since Kristallnacht, it seemed that everyone was different. She even remembered Peter talking to him a few times about the weather or fishing or something. It was hard to believe that underneath all that, there was such hatred. Neighbours, people on the street, children even, seemed to have turned against all Jews. Liesl and Erich were scared all the time. Liesl tried to put a brave face on it – she was such a wonderful child – but she was only ten. Erich looked up to her so much. At seven, he thought his big sister could fix everything.

It was her daughter's birthday next month but there was no way to celebrate. Ariella thought back to birthdays of the past, cakes and friends and presents, but that was all gone. Everything was gone.

She tried to swallow the by-now-familiar lump of panic. Peter had been picked up because he and his colleague, a Christian, tried to defend an old Jewish lady the Nazi thugs were abusing in the street. Ariella had been told that the uniformed guards beat up the two men and threw them in a truck. That was five months ago. She hoped every day her husband would turn up, but so far, nothing. She considered going to visit his colleague's wife to see if she had heard anything, but nowadays, it was not a good idea for a Jew to approach an Aryan for any reason.

At least she'd spoken to the children in English since they were born. At least that. She did it because she could; she'd had an English governess as a child, a terrifying woman called Mrs Beech who insisted Ariella speak not only German but English, French and Italian as well. Peter smiled to hear his children jabbering away in other languages, and he always said they got that flair for languages from her. He spoke German only, even though his father was Irish.

She remembered fondly her father-in-law, Paddy. He'd died when Erich was a baby. Though he spoke fluent German, it was always with a lovely lilting accent. He would tell her tales of growing up in Ireland. He came to Germany to study when he was a young man, and saw and fell instantly in love with Christiana Berger, a beauty from Bavaria. And so in Germany he remained. Peter was their only child because Christiana was killed in a horse-riding accident when Peter was only five years old. How simple those days were, seven short years ago, when she had her daughter toddling about, her newborn son in her arms, a loving husband and a doting father-in-law. Now, she felt so alone.

Relief. It was Frau Braun. But she walked past the building.

Ariella fought the wave of despair. She should have gotten the letter Ariella had posted by now, surely. It was sent three weeks ago. Ariella tried not to dwell on the many possibilities. What if she wasn't at the address? Maybe the family had moved on. Peter had no contact with his only first cousin as far as she knew.

Nathaniel, Peter's best friend, told her he might be able to get Liesl and Erich on the Kindertransport out of Berlin – he had some connections apparently – but she couldn't bear the idea of them going to strangers. If only Elizabeth would say yes. It was the only way she could put her babies on that train. And even then… She dismissed that thought and refused to let her mind go there. She had to get them away until all this madness died down.

She'd tried everything to get them all out. But there was no way. She'd contacted every single embassy – the United States, Venezuela, Paraguay, places she'd barely heard of – but there was no hope. The lines outside the embassies grew longer every day, and without someone to vouch for you, it was impossible. Ireland was her only chance. Peter's father, the children's grandfather, was an Irish citizen. If she could only get Elizabeth Bannon to agree to take the children, then at least they would be safe.

Sometimes she woke in the night, thinking this must all be a nightmare. Surely this wasn't happening in Germany, a country known for learning and literature, music and art? And yet it was.

Peter and Ariella would have said they were German, their children were German, just the same as everyone else, but not so. Because of her, her darling children were considered *Untermensch*, subhuman, because of the Jewish blood in their veins.

To continue reading this story, click here
https://geni.us/TheStarandtheShamrocAL

ABOUT THE AUTHOR

Jean Grainger is a USA Today bestselling Irish author. She writes historical and contemporary Irish fiction and her work has very flatteringly been compared to the late great Maeve Binchy.

She lives in a stone cottage in Cork with her husband Diarmuid and the youngest two of her four children. The older two show up occasionally with laundry and to raid the fridge. There are a variety of animals there too, all led by two cute but clueless micro-dogs called Scrappy and Scoobi.

f

ALSO BY JEAN GRAINGER

To get a free novel and to join my readers club (100% free and always will be)

Go to www.jeangrainger.com

The Tour Series

The Tour

Safe at the Edge of the World

The Story of Grenville King

The Homecoming of Bubbles O'Leary

Finding Billie Romano

Kayla's Trick

The Carmel Sheehan Story

Letters of Freedom

The Future's Not Ours To See

What Will Be

The Robinswood Story

What Once Was True

Return To Robinswood

Trials and Tribulations

The Star and the Shamrock Series

The Star and the Shamrock

The Emerald Horizon

The Hard Way Home

The World Starts Anew

The Queenstown Series

Last Port of Call

The West's Awake

The Harp and the Rose

Roaring Liberty

Standalone Books

So Much Owed

Shadow of a Century

Under Heaven's Shining Stars

Catriona's War

Sisters of the Southern Cross

Printed in Great Britain
by Amazon